Dear Reader,

No matter how busy your day, there'll *always* be time for romance. TAKE 5 is a new way to indulge in love, passion and adventure—and still be on time to pick up the kids! Each TAKE 5 volume offers five condensed stories by top Harlequin and Silhouette authors. Now you can have the enjoyment and satisfaction of a full-length novel, but in less time—perfect for those days when it's difficult to squeeze a longer read into your hectic schedule.

This volume of TAKE 5 features five tender love stories...five *sweet* escapes! *New York Times* bestselling author Debbie Macomber tantalizes readers with a marriage of convenience in *Yesterday Once More*, and in *Adam's Image* an editor plots her very own happy-ever-after. Powerful heroes meet their match in *Roomful of Roses* and *Woman Hater*—both by top Silhouette author Diana Palmer. And secret love is at the heart of *Always a Bridesmaid* by beloved author Patricia Knoll.

Why not indulge in all four volumes of TAKE 5 available now—tender romance, sizzling passion, riveting adventure and heartwarming family love. No matter what mood you're in, you'll have the perfect escape!

Happy reading,

Marsha Zinberg
Senior Editor and Editorial Coordinator, TAKE 5

Debbie Macomber always enjoyed telling stories—
first to her baby-sitting clients and then to her own
four children. As a full-time wife and mother and an
avid romance reader, she dreamed of one day sharing
her stories with a wider audience. In the autumn of
1982 she sold her first book, and that was only the
beginning. Debbie became a *New York Times* bestselling
author with the publication of *Promise, Texas,* and she
has been making regular appearances on the *USA Today*
bestseller list—not surprising, considering that there are
over 40 million copies of her books in print worldwide.

Diana Palmer is a prolific writer of women's fiction
who got her start as a newspaper reporter. As one of
the top ten romance writers in America, she has a gift for
telling the most sensual tales with charm and humor. Her
readers have grown to treasure her emotional style. This
popular author has over 10 million copies of her books
in print, and is the recipient of eleven national bestseller
awards and numerous readers' choice awards!

Patricia Knoll began writing romances a number of years
ago when she was faced with birthday number thirty and
the impending arrival of baby number four. Convinced
that she would be forever confined to the house changing
diapers, she found escape in a popular-fiction-writing
class being offered locally. Several class members were
interested in writing romances, and Patricia, wanting to
see what they were all about, quickly became hooked.
She has now written over twenty books, and especially
likes creating quirky characters and funny situations.

TAKE5

Quick Reads. Great Escapes.

**NEW YORK TIMES
BESTSELLING AUTHOR**

Debbie
Macomber

Diana
Palmer

Patricia
Knoll

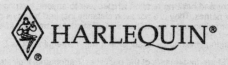

HARLEQUIN®

TORONTO • NEW YORK • LONDON
AMSTERDAM • PARIS • SYDNEY • HAMBURG
STOCKHOLM • ATHENS • TOKYO • MILAN • MADRID
PRAGUE • WARSAW • BUDAPEST • AUCKLAND

ISBN 0-373-83492-6

TAKE 5, VOLUME 1

Copyright © 2001 by Harlequin Books S.A.

The publisher acknowledges the copyright holders of the individual titles as follows:

YESTERDAY ONCE MORE
Copyright © 1998 by Debbie Macomber

ADAM'S IMAGE
Copyright © 1985 by Debbie Macomber

ROOMFUL OF ROSES
Copyright © 1984 by Diana Palmer

WOMAN HATER
Copyright © 1987 by Diana Palmer

ALWAYS A BRIDESMAID
Copyright © 1989 by Patricia Knoll

CONTENTS

YESTERDAY ONCE MORE

Debbie Macomber

anxious when she'd be in town. The rest of the left for hurrying the rose—...

Julie Houser pushed the elevator button and stepped back to wait, absently glancing at her watch; she'd have plenty of time to finish unpacking tonight.

The giant metal doors swooshed open and Julie moved right to the rear, anticipating the five-thirty rush. By the time the car reached the bottom floor it would be full.

The next floor down it stopped again. This time three men boarded, then another.

As Julie squeezed into the far corner, her purse strap slid off her shoulder. Easing it back up, she felt someone's eyes roam over her. Accustomed to the appreciative gaze of men, Julie at first ignored the man. But after one look at her admirer, she nearly choked.

"Daniel." The name slipped from her lips as their eyes met and held. His dark eyes narrowed, an impassive expression masking his handsome features.

Unable to bear his gaze any longer, Julie lowered her eyes.

The elevator stopped and everyone filed out until she stood alone in the empty shell, her breath coming in deep, uneven gasps. So soon? She'd only been back to Wichita six days. To see Daniel so quickly! And in the building where she worked. Was his office here? Oh, please, she begged, not yet. I'm not ready.

The downtown sidewalks were filled with people and Julie weaved her way through the crowds. Ten minutes later her hand trembled uncontrollably as she unlocked her car door.

Her heart felt as if she'd been running a marathon as she slipped into the driver's seat. Three long years had passed since she'd seen Daniel. Years of change. She'd only been nineteen when she'd fled in panic. The regret she felt for hurting the man she loved so intensely was almost more than she could bear. And she had loved Daniel. The evening he'd slipped the diamond engagement ring on her finger had been the happiest of her young life.

Julie let her thoughts drift back to that night as she started her car. Daniel had taken her to an elegant French restaurant. Flickering candlelight had sent shadows dancing over the white linen tablecloth.

"Happy?" he asked.

Julie glanced over the top of the gold-tasseled menu and nodded shyly.

Daniel set his menu aside. Julie noticed that from the moment he'd picked her up that evening he'd been unnaturally quiet.

"Daniel, is something the matter?" she ventured.

He stared at her blankly and shook his head.

"I'm not wearing the right kind of dress, am I?" She'd changed outfits three times before he'd arrived.

"You're beautiful," Daniel whispered. "Is it any wonder I love you so?" He reached for her hand, gripping her fingers with his. "I've been trying to find a way to ask you a question."

"But, Daniel, all you need to do is ask."

He sighed. "It's not that simple, my love."

Julie couldn't imagine what was troubling him.

"I've been accepted into the law practice of McFife, Lawson and Garrison."

Julie smiled. "That's wonderful news. Congratulations."

"It's only a junior partnership."

"But, Daniel, that is the firm you were hoping would accept you."

"Yes, it is, for more reasons than you know."

"We're here to celebrate, then."

"Not quite yet." He leaned forward and clasped her

hand with both of his. "Honey, these last months have been the happiest of my life."

"Mine, too," she whispered.

"I know you're only nineteen, and I probably should wait a couple of years…"

Julie's heart was pounding so loudly she was afraid he could hear it. "Yes, Daniel?"

"What I'm trying to say is…I love you, Julie. Now that I can offer you a future, I'm asking you to marry me."

Julie bit into her bottom lip, convinced if she said anything, she'd start to cry.

"Julie," he pleaded.

She nodded wildly.

"Does that mean yes?"

The words trembled from her lips. "Yes, Daniel, yes! I love you so much. I can't think of anything that would make me happier than to spend the rest of my life with you."

The loving look in Daniel's eyes was enough to melt her bones. He pulled a jeweler's box from his pocket. He opened the lid and the size of the diamond made Julie gasp.

"Oh, Daniel." Unbidden tears blurred her gaze. "It's the most beautiful ring I've ever seen."

"Here." He slowly slipped the diamond onto her finger, his eyes alight with a heart full of love.

Battling to put an end to the memories, Julie pulled into the apartment parking lot and sat for several moments. She toyed with the gold chain around her slender neck, seeking the diamond. She would keep the engagement ring there until it was back on her finger where it belonged. But after seeing Daniel today, Julie realized how difficult the task was going to be. He wouldn't forgive her easily.

The most difficult decision she'd ever made was to flee Wichita three years ago. The second hardest was to come back. But love had demanded that she return and set things right—if possible.

When she reached her apartment, Julie hung her purse on the bedroom doorknob and placed her coat in the closet. Several large boxes littered the living room floor, but she felt exhausted, and it had nothing to do with physical exertion.

Everything had happened just as she'd hoped. The job had been lined up even before the move, then she'd located an apartment within her budget. But inadvertently running into Daniel so soon seemed unreal.

She located the box that held their engagement portrait and stared at the two smiling faces. They'd been so much in love. Tears filled her eyes as her fingers lovingly traced Daniel's face. He looked more mature now. Even the sandy-colored hair that had always seemed wind tousled was urbanely styled. The powerful male features were more pronounced now. Her finger idly moved over the lean, proud jaw and paused at the tiny cleft in his chin.

She had loved to kiss him there. To tease him unmercifully with her lips. And he had been so wonderful. Conscious of her innocence, Daniel had held his desire in a tight rein. Julie wondered if he regretted that now.

EARLY THE NEXT morning Julie arrived at work intent on checking the occupant listings of the office complex. Daniel Van Deen, Attorney, seemed to leap off the register at her. Only one floor separated them.

Unexpectedly a tingling sensation swept through her, and she didn't need to be told that Daniel had entered the building. Slowly she turned her head to see him walk to the elevator. Stepping inside, he turned around. Their eyes locked.

Shivering, she watched an angry frustration sweep over his features. His magnetic dark eyes narrowed as he stared back at her. Then the door glided shut.

Julie released a quivering breath. Daniel's look said he hadn't forgotten or forgiven her.

Her legs felt unsteady as she rode up to the office of Cheney Trust and Mortgage Company. Grateful that she was the first one in, Julie sat at her desk, striving to regain her usual poise.

Sherry Adams, a pert blonde, strolled in about fifteen minutes late. Their employer, Jack Barrett, had arrived earlier and pointedly stared at her empty desk. Julie had only been working there a few days, and although Sherry had her faults, it was easy to see that the young woman was a valuable asset.

"Morning," Julie responded to her co-worker.

"Did Mr. Barrett say anything about me being late?" she asked, but didn't look concerned.

"Not to me he didn't."

"One of these days, old Barrett is going to fire me."

"I doubt that," Julie commented.

The remainder of the morning was peaceful. The two women took turns answering the phone. Julie still relied on Sherry for help, which she supplied willingly.

A couple of minutes after noon, Jack Barrett strolled into the outer room. "Are you going out for lunch?" he asked Julie.

"Shall I get you something?" she asked.

"Not today." He handed her a large manila envelope. "But would you mind dropping this off at Daniel Van Deen's office?"

Julie forced a smile and walked out. The palms of her hands felt clammy as she entered Daniel's plush office.

A round-faced secretary glanced up and smiled. "Can I help you?"

"I...have an envelope from Jack Barrett," she managed.

"Agnes, did you find—" Abruptly, Daniel stopped mid-sentence when he saw Julie. The hard look in his eyes was solely for her.

Then unexpectedly his gaze softened and an emotion Julie couldn't define came over his features.

"Mr. Barrett sent the papers you asked about this morning," Agnes supplied, and her sharp gaze went first to Julie then to Daniel. "Was that all?"

"Pardon?" Julie tore her attention from him.

"Was there something else?"

"No," she mumbled. "Thank you."

A puzzled look marred the woman's brow. "Thank you for bringing them," she murmured.

Julie left the office with her head held high.

The remainder of the day passed in a blur and by the time she returned home that night, Julie felt drained. She decided to call her mother.

Margaret Houser lived in a retirement community in Southern California. None of Julie's family was in Wichita anymore.

"Have you looked up any of your old high school friends?" her mother asked.

"Not yet." Actually Julie doubted that she would. "Mom." She took a deep breath. "I've seen Daniel."

Instantly her mother was concerned. "How is he?"

"We...we haven't talked. But he's changed. He's not likely to understand why I came back."

"Don't be so sure, sweetheart," Margaret said. "He's been hurt, and the years are bound to have changed him."

"Mom, I don't think he will talk to me."

"I've never known you to be a defeatist," her mother said. "But I worry about Daniel's mother. Be careful of her."

"I will." Idly Julie's fingers flipped through the white pages of the telephone directory after she'd hung up. Clara Van Deen's phone was unlisted. But Daniel's was there.

From the beginning, Julie had known that Daniel's mother wanted him to marry a more socially prominent girl. But to her credit, Clara Van Deen accepted Julie as Daniel's choice. Then she set about making her into something she would never be. Clara had Julie's hair cut and styled, then she purchased an entire wardrobe for her.

Julie swallowed her pride a hundred times and tried to do exactly as Mrs. Van Deen wished. She did so want to make Daniel proud.

But the wedding plans were what had finally caused Julie to buckle and run. She had wanted a simple ceremony with only their immediate families. Daniel's mother issued invitations to four hundred close and intimate friends she couldn't possibly insult by not inviting.

"But, Daniel," Julie had protested, "I don't know any of these people."

"Don't worry about it," Daniel had said. "They'll love you as much as I do."

Daniel had negated any further protests with a searing kiss.

As the date drew closer, Julie was the focus of attention at a variety of teas and social events.

After each one, Mrs. Van Deen would run through a list of taboos that Julie had violated. No matter how hard Julie tried, there was always something she'd done wrong or shouldn't have said. Someone she might have offended.

"I can't take it anymore," Julie cried to her mother at last.

"Say something," her mother advised.

"Don't you think I've tried?" Julie shouted.

Every day the pressure mounted. The whole wedding had grown into a monster that loomed ready to devour Julie. The caterers, musicians, soloist, organist. The flower girl, the dresses, the bridesmaids. Mrs. Van Deen even booked their honeymoon.

"Daniel, please listen to me," Julie had begged a week before the wedding. "I don't want any of this."

"Honey, I know you're nervous," he'd whispered. "But everything will be over in one day and we can go on with the rest of our lives as we wish."

But Julie doubted that they could. Her suspicions were confirmed when Mrs. Van Deen made a large down payment on a house for them.

"It's her wedding gift to us," Daniel explained. But the house was only a few minutes from his mother's, and the handwriting was bold and clear on the freshly painted walls.

"Doesn't it bother you the way she's taken over our lives?"

In that second, she saw that Daniel did care, but would do nothing.

"For the first time since Dad died, my mother's got a purpose. She's loving every minute of it. Can't you see the difference our wedding has made in her?"

All Julie could feel was a growing case of claustrophobia. That night she couldn't sleep. By early the next morning, she had packed her bags.

"You can't do this," Margaret Houser argued.

"I've got to," Julie cried, her eyes red. "I'm not marrying Daniel. I'm marrying his mother."

"But the wedding's in five days."

"There will be no wedding," Julie replied.

"But Julie—"

"I know what you're going to say," she interrupted. "This is far more than pre-wedding jitters."

"Talk to Daniel, dear. Explain how you feel. At least do that much."

Julie went to Daniel's office. They met as he was on his way out the door.

"I need to talk to you." Her hands were clenched tightly in front of her.

Daniel glanced at his watch. "Honey, can't it wait?"

"No." She shook her head. "It can't wait."

Daniel led her into his office. "I know things have been hectic lately, but it's bound to get better once we're married. We'll have lots of time together then, I promise."

"That's just it, Daniel," Julie informed him. "We aren't going to be married."

Daniel inhaled sharply. "What do you mean?"

"I can't marry you, Daniel." She slipped the diamond off and held it out to him in the palm of her hand.

"Julie!" He was stunned. "I don't understand."

"I don't imagine you do." Julie bowed her head. "Do you remember last week when I suggested we drive across the border and get married? You laughed." Her voice wobbled. "But I was dead serious."

"Mother would never forgive us if we did something like that."

Julie released a short, harsh breath. "That's just the point. You wouldn't dream of crossing your mother, but it doesn't seem to matter what all this is doing to me."

"But she loves you."

"She loves the woman she's created. I'm slowly being molded into what she thinks is the picture of the right woman for you. I've had it. I can't take it anymore."

"Why don't you stand up to her?" Daniel said.

"Do you think I haven't tried? But no one listens to me. Not even you, Daniel. I'm…not sure how I feel about you anymore."

"Is that so?" He exhaled a sharp breath.

"That's right," Julie insisted huskily. "I want out. Here." Again she tried to return the ring.

For an agonizing moment Daniel stared at her and then the ring. Then he stalked to the far side of the room and looked out the window, his back to her. "Keep it."

"But Daniel," she pleaded.

"I said keep it," he grated. When he turned around, his mouth was a rigid line. The piercing dark eyes clouded with pain. "Now get out of my life and stay out."

That had been three years ago. She'd driven to her aunt's home in California. Every night since, she'd wondered she'd done the right thing.

Now she'd come back to ask Daniel's and Mrs. Van Deen's forgiveness. She wouldn't leave without it.

*

THE NEXT morning Julie stood inside the Inland Empire foyer and waited until Daniel entered the building. She longed to talk to him.

When she saw him advance toward the elevator, she moved behind him so that when the metal doors opened she could enter, too. But there were two other people inside.

If Daniel was aware of her presence he refused to react. But Julie had never been more aware of anyone in her life. Daniel's tall, handsome figure, looming beside her, seemed to fill the elevator. The years had been good to him. He'd been boyishly good-looking three years ago; now he was devastating.

The two strangers exited on the fifth floor and a surprised Julie found herself alone with Daniel. This was exactly what she'd planned, yet her tongue felt uncooperative.

"Hello, Daniel," she managed, but he ignored her, staring straight ahead.

"We need to talk." Her voice was a whisper.

Silence.

Gently she laid her hand on his forearm. But the hopelessness of the situation overwhelmed her. As stinging tears filled her eyes, the tall figure became a watery blur, and Julie dropped her hand. The elevator stopped and he left. Daniel had refused to look at her.

WHEN JULIE woke Saturday morning the sun was shining and the early spring day was much too beautiful to spend indoors. She recalled how Daniel's mother loved to work in her flower garden. Clara Van Deen had grown the most gorgeous irises.

Julie's intention had been to drive to the paint store, but

instead she found herself on the street that led to Clara's house.

She pulled to a stop across the street and stared at the lovely two-story home with its landscaped front yard. A fancy sports car was parked in the driveway. Julie debated whether she should gather her courage and approach Mrs. Van Deen.

But no. Now wasn't the time. Not when she was dressed in jeans and a sweatshirt. When she faced Mrs. Van Deen she would need to look and feel her best. She shifted gears and headed for the shopping center.

The paint she chose for the living room was an antique white that was sure to cheer the drab room. She actually looked forward to spending a quiet afternoon painting.

First she took down the drapes and carefully laid them across the back of the sofa. Intent on spreading out newspapers, she jerked upright as the sound of the doorbell caught her off guard.

Daniel's tall figure filled the doorway. The look on his face sent a cold shaft of apprehension through her.

"Leave my mother alone."

Julie stared at him.

"I saw you this morning parked in front of her house. Stay away, Julie, I'm warning you."

Inwardly Julie flinched, but she jutted her chin out in a gesture of defiance. "Daniel, I've come a thousand miles to talk to you and your mother."

"Then you've wasted your time. Neither of us care to see you."

Levelly, Julie met his gaze. "I've come to make amends."

"Amends? Do you think you could ever undo the humiliation I suffered when you walked out?"

"I'd like to try. A thousand times I've regretted—"

"Regretted." He turned to face her. "I used to dream you'd say that to me. Now that you have, it means nothing.

I look at you and I don't feel a thing. You came back to apologize, then fine, you've made your peace. Just don't go to my mother, bringing up the past. She has no desire to see you. Whatever you and I shared is over and done with."

Julie closed her eyes at the sting in his voice. She wouldn't be easily swayed from her goal. "Oh, Daniel," she whispered. "You don't mean that."

"Does that bother you?" he asked. "You taught me a lot of things. I've blocked you from my mind, but unfortunately my mother has never been the same. I can't forgive you for what you've done to her."

"But that's the reason I've come back," she said.

He looked right through her and Julie knew he was lost to another world.

Impatiently he reiterated, "Leave my mother alone. Do you understand?"

"I'm sorry." Julie hung her head. "I promise not to do anything to hurt her. Can you trust me for that, at least?"

"I shouldn't." A nerve moved in his jaw and without another word, he turned and walked out of the apartment.

Numb, Julie stood exactly where she was for what could have been a split second or a half hour. Her hands felt moist with nervous perspiration. Forcing herself into action, she opened the first gallon of paint.

Julie worked until well past midnight. When she finished, the old room was barely recognizable. The feeling of accomplishment helped lift her heavy heart. Had she thought confronting Daniel and his mother would be easy? No. She'd known what to expect.

As she worked, Julie remembered Daniel's words. Maybe contacting Clara Van Deen now could do more harm than good.

Hours later, lying in bed, Julie couldn't let the thought go. Although she was physically exhausted, she hadn't been able to sleep. Pounding her pillow, Julie rolled over and faced the wall.

Write her.

The idea flashed through her mind like a laser beam. Instantly, Julie sat up and threw back the covers and searched for a pen and pad.

A WEEK PASSED before she heard from the older woman. Her fingers shook as she took the single sheet of stationery from its envelope.

It read simply: Saturday at four.

"That's today." Julie spoke out loud and shot a look at the kitchen clock. Just after one. She had only three hours to prepare herself. Mrs. Van Deen had done that deliberately, hoping to catch her off guard. But Julie was prepared for this confrontation.

She chose a simple business suit of blue gabardine, the same one she'd worn to the job interview with Mr. Barrett. She wanted to show Mrs. Van Deen that she wasn't an awkward teenager any longer. At precisely four o'clock, Julie pulled into the curved driveway.

The doorbell was answered by Mrs. Batten, the elderly cook who had been with the family for years. If she recognized Julie, she said nothing.

The interior of the house hadn't changed. To her left was the salon, as Mrs. Van Deen called it. At one time Julie had thought of it as a torture chamber. To her right was a massive dining room.

"This way," Mrs. Batten instructed, and she was led through the house to the back garden.

"You may wait here." She gestured to a heavy cast-iron chair separated from an identical one by a small table.

Fifteen minutes passed and still Julie sat alone. Then the sound of soft footsteps behind her caused her to tense.

"Hello, Julie." The words were low and trembling.

Julie stood. Daniel's mother was frail and obviously

weak. She leaned heavily upon a cane, yet she was elegant as ever, her hair completely white now. She was far thinner than Julie remembered.

"Sit down." Mrs. Van Deen motioned, and took the seat opposite her. "To say I was surprised to receive your letter would be an understatement."

"I imagine it was."

"Does Daniel know you're back?"

She nodded. "We work in the same building."

"You have a Wichita address?"

"Yes, I moved back." Her voice quavered slightly.

"Why?"

"Because—I wanted to make amends, and I didn't think I could do that if I flew in for a weekend."

"That was wise, dear."

"I came because I deeply regret my actions. I—"

"Do you still love my son?" Clara Van Deen asked.

"Yes," she admitted. "Yes, I do, but I…"

"But you hate me?"

"Oh, no. The only person I've hated over the years was myself."

The old woman's smile was wan. "There comes a time in a woman's life when she can look at things more clearly. In my life it comes as I face death. As you've probably guessed, I'm not well."

Tears filled Julie's eyes. She hadn't expected Daniel's mother to be kind or understanding.

"There's no need to cry. I've lived a full life, but my heart is weak and I can't do much of anything these days. Ill health helps one gain perspective."

"Then you do forgive me?" Julie whispered.

Her hand tightened around the cane. "No."

Julie closed her eyes to the disappointment and hurt. "What can I do?" she asked softly.

"I want you to forgive me." Daniel's mother reached across and patted Julie's hand. "I was the reason you left.

All these years I've buried that guilt deep in my heart. I behaved like an interfering old woman.''

Julie noticed a tear slide down the weathered cheek, followed by several more. Her own face was moist.

"We've both been fools."

"But there's no fool like an old one." Clara Van Deen wiped her cheek. She looked pale and tired, but a radiance came from her eyes.

As if on cue, Mrs. Batten carried in a silver tray with a coffeepot and two china cups.

"Tell me what you've done with yourself all this time." Mrs. Van Deen looked genuinely interested.

"I went to school for a while in California and lived with my aunt. Later my mother joined me and I got a job with a bank. Then with a trust company. Nothing very exciting."

"What about men?"

"I...dated some."

"Anyone seriously?"

Julie shook her head. "No one. What about Daniel?"

The former radiance dimmed. "He never tells me."

"He's changed."

"Yes, he has. And not for the good, I fear. He's an intense young man. Some days he reminds me of..." She paused.

"Mrs. Van Deen, are you feeling all right?"

"I'm fine, child. You're beginning to sound like Daniel. And please, call me Clara."

Even when engaged to Daniel, Julie had never had that privilege. It was a confirmation of their new understanding.

"All right, Clara."

"I do have regrets." The older woman looked far away. "I would so have liked to hold a grandchild."

Julie took a sip of her coffee.

"I know what it's cost you to come to me," she continued. "You have far more character than I gave you credit—'' The woman's tired eyes widened and she paused. ''I'm sorry, Julie, but I'm not feeling well.'' The older woman's hand covered her heart. ''I think you should call Mrs. Batten.''

Panic filled Julie. Daniel's mother was a lot more than weak and unwell. ''Mrs. Batten,'' she cried as she ran toward the kitchen. ''Call Medic One and tell them to hurry.''

THE HOSPITAL was a whirlwind of activity when Julie arrived. Daniel was pacing the small waiting area. He turned toward her.

''Don't ask me to leave,'' she pleaded.

He rammed his fingers through his hair. ''The ambulance driver told me you were responsible for calling them in time to save her life.''

Julie didn't answer. Her arms cradled her stomach as she paced the enclosure with him. They didn't speak. They didn't touch. But Julie couldn't remember a closer communication with anyone.

The whole universe seemed to halt when the doctor stepped into the room. ''She's resting comfortably,'' he announced.

''Thank God,'' Daniel said.

''Your mother's a stubborn woman. She insists on seeing both of you. But only take a minute.''

Julie glanced at Daniel. ''You go.''

''Both,'' the doctor repeated.

Clara Van Deen looked as pale as the sheets she was lying against in the intensive care unit.

She opened her eyes and attempted to smile. ''My dears,'' she began, ''I'm so sorry to cause you all this worry.''

''Rest, Mother,'' Daniel whispered.

''Not yet.'' She fluttered her eyes open. ''Julie, you said you'd do anything to gain my forgiveness?''

''Yes.''

"And Daniel, will you do one last thing for me?"

"Anything, you know that."

The tired old eyes closed and opened again. "My dears, won't you please marry...for my sake?"

JULIE WOKE in the gray light of early morning. She hadn't slept well and imagined Daniel hadn't, either. They'd hardly spoken as they left the hospital. The line that was Daniel's mouth had revealed his feelings in the matter of any marriage between them. Words had not been necessary.

When she'd arrived home Julie had undressed and made herself a cup of strong coffee. Her thoughts were troubled and confused. Clara was so different from what she'd imagined. Julie had braced herself for a confrontation, but she'd discovered a sick, gentle woman with many regrets. Deep within her, Julie longed to ease Clara's mind. She lay facing death. She needed the assurance that her son would be happy.

But Daniel resented her too much.

Yet she loved him, had loved him when she ran away all those years ago and, if possible, loved him even more now. Every time she looked at him, her heart ached with that love. Closing her eyes, Julie reminded herself over and over again of why she'd returned to Wichita.

EVEN AT midmorning the hospital parking lot was full. Although Julie hadn't reached a decision, she had peace in her heart. She'd talk to Daniel, and together they would decide what to do.

Daniel was in the waiting area outside the intensive care unit. He glanced up as Julie approached.

"Good morning," she said. "How's Clara?"

"My mother," he returned, "is resting comfortably."

Julie took the seat opposite. "Can we talk?" Sitting on the edge of the cushion, Julie leaned forward.

"The doctor's with her now."

"Daniel." Julie found it hard to speak. "What are we going to do?"

His laughter was mirthless. "What do you mean, *do?* My mother didn't know what she was saying. They'd given her so many drugs yesterday she wasn't thinking straight. Today she won't remember."

Julie didn't believe that any more than Daniel did, but clearly he wished to avoid the issue.

They both looked up expectantly when the doctor entered the room.

"How is she?" Daniel spoke first.

"She's incredibly weak, but better than we expected." The doctor paused to study them both. "Your mother seems to have decided she wants to live. And since she's come this far the possibilities of her making a complete recovery are good."

Julie bit her lip to keep from crying out with relief.

"She's resting now and both of you should do the same."

Daniel nodded. "I didn't want to leave until I was sure she was going to be all right."

The doctor shook his head. "I don't know what she said to you last night, but it has made the world of difference in her attitude. From that moment on, she started to recover."

Julie's eyes clashed with Daniel's.

"Now go home and get some rest. There's nothing you can do here. I'll phone you if there's any change."

"Thank you, Doctor," Daniel said.

"Can I drop you off at your place?" Julie asked quietly. Daniel didn't look as if he should drive.

He shook his head. "No."

"You'll phone me if you hear anything?"

"Yes. Now please go. I'm going to stay here a little longer."

Julie nodded, then walked down the corridor and outside to her car.

Once she was home, she stretched out on the sofa, relieved that some of her tension had dissipated. She felt her body relax and her mind still. The next thing she knew someone was knocking on the door.

Julie glanced at her wristwatch, shocked to see that it was after two. She must have dozed off.

"Just a minute," she called. "Who is it?" she asked before releasing the lock.

"Daniel," came the taut reply.

Julie threw open the door. "Is she all right?"

"She's doing remarkably well."

"Thank God," Julie whispered.

"I do," Daniel murmured. "Did I wake you?"

Julie nodded. "It's a good thing you did."

"They let me see her for a few minutes." He stood uneasily in the center of the room.

"And?" Julie prompted.

"She asked when we were planning to have the wedding."

Julie sat down. "I was afraid of that."

Daniel remained standing. "The head nurse told me she firmly believed the fact you and I are going to be married was what kept mother alive last night."

"And," Julie finished for him, "you're afraid telling her otherwise could kill her."

"I talked to the doctor again. He explained that if Mother can grow strong enough in the next few months, heart surgery might correct her condition."

"That's wonderful news."

The hard look in his dark eyes raked over her. "Yes, in some ways it's given me reason to hope. But in others..." He shook his head. "Why did you come back, Julie? Why couldn't you have left well enough alone?"

"I already explained," she answered quietly. "I need

your forgiveness. I won't leave until I've accomplished that.''

"You have a long wait."

"I didn't expect it to be easy."

He muttered a curse under his breath. "A marriage between us would never work. The possibility of a life together ended when you left. But my mother's health—''

"Daniel," she said. "You may find this hard to believe, but I never stopped loving you."

His eyes hardened. "If you had loved me, you would never have walked out. You don't know what it is to love, Julie."

Her mouth trembled with the effort to restrain stinging tears. "If you honestly believe that, there's no point in having this discussion." Abruptly she stood, but he gripped her arm.

"You're marrying me, Julie, as soon as I can make the arrangements."

"I'd be crazy to marry a man like you."

His laughter was harsh. "Can you carry the guilt of my mother's death on your shoulders? Are you ready to face that, Julie? Or don't you care?"

Julie pulled herself free from his grip. "Daniel," she pleaded, "marriage is sacred."

"Not in this instance. It'll be one of convenience."

"Will it remain that way?" Her eyes sought his.

His gaze didn't flicker. "I couldn't touch you."

Julie struggled not to reveal the hurt. It shouldn't matter to her. The way he felt about her, Julie didn't want Daniel to make love to her. "And after your mother…" She couldn't speak of the possibility of Clara's death.

"You will be free to go, no strings attached. An annulment will be fairly simple."

"I don't know," Julie said. "I need time to think."

"No," Daniel said. "I need to know now."

In some ways he was right. What choice did she have?

"All right, Daniel, I'll marry you, but only for your mother's sake."

Unfastening the chain from around her neck, Julie handed him her original engagement ring.

"You kept it?" He sounded shocked.

Julie gave him a gentle smile. "I couldn't bear to part with it. I wore it all these years. Close to my heart."

"It must have given you a sense of triumph to have kept it. To be honest, I'm surprised there's only one. In three years I would have expected you to add at least that many more."

"No," she answered, lowering her gaze, "there was never anyone but you."

"You don't expect me to believe that, do you?"

"It doesn't matter what you believe."

"Keep the ring around your neck. It represented a lot of devotion I don't have now. I'll buy another one."

"If that's what you want," Julie whispered.

"I'll make the arrangements and get back to you with the details."

"Fine."

Daniel left and she shut the door after him. Julie's legs trembled as she made her way to the couch. She took a deep breath to steady her hands, then refastened the diamond necklace. The familiar weight around her neck calmed her.

"I'm once again about to become Mrs. Daniel Van Deen," she uttered. "But this time he doesn't love me." Julie knew there was only one way she could live with their arrangement—she had to ignite his former feelings. But how?

JULIE'S MOTHER was shocked but pleased, and planned to fly in for the wedding. Unfortunately Margaret Houser had to get back for volunteer work the next day. Julie was relieved that her mother's stay would be cut short. She wasn't

sure how effectively she could act out the role of a happy
bride, but of one thing she was certain: right or wrong, she
wouldn't walk out on Daniel a second time.

Daniel met Julie and her mother at the church door. His
eyes roamed over the white street-length dress Julie had
chosen and something unreadable flickered across his face.

His casual "Are you ready?" stirred the sense that she
was making a terrible mistake, but Julie decided to ignore
it.

The ceremony was short. Daniel's steady voice responded to the minister's instructions as if the words held
no meaning for him. In contrast, Julie's strained speech
wobbled uncontrollably.

Daniel glanced at her when she pledged her love and a
glint of challenge entered his gaze.

Her fingers trembled slightly as he slipped a plain gold
band on her slim finger. The simplicity of the ring suited
her, but she was sure Daniel had chosen something so plain
as a contrast to the beautiful diamond. Julie was confident
the contrast didn't stop there.

Julie's mother hugged them both, her eyes shining. All
three rode to the hospital together and were allowed a short
visit with Daniel's mother.

Clara Van Deen smiled as a tear of happiness slipped
from the corner of her eye.

"Trust me, Julie," she whispered. "Things will work
out."

Julie nodded, smiling feebly as she kissed the wrinkled
brow.

From the hospital, Daniel and Julie drove her mother to
the airport. Margaret Houser insisted on paying for everyone's lunch before her plane arrived. If she noticed the
silence between the groom and bride, she said nothing.

Julie would have liked to visit longer with her mother,
but Daniel was clearly in a hurry and after a few abrupt
words, he ushered Julie back to the car.

Neither spoke again until Daniel had parked at his condominium, located in Wichita's most prestigious downtown area. The tiled entryway led to a sunken living room carpeted in a plush brown pile. Two huge picture windows overlooked the skyline and Julie paused to admire the fantastic view from fifteen floors up.

Daniel moved around her and briskly delivered her suitcase to what was apparently to be her bedroom. He stopped outside the door in the wide hallway.

"This is your room," he called abruptly, and a glance inside confirmed that this had been a guest room. Fitting, Julie realized, since she was little more than an unwelcome guest in Daniel's life.

*

"MARRIED LIFE doesn't seem to agree with you," Sherry commented, watching Julie work.

"What do you mean?" Julie knew she wasn't doing a good job of hiding her feelings. Another week had passed and just when she thought the tension was lessening between her and Daniel something would happen to set them back. They hardly spoke in the mornings. Even during the drive downtown he was strangely quiet. In the evenings they visited his mother, came home and ate dinner. Then he'd hole up in his den. Sometimes Julie wondered if he was aware of her at all. He treated her more like a roommate than a wife.

"Maybe I should keep quiet," Sherry continued, "but you don't have the look of a happy bride."

Julie bit her lip. "I don't feel much like a bride."

"But why?"

A tear traced a wet trail down Julie's pale cheek. "Daniel's busy right now. I hardly see him."

Sherry rolled her chair close to Julie's and handed her friend a tissue. "Believe me," she said, "I know that feeling well. That's how all my problems with Andy started. He worked so many long hours that we didn't have time to be a couple anymore. Eventually we drifted apart. It got to be that he was home so little that I'd been gone a week before he even knew I was missing.''

Julie tried to laugh but just then their employer came out of his office. He started to say something before noticing Julie blowing her nose. He paused and quickly retreated. The two women broke into helpless giggles.

Ten minutes later, Mr. Barrett returned. ''I was wondering….'' he said, ''would you two like to take an extra half hour for lunch today? It's been a hectic week.''

''We'd love it. Right, Julie?'' Sherry winked.

The long lunch with Sherry proved to be just the tonic Julie needed to raise her sagging spirits.

''You know,'' Sherry said between bites of her salad, ''if I had to do it all over I'd make it so Andy never wanted to leave the house again.''

Julie stirred her clam chowder without much interest. ''How do you mean?''

''Think about it.'' Sherry's eyes sparkled. ''We're both reasonably attractive women. There are ways for a wife to keep a husband home nights.'' Demurely she lowered her thick lashes. ''Subtle ways, of course.''

''Of course,'' Julie repeated, her thoughts spinning. Sherry didn't know the details of her problems with Daniel, but her co-worker was amazingly astute.

As the day progressed, Julie gave more thought to Daniel's actions. In the weeks since their wedding, Daniel had only touched and kissed her a few times and yet she'd seen the desire in his eyes. He wanted her. He spent the evenings avoiding her for fear of what would happen. His male pride was punishing them both.

A secret smile touched Julie's eyes as she recalled the pearly white satin nightgown she'd recently admired in a department store window. Since she had a long lunch hour she could walk across the street and buy it. Perhaps she could lure her husband to her bed without injuring either of their sensitive egos. The more she contemplated such an action, the more confident she became.

After work that evening Julie and Daniel drove silently to the hospital. Mrs. Van Deen was sitting up in bed and smiled warmly, holding out her hand to Julie.

"My dears," she murmured, "it's so good to see you."

"Mother." Daniel kissed her wrinkled cheek and held Julie close to his side.

"Julie, you're looking especially pretty."

A smile touched Daniel's eyes. "She certainly does," he said.

"How are you feeling?" Julie centered her attention on Clara.

"Better," she said with a sigh. "The doctor said he'd never seen a woman make a swifter recovery. But I told him I have something to live for now. My son has the wife he's always wanted and I shall soon have the grandchildren I've dreamed about holding.

"My grandchild will have the bluest eyes," she continued, oblivious to the tension in the room. "My husband's eyes were so blue I swear they were deeper than any sea. I wish you'd known him, Julie," she continued. "He would have loved you just as I do. He was a fine man."

"I'm sure he was," Julie replied.

"A lot like Daniel."

Julie glanced up at her husband; her eyes were captured by the warmth of his look. Clara continued reminiscing about her life with August Van Deen.

When Julie and Daniel returned to the condominium that evening, she changed clothes while dinner was cooking. In tight navy blue cords and a thin sweater that outlined the ripe fullness of her breasts, she refreshed her makeup and dabbed on Daniel's favorite perfume, then returned to finish preparing dinner.

Daniel looked surprised as he joined her in the kitchen.

"I didn't want to spill anything on my dress," she told him, hiding a smile.

He nodded, but he couldn't seem to keep his eyes off her as she deftly moved around the tiny kitchen.

He didn't talk much while they ate, but that wasn't unusual. Perhaps Julie was reading too much into his actions. After so many years of living alone he could simply prefer to keep his thoughts to himself.

With seduction plots brewing in her head, she placed her plate in the dishwasher.

"I thought I was doing dishes."

"There are only a few things."

"Hey, we made a deal. When you cook, I wash the dishes," he said. "Now scoot."

Julie sat watching television, but her mind was not on the situation comedy.

Daniel worked in the kitchen, but several times she felt his eyes rest on her.

"A penny for your thoughts," he said, bringing her a cup of fresh coffee.

"You wouldn't want to know," she teased. "You'd run in the opposite direction."

"That sounds interesting."

"I promise you it is."

Daniel surprised her by sitting beside her. "Julie." He muted the television. "Can we talk a minute?"

"Sure." She turned toward him.

"I haven't been the best of company lately."

"There's no need to apologize," she told him. "You've been working yourself half to death this last month." Crossing her legs, Julie leaned back. "And then this evening your mother started talking about grandchildren and neither one of us has the courage to tell her we aren't sharing a bed." It was on the tip of her tongue to admit how much she wanted that to change, how much she longed to be his wife in the full sense of the word and give life to his children.

"Julie, listen." His voice was filled with emotion.

The phone rang in the kitchen.

"I'll get it," Julie volunteered. Whoever it was, she'd get rid of him in a hurry. For the first time Julie felt as if they were making giant strides in their marriage. "Hello," she said.

"Who's this?" the husky female voice returned.

"Julie Van Deen," she answered.

"So it's true," came the hushed words.

"And you're…?" Julie squared her shoulders.

"Kali Morgan," the woman answered.

An icy chill raced up Julie's spine. "Would you like to talk to Daniel?"

Kali paused. "No. Just…give him my best…to you both."

"Thank you." Julie replaced the phone.

"Who was it?" Daniel was looking at her.

Twisting around, Julie clasped her hands together behind her back.

"Someone named Kali Morgan who obviously didn't know you had a wife."

Slowly Daniel took a step toward her. "Julie, don't look at me like that."

Paralysis gripped her throat as she moved down the hall. The bag containing her lovely new nightgown rested on her bed. She stared at it in disbelief. Only minutes before she'd plotted to seduce her husband.

Daniel followed her. "Julie, be reasonable. Surely you didn't think I've lived the last few years like a priest."

Everything went incredibly still as hot tears filled her eyes. "For three years my heart grieved for you until I couldn't take it anymore…and I came back be-cause…facing your bitterness was easier than trying to for-get you."

''Julie.'' His voice took on a soft, pleading quality. ''Kali and I had been dating for several months,'' he said. ''But she's in the past. I haven't touched her since the day I saw you in the elevator.''

''Touched her,'' Julie repeated. ''Is that supposed to reassure me? You haven't touched me, either!''

''What did you expect me to do the rest of my life?'' Daniel shouted. ''You walked out on me!''

Julie raked her eyes over him with open disdain. ''You didn't tell her we were married!''

''Don't tell me that there hasn't been anyone in—''

''Yes,'' she shouted. ''I seldom dated. You were the only man I could ever love.''

''Julie,'' he pleaded softly, a gentle hand on each of her shoulders.

''Don't touch me,'' she shouted, and shrugged to break his light hold. ''You must find me incredibly stupid to have cherished the belief you still care.''

He pulled her into his arms. ''You're going to listen to me, Julie. Perhaps for the first time since we met, we're going to have an honest discussion.''

Julie was in no mood to be reasonable. ''No,'' she cried. Grabbing the package from her bed, she shoved it at him. ''Here. Once I'm gone you might find this useful for one of your other women.'' With that she slammed the door, and collapsed into tears.

DANIEL WAS already in his den when Julie returned the next evening. Clara had let it slip that her son had been by earlier to visit. Her astute mother-in-law studied the dark shadows under Julie's eyes, but didn't comment. Julie was grateful.

Hanging up her jacket, she headed for the kitchen. A package of veal cutlets rested on the countertop.

''I thought it was my turn to cook,'' Daniel said heavily from behind her.

"All right," she murmured. "But I'm not very hungry. I think I'll lie down for a while."

"Okay," he said. "I'll call you when dinner's ready."

"Fine." They were treating each other like polite strangers. Worse. They seemed afraid even to look at each other.

It seemed only minutes later when Daniel knocked softly against the open bedroom door. "Dinner's ready."

She toyed with the idea of telling him she wasn't feeling well, but decided it was better to face him. Things couldn't get much worse.

The table was already set when Julie pulled out the chair and sat. Daniel joined her.

"Your mother looked better tonight."

Daniel nodded. "Her physician says she's healthy enough for surgery. He wants to schedule it soon."

"That's marvelous." Julie smiled, then looked away.

Five minutes passed and neither spoke. Julie looked out the window and Daniel's gaze followed. "It looks like rain."

Julie nodded. Since it seemed they had no shared interests, there was little to discuss beyond his mother and the weather.

Another awkward silence filled the kitchen until Julie stood and started to load the dishwasher.

That took all of ten minutes. The hum of the dishwasher followed her into the hallway. Daniel had disappeared to his den and Julie doubted that she'd be seeing him again that evening.

Deciding to read, she returned to her room. As she turned, a glimmer of satin caught her attention. Setting the book down, she discovered that the lovely, alluring gown she'd shoved at Daniel was hanging in her closet. She touched the silky smoothness as tears jammed her throat. She'd so wanted things to be different.

"Julie." Daniel spoke from outside her room. "Are you all right?"

Angrily she turned on him. "I'm wonderful. Just leave me alone." And she closed the door.

For a stunned moment nothing happened. Then her door was knocked open with such force that it was a wonder it wasn't ripped from the wall.

Julie gasped as Daniel marched in and hauled her into his arms.

"Put me down," she cried, kicking, but her efforts only made him tighten his grip.

"You're my wife, Julie Van Deen. And I'm tired of playing a game in which I am the loser." With that he carried her to his bedroom, slamming the door closed with his foot.

Furiously Julie wiped the tears from her face. "You didn't even tell Kali you were married," she shouted.

"I couldn't," he shouted back. "She was in England on a business trip. Anyway, we're married. What the hell has she got to do with us now?"

"Nothing," she whispered, laughing softly. "Nothing at all."

"What's so amusing?" he barked, and sank onto the side of his bed, his hold on her loosening.

"You wouldn't understand," she murmured. "Never mind." Gently she covered his mouth with hers.

"Julie," he groaned, his hands folding her in his embrace.

"Are you really tired of playing games?" she asked, spreading a series of sweet kisses over his face. Her eager lips sought his temple and nose, slowly progressing downward toward his mouth, teasing him with short, playful kisses along the way.

"Yes," he moaned, directing her lips to his. "Oh, yes."

A pervading warmth flowed through her. "Oh, Daniel, what took you so long?"

Slowly his hands slid across her breasts as he began unfastening the tiny buttons of her blouse. All the while his mouth moved over hers in eager passion. Frustrated, he abandoned the effort and broke the kiss long enough to try to pull the blouse over her head.

Breathless and smiling softly, Julie stopped him. "You've waited a whole month for me. Another thirty seconds shouldn't matter."

As she freed her blouse, Daniel cupped the soft mounds of her breasts and buried his face in the fragile hollow of her throat. "I couldn't live another month like the last one," he told her. "I couldn't sleep knowing you were just down the hall. Every time I closed my eyes all I could see was you. The only thing that helped was working until I was ready to drop."

"Oh, love, and I wanted you so much." Sliding her hands up and down his muscled shoulders, she felt the coiled tension ease out of him.

Hungrily he devoured her mouth. "You're my wife, Julie, the way you were always meant to be."

"I know, love, I know." Her heart singing, Julie gave herself to the only man she had ever loved.

"WAKE UP, sleepyhead," Daniel whispered. "It's morning."

"Already?" Julie groaned, resting her head in the crook of his arm. Her eyes refused to open.

"Are you happy?" Daniel asked, kissing the crown of her head.

"Oh, yes."

"Me, too." In long soothing movements, he stroked her bare arm. "I never stopped loving you, Julie. For a time I convinced myself I hated you. But the day I saw you in the elevator, I knew I'd been fooling myself. One look and I realized I'd never love another woman the way I love you."

Raising her head, Julie rolled onto her stomach and kissed him with infinite sweetness.

The hunger of his response surprised her. Quickly he

altered their positions so that Julie was on her back looking up at him. His eyes burned into hers.

"Daniel," she protested, "we'll be late for work."

"Yes, we will," he agreed. "Very late."

AN HOUR LATER, while Julie dressed, Daniel fried their eggs, humming as he worked.

"My, you're in a good mood this morning," she teased, sliding her arms around his middle.

Daniel chuckled. "And with good reason." He pulled her into his arms, kissing her. "I love you."

Her eyes drank in the tenderness in his expression as she slowly nodded. "I know."

"I think it's time we took that diamond ring and put it on your finger, where it belongs," he told her gently. She unhooked the necklace and handed the ring to Daniel. He slid the solitaire onto her finger with a solemnness that told her how seriously he took his vows. "I wanted you the minute the minister pronounced us man and wife," he admitted.

"And I thought—"

"I know what you thought," he said, taking her back into his embrace. "It was exactly what I wanted you to believe. My ego had suffered enough. I couldn't tolerate it if you knew how badly I wanted to make love to you then."

"Really?" she asked, her eyes sparkling.

"Yes, darling," Daniel said, and when he pulled her into his embrace, Julie knew she was finally his wife in every way.

THE WORKDAYS flew by and after a wonderful weekend spent enjoying each other's company and visiting Clara, Julie and Daniel were back at the hospital, awaiting the results of his mother's heart surgery.

Daniel paced the waiting room as Julie sat attempting to

read. Repeatedly, her concentration wandered and she glanced at her wristwatch.

"What time is it?" Daniel inquired.

What he really wanted to know, Julie realized, was how much longer it would be. The doctor had assured them the procedure would take at least five hours.

"Anytime now," Julie answered softly. They'd been in the waiting room most of the day. A nurse came at noon and suggested they have lunch. But neither was hungry.

Daniel took the seat beside her and reached for her hand. "Have I told you how much I love you?" His eyes filled with tenderness.

Before Julie could answer, the doctor, clad in a green surgical gown, walked into the room. He looked as exhausted as she felt. Automatically, both Julie and Daniel stood.

"Your mother did amazingly well," the doctor began. "Her chances appear to be excellent."

Julie smiled brightly at her husband, feeling as if the weight of the world had been lifted from her back.

"Can we see her?" Daniel inquired.

"Yes, but only for a few minutes. You both can go in. She'll be in intensive care for a few days, then if everything goes well, on the surgical floor."

"How long will it be before she can come home?"

The doctor shook his head. "Hard to say. As soon as two weeks, or as long as a month."

"Thank you, Doctor." Julie smiled. "Thank you very much."

With their hands linked, Julie and Daniel were led into the intensive care area.

Clara Van Deen's eyes fluttered open and she attempted to speak, but the words were slurred. She tried to lift one hand, but it was taped to a board to hold the IV in place.

Lovingly Daniel laid his hand over his mother's.

"I'm afraid I'm going to have to ask you to leave," the

nurse requested softly a couple of minutes later. "You're welcome to come back tomorrow, but for now Mrs. Van Deen needs to rest."

Julie thanked the nurse and watched an expression of tenderness move across her husband's face.

"We'll be back, Mother," he whispered softly.

The air outside the hospital felt fresh and clean. Julie paused to inhale several deep breaths before getting in the car. She was exhausted. With her head resting against the back of the seat, she closed her eyes as Daniel drove the short distance home.

"Julie. Wake up. We're home."

"My goodness, I don't know why I should be so tired."

"We didn't get much sleep last night," he reminded her with a roguish grin. "And the way I feel right now we may not tonight, either."

Daniel led her directly into the bedroom. "I want you to take a nice long nap and when you're rested Mother has ordered us to have a night on the town. We had a long talk yesterday, and she suggested that after we spent today at the hospital we should go out."

"Aren't you going to rest?" Julie wanted to know.

"Honey, if I crawl into that bed with you it won't be to sleep." He brushed the hair from her temple. "Actually I've got some papers to go over. That should take an hour or two. Just enough time for you to catch up on some sleep."

The next thing she knew, Daniel was beside her, holding her close.

"Is it time to get ready for dinner?" she muttered.

"I think breakfast is more in order."

"Breakfast?" Her lashes flew up. "I couldn't have slept through the night. Could I?"

"I paraded a marching band through here late yesterday afternoon and you wouldn't budge."

Wiping the sleep from her face, Julie sat up. "I can't believe I was dead to the world for fifteen hours or more."

"I imagine you're starved."

Strangely, she wasn't at first, but once she ate breakfast, she realized how famished she actually had been.

"I'm sorry I ruined your night."

Daniel looked up from his plate and smiled tenderly. He reached out and traced the delicate line of her jaw. "You didn't ruin anything," he whispered. "Do you know how beautiful you are in your sleep? I could have watched you for hours. In fact, I did."

Somewhat embarrassed, Julie shook her head.

"I lay awake last night, my heart full of love, and I realized I'm the luckiest man in the world."

"Yesterday was a day to think that. Your mother survived the surgery, and we've been given a second chance to build a solid marriage."

"Yes, we have," Daniel whispered, "a marriage to last a lifetime."

*

A WEEK AFTER the open-heart surgery, Clara Van Deen was sitting up in bed looking healthier than Julie could remember since returning to Wichita.

"I can't tell you how grateful I'll be to go home," she said. "Everyone's been wonderful here, but I do so miss my garden."

"And your garden misses you," Julie said with a wink to her husband.

"That's right, Mother." Daniel shook his head. "Weeds all the way up to my knees."

Clara grimaced. "I can't bear to think of what months of neglect have done to my precious yard."

Unable to continue the game any longer, Julie patted her

mother-in-law's hand reassuringly. "Your garden looks lovely. Now don't you fret."

"Thanks to Julie," Daniel inserted. "She spent a good portion of the weekend weeding."

"I should have been thinking of ways to torture a husband with a loose tongue," Julie admonished. "It was supposed to be a surprise."

"My dear, Julie. You didn't really?"

"She has the blisters to prove it," Daniel inserted.

"Daniel! I didn't know your mouth was so big."

He gently squeezed her shoulder. "All the better to kiss you with, my dear."

Julie tried to hide a smile. "It's times like these that I wonder what kind of family I married into."

"One that loves you," Clara replied. "Say, Julie, isn't it today you were meeting with—"

"No," she interrupted, warning her mother-in-law to say nothing more. Jim Patterson, a colleague of Daniel's, had let Julie know that Daniel's country club had voted him Man of the Year. She had shared the good news with Clara, who had clearly forgotten that the award was supposed to be a surprise.

Daniel made a show of glancing at his watch. "What's this about Julie meeting someone?"

"Nothing," Julie returned hastily.

"It's a surprise, son. Forgive an old woman, Julie."

"There's nothing to forgive."

"Will you two kindly let me know what's going on?"

"My lips are sealed," Julie taunted.

"Mine, too," Clara chimed in. "It's sometime this week, isn't it?"

Julie knew Clara was referring to her meeting with Jim. "Yes, over lunch. I'll let you know how everything goes." Jim wanted some details about Daniel for the skit they would perform on the award night.

On the way to the hospital parking lot, Daniel's expression altered from amused to concerned. "You're not going to tell me, are you?"

"Nope."

"At least let me know whom you're meeting with."

"Never." He looked so handsome that she couldn't resist stealing a kiss.

"What was that for?"

"Because I love you."

A brief look passed over his features. One so fleeting that Julie was almost sure she'd imagined it. But she hadn't. Daniel doubted her.

On the ride home, Julie was introspective. They'd traveled this way so many times over the past six weeks that sights along the way blended into one another.

"Daniel?" Julie sat upright.

"Hmm?"

"Take a right here," she directed. "There's a house on the corner that's for sale." They must have passed the place a thousand times. Julie had noted the Realtor's sign but now something about the house reached out to her.

Daniel eased to a stop at the tree-lined curb in front of a two-story Colonial home. The paint was peeling from the white exterior and several of the green shutters were hanging by a single hinge. "Julie," he groaned, "it doesn't even look like anyone lives there."

Julie glanced around at the neighboring homes. They were family oriented and well maintained. "All this place needs is a bit of tender, loving care."

"It's the neighborhood eyesore," Daniel said.

"I'd like to see the inside," Julie said, undeterred. Something told her this was the family home she'd been dreaming of.

THAT SAME evening they met with James Derek, the Realtor. "I'm afraid this place has been vacant for several months," he told them.

"What did I tell you?" Daniel whispered. "This isn't for us—"

Julie climbed out of the car. "But I like it. I like it very much."

"Julie," Daniel moaned as he joined her.

The entryway was small and led to an open stairway and a long mahogany banister that rounded at the top. To her right was a huge family living room and to her left a smaller room obviously meant as a library or a den. Dust covered everything and a musty smell permeated the house. The hardwood floors were badly in need of buffing.

The formal dining room had built-in china cabinets and a window seat. The kitchen was huge with a large eating area. The main level had two bedrooms and the upstairs had three more. The full basement was ideal for storage.

Desperately Julie hoped that Daniel could see the potential of the house. "It's perfect. Right down to the fenced backyard, patio and tree house."

"Perhaps you'd care to make a few comparisons with some other homes," James interjected.

Determined, Julie shook her head. "I wouldn't." Her eyes met Daniel's. She understood his doubts. This house would require weeks of expensive repairs, but the asking price was reasonable.

"In all fairness I feel you should be aware of several things."

The Realtor's voice seemed to fade into the background as Julie sauntered from one room to the next.

"Julie." Daniel found her and placed a hand on her shoulder. "I think we should go home and think this over before we make our final decision."

"What's there to decide? If we don't put down earnest money now, someone else will."

"That's highly unlikely, Mrs. Van Deen," James interrupted. "This place has been on the market for six months."

On the drive back to the Realtor's office it was all Julie could do to keep quiet. Then, before they climbed into their own car, Daniel and James scheduled a time to look at other houses.

Julie closed her car door and stared straight ahead.

"Why'd you set up another appointment?" she demanded.

"To look at houses—"

"But I've found the one I want," she declared. "Daniel, I love that house. Best of all it's only a few blocks from your mother's. It's got a den for you and..."

"The repair cost alone would be more than the value of the house. The roof's got to be replaced. There's dry rot in the basement."

"I don't care," Julie stated.

"I'm not going to fight with you about it. If we're going to buy a house then it's one we both agree on."

Julie had no argument. That house was everything she wanted. Hot tears blurred her vision. Something was definitely the matter with her lately. She couldn't believe she would cry over something as silly as a house.

THE DAY Clara Van Deen came home from the hospital was the happiest Julie could remember.

Although weak, the smile on her mother-in-law's face was reward enough for Julie's long hours in her much-loved garden.

Mrs. Batten arranged huge floral bouquets around the living room and cooked a meal of roast beef, potatoes and fresh strawberry shortcake.

Sitting with Clara on the patio, in the late-afternoon sun, Julie lifted her face to its golden rays.

"Is everything all right with you, dear?"

"Of course. What could possibly be wrong?"

Clara sipped tea from her delicate china cup. "I'm not

sure, but you haven't been yourself the last couple of weeks. Has this house business got you down?''

''Not really.'' Julie straightened. The question struck a raw nerve. ''Daniel and I have agreed to wait. There's no rush.''

''But there was one house you liked?''

Julie knew the smile of reassurance she gave her mother-in-law spoke more of disappointment than any confidence. ''We agreed to disagree.''

Clara didn't answer; her look was thoughtful. Daniel's look was almost identical when he unlocked the front door of the condo an hour later.

''Is something bothering you?'' Julie asked him.

Daniel smiled wryly. ''I thought we agreed not to take our disagreements to my mother?''

Julie blanched. Clara had spoken to Daniel about the house. ''We did,'' she admitted.

''Mother had a talk with me before we left.''

''I know what it sounds like,'' Julie cut in, ''but I didn't do anything more than mention it.''

A brooding silence followed and Julie watched as her husband's mouth thinned with impatience.

''If anything,'' she said, ''I think I should have a talk with your mother. She'll have to learn that although we love her dearly, she can't become involved in our lives to the point that she takes sides. Okay?''

''Definitely.''

Julie walked across the room, her arms cradling her middle in an instinctively protective action.

Daniel cleared his throat and came to stand behind her. ''I can see that this house issue could grow into a major problem.''

Julie shook her head. ''I won't let it. All I want is to be your wife. It doesn't matter where we live.''

He gathered her close. ''I've been giving the house you wanted considerable thought,'' he whispered.

"And?" It was difficult to maintain her poise.

"I think we should be able to come up with a compromise." He drew back, his hands linked at the small of her back as he smiled at her. "I'll buy it if you agree to quit your job."

"Quit my job?" Julie repeated. "You must be joking."

"That house is going to need extensive remodeling. Someone should be there to supervise the work."

Her wide, troubled eyes searched his face. "It isn't remodeling the house needs, but repairs, most of which will have to be done before we move in." Breaking from him, Julie crossed the room. "I've seen it in you several times, but didn't bring it up—"

"You're speaking in riddles," Daniel countered.

"The house isn't the real reason—"

"I want you to be my wife."

"And I'm not now?" she responded. "I enjoy my job." Her hand made a sweeping gesture. "I've seen it in your eyes, Daniel. You think I'm going to walk out on you again. It's almost as if you're waiting for it to happen."

"You're being ridiculous."

"Am I?" she asked softly.

"I saw you with Jim Patterson last week," Daniel announced harshly.

"And you immediately jumped to conclusions."

"No." He turned around and Julie noted the heavy lines of strain around his eyes. She'd known something was wrong for days.

"Will you tell me why you and Jim found it necessary to have lunch together?"

"I can't," she whispered. "But I'm asking you to trust me. Surely you don't believe Jim and I are involved in any way?"

"I've tried. A hundred times I've told myself that you must love me. You wouldn't have come back or married me if you didn't."

"I do love you," she cried. "What makes you think I would even look at another man?"

Daniel lowered his gaze and ran a hand over his weary eyes. "Sometimes I hate myself."

"You don't trust me."

His returning look confirmed her worst suspicions. A sob rose to her throat, but she forced it down. "I love you so much I could never think about another man—or leave you. How can I convince you of that?"

Daniel couldn't meet her eyes. "I don't know." He paced the carpet. "When I first saw you with Jim, I felt sick inside, then explosive. Even though I'd heard you joke with my mother about this meeting, I couldn't believe I'd see my wife and a good friend together. I expected to wake up and find you gone."

"You actually believe that I'd run away with Jim Patterson?"

"Why not? You ran away from me before."

Julie closed her eyes. "I haven't even thought about anyone else since I moved to Wichita."

"But you had lunch with my friend. And you won't tell me why you met him." He scowled.

"No. I'm asking you to trust me."

His dark eyes narrowed. "I'm trying. Lord knows I want to, but I don't know if I can," he whispered.

"JULIE, YOU don't look as if you slept at all last night," Sherry told Julie the following morning.

"I didn't."

"Why not?"

Julie had felt the weight of the world pressing down on her when they'd gone to bed after their discussion. Daniel stayed on his side of the mattress, but he could have been on the other side of the world for all the warmth and comfort they shared.

"What would you think if I told you that Daniel wants me to quit my job?" she finally asked.

"Does he?" Sherry's eyes rounded with concern.

"Let's make this a hypothetical question."

Julie wondered if, without knowing the background of her relationship with Daniel, Sherry would read the same meaning into his behavior.

"Well," Sherry said, "my guess is that he's insecure about something. But it's obvious to anyone how much you love him."

"I only wish Daniel recognized that."

"You're not going to quit working, are you?" Sherry asked. "I'd miss your friendship."

"No, I'm not going to do it. How's everything between you and Andy?"

"I get depressed so easily." Sherry lowered her gaze. "Who would have thought wooing my husband back could be so difficult?"

Julie smiled secretly to herself. She knew exactly what Sherry meant.

The phone buzzed and Sherry looked up. Suddenly pale, she motioned for Julie to answer it as she rushed into the bathroom. Not for the first time lately, Julie suspected her friend was pregnant.

Julie was off the phone when she returned. "Are you going to tell me or are you going to make me ask?"

"How'd you know?" Sherry protested.

"Sherry, honestly. I can't believe you sometimes. Does Andy know?"

Bright tears sparkled from her eyelashes. "No. If we do get back together, I want it to be because he loves and wants me. Not because of the baby."

"The divorce proceedings were halted, weren't they?"

Sherry nodded. "But only because Andy and I felt we needed time to think things out. We're not living together."

"You won't be able to hide it from him much longer."

Sherry shrugged. "I know. That's why I've given him three weeks to decide what he wants."

"How does Andy feel about an ultimatum?"

Sherry giggled. "Andy doesn't know."

"Oh, Sherry," Julie groaned.

A tear slid down her friend's cheek. "I realize this sounds crazy, but I've thought everything out. If Andy found out about the baby and we reconciled, I'd never be sure. This way I'll have the confidence I need that he really loves me and wants to make this marriage work."

The phone rang and the two were quickly involved in business again.

Not until that night when Julie took pains to cook Daniel's favorite dinner did she stop thinking about Sherry's predicament.

"Did I miss something?" Daniel asked teasingly as she entered the kitchen.

"Miss something?"

"It's not my birthday, is it? I've got it! You overdrew the checking account. Right?"

"Just because I cook stroganoff does it mean I'm up to something?" Julie inquired.

"In my short experience as a husband, my immediate reaction is...yes!"

"Well, you're wrong. I've bought a cookbook. I can't have my husband fainting away from lack of nourishment."

"Would you like me to demonstrate how weak I am?" he asked, slipping his hands over her breasts and pulling her against him.

"Daniel, not now."

"Why not?" he growled against her neck.

"I thought you were hungry."

"I am. Come to bed and I'll show you how hungry."

Julie switched off the stove and turned into her husband's arms, meeting the urgency of his kiss with a willingness that surprised even Julie. She did love this man. Someday he'd realize how much.

Daniel broke their kiss and looked down at Julie, love blazing in his eyes. "I'll be happy when you're pregnant," he whispered.

Involuntarily Julie stiffened. "Why?"

"I thought you wanted a family?"

"I do." But first she wanted them secure in their marriage.

"Then why the questions?"

"I want to know why you want a baby." Her greatest fear was that he would see a child as the means of binding her to him.

"For all the reasons a man usually wants to be a father. As I recall, we agreed that when you were pregnant, you'd quit your job."

Julie stepped from his embrace. "I think you should know I've made an appointment with the doctor."

The silence grew and grew.

"So you think you might be pregnant?"

"No, I want to make sure that doesn't happen."

AS THE DAYS passed Julie had never been more miserable. Daniel treated her with icy politeness, and if she'd thought the first days of their marriage were a test of her love it was nothing compared to this.

Daniel threw himself into his work, and Julie did her best to give the outward appearance that everything was fine. All week he had failed to show up for dinner or to call and inform her when he expected to come home. Exhausted with another night of worry, Julie soaked in a tub filled with hot water and perfumed bubble bath. She had no idea where Daniel was. Although it was Saturday, he'd left early that morning.

Julie had hoped that a bubble bath would raise her spirits. She'd been so tired lately. It was ridiculous. It seemed she went to bed every night before Daniel and had trouble dragging herself up in the morning. That wasn't like her. Nor was her unbalanced appetite. She was starving one moment and feeling as if she'd overeaten the next. Her appointment with the doctor was next week; she'd mention it to him.

Abruptly, Julie sat up in the tub. In a flash she knew. She was pregnant. So much had been happening that she'd completely lost track of time. Biting into her trembling bottom lip, Julie leaned back and placed a hand on her flat stomach. Daniel would be pleased, and despite her misgivings, Julie's heart swelled with joy. Just as quickly, tears flooded her eyes. Desperately she wanted this child, but she wanted the baby to come into a warm, secure marriage and not one torn by tension and mistrust. Sniffling, she wiped the moisture from her face.

Dripping water and bubbles over the bathroom floor, Julie wrapped a towel around her body. Mixed emotions flew at her from all directions until she wanted to thrash out her arms to ward them off.

Sitting on top of their bed, she reached for the phone and dialed Daniel's office where she suspected he'd be. The phone rang twice before she cut the connection. What could she possibly say?

Sniffling anew, Julie dialed again and waited several long rings. "Sher-ry," she said, relieved that her friend was home. "Congratulate me, we're both pregnant." With that she burst into sobs.

"HERE," Sherry said, handing Julie another tissue. "You're going to need this."

A dry-eyed Julie glanced at the tissue, then back to her friend. "I'm through crying. It was a shock, that's all." Within fifteen minutes of receiving the call, Sherry had arrived, flushed and excited.

"Discovering I was pregnant was a shock for me, too,

if you recall. At first I was ecstatic, then I had doubts. Three days later I leveled out at 'great.' ''

Julie's smile was wan. ''A baby is exactly what Daniel wants.''

''But for all the wrong reasons,'' Sherry claimed heatedly. ''If Andy knew about me, I suspect he'd be thrilled, but again for all the wrong reasons.''

Julie nodded, feeling slightly ill. She hadn't eaten since breakfast.

''What did Daniel say?'' Sherry asked.

''He doesn't know yet.''

''What are you going to do?''

''I don't know. He has to be told, but I don't know when. He's...hardly around anymore.''

''So he's pulling that trick again,'' Sherry huffed.

''He's working himself to death.''

''Or he could be out having the time of his life as Andy did.''

Julie doubted that. ''I don't think so.''

''Ha! That's what I thought about Andy. But I won't let you sit here and sulk. Come on, I'm taking you out.''

''Sherry, honestly, the last thing in the world I want is to be seen in public. I look a mess.''

''So, it'll take a bit of inventive application with your makeup. My friend, I'm going to let you in on one of life's important secrets.''

''Oh?'' Julie was dubious.

''When the going gets tough, the tough go shopping.''

''Sherry,'' Julie groaned. ''I don't feel up to—''

''Trust me, you'll feel a hundred percent better. Afterward I'll treat you to dinner.''

''But Daniel...''

''Did he bother to tell you he wouldn't be home for dinner the last three nights?''

''No.'' She lowered her gaze to disguise the pain.

"Then it's time you quit moping around and do something positive for yourself."

"All right," Julie agreed, "I'll go."

It took an hour to get ready, but Sherry was right—she felt better for it. Before they left, Julie penned Daniel a short note, telling him whom she was with. He might not want to know, but Julie felt better for having done it.

Sherry seemed intent on having a good time. First they visited the mall stores, scouting out baby items and trying on maternity dresses.

Next they took in a movie, and had an Italian dinner afterward. On the way home, Sherry insisted that they stop off at her house so Julie could see the baby blanket she was knitting.

"I think I'd better call Daniel," Julie said, sipping her cup of tea. Already it was after eleven and although she had left the note, he might be worried. She *hoped* he'd be worried.

"Don't," Sherry chastised. "He hasn't phoned you lately, has he?"

"No," Julie admitted. She had barely seen him.

"I think I'll put on some soothing music."

"Good idea," Julie chimed in. She knew she sounded pleasant enough, but inside she desperately missed her husband.

THE NEXT thing Julie knew, she was lying on the sofa, wrapped in a thick comforter. Struggling to sit upright, she glanced at her watch.

"I was wondering what time you'd wake up," Sherry called. "How do you want your eggs?"

"It's morning?" Julie was incredulous.

"Right, and almost ten. You were tired, my friend."

"Oh, good grief." She stood up. "I'd better call Daniel."

"Go ahead. The phone's on the counter."

While Julie dialed, Sherry handed her a small glass of orange juice and two soda crackers. Julie smiled. Her stomach had been queasy for several mornings.

Ten rings later, she hesitantly replaced the receiver.

"No answer?" asked Sherry.

"No. Maybe he was in the shower."

"Maybe. Try again in five minutes."

"At least he knows whom I'm with. If he was worried he would have called."

Sherry turned back to the stove. "He didn't know."

"I left a note."

"I stuck it in my pocket before we left your place. Heavens, I didn't know you were going to fall asleep on me and spend the night. I thought if Daniel worried a little it would be good for him."

"Oh, Sherry."

"It was a rotten thing to do. Are you mad?"

Julie shook her head, feeling defeated. Sherry had no idea that she had walked out on Daniel once and he was sure to believe she'd done it again.

But fifteen minutes later, Julie used her key to open her front door. The room was dark, and she walked over to open the drapes.

"Julie?"

Abruptly, she swiveled around to find Daniel sitting in a chair, his dark eyes wide and disbelieving.

"Hello, Daniel." He looked so utterly dejected that she fought back the tears.

Quickly the proud mask he wore slid into place and he stood. "I suppose you came back for your things."

"No." Somehow she managed to let the lone word escape. His clothes were badly wrinkled and his hair was rumpled.

Apparently he didn't hear her. "Well, go ahead and get them. Don't let me stop you."

"You want me to leave?" she asked.

"I won't stop you."

She dropped her gaze as the pain washed over her. "I see." Julie took a step toward the hallway.

Daniel jerked his head up as she moved. "Julie."

Their eyes met and held. Neither seemed willing to break the contact. The tears filled her eyes and she wiped them aside with the back of her hand.

"I don't blame you for walking out on me," he spoke at last. "I drove you to it." He jerked his hand through his hair. "I let you out of my life the first time and blamed you for it. God help me, I can't do it again." He took a tentative step toward her. "Once you're gone, there won't be any more sunshine in my life—don't leave me," he pleaded. "Let me make up for all the unhappiness I've caused you."

With a cry of joy, Julie reached out to him and Daniel crushed her into his embrace. He took deep breaths as he struggled with emotion.

"It doesn't matter why you saw Jim or any other man. I was a fool to think everything would be solved by having you quit your job."

"Daniel, listen—"

"I love you, Julie, you're the most important person in my life. I can't let you go."

Julie spread tiny kisses over his face. "Would you kindly listen to me for one minute? I'm not leaving and never was. That was all a mix-up that we have to thank Sherry for. And as for my job, I plan to work for about another six months and then think about quitting."

"That sounds fair," he said. "Why six months?"

"Because by then the baby—"

"The baby?" Daniel repeated, stunned. His frown deepened. "Julie, are you telling me you're pregnant?"

Twenty-four hours ago, Julie would have been just as shocked had anyone mentioned her condition.

"How? When?" He looked completely flustered.

"You don't honestly need an answer to that, do you?"

"No," he agreed, his eyes shining. "All these weeks I'd hoped you would be. I wanted a child to bind you to me. Now I realize you've always been with me. Even while you lived in California, you were here in my heart."

Slipping her arms around her husband's neck, Julie smiled into the loving depths of his tender gaze. "We're already bound."

"By our love," he finished for her. When his mouth sought hers, Julie surrendered to her husband's deep hunger, secure in his love. "You needn't worry, Julie. I learned some valuable lessons about myself last night while I sat here alone. I was convinced my selfishness had driven you away a second time. Now I feel like a fool who's been given a third chance at happiness. Believe me, this time I'm not going to blow it."

One year later

"WE'RE HOME," Julie said gently as she saw her mother-in-law rocking her three-month-old son. She paused in the living room. Daniel had bought the house she'd loved, and made extensive repairs. "You know who you remind me of?" Julie asked, lifting the sleeping baby from Clara's arms.

"Probably Whistler's mother," the older woman answered. She had spent the evening with little Ted while Julie and Daniel attended a banquet at the country club.

"Was Jim surprised to be named Man of the Year?" Clara asked.

"No more than I was last year," Daniel chuckled. "But then last year was a very good year."

"It was indeed," Clara murmured. "I was given a new lease on life."

"So was I." Daniel slipped an arm around his wife's trim waist and lovingly kissed his son's brow.

Julie smiled down on her baby. "Was he good?"

"Not a peep. I must admit to being a bit frightened by him yet. He's so small. Theodore August Van Deen seems such a big name for such a tiny baby."

"He'll grow," Daniel said confidently. "And be joined by several more if his mother agrees."

"Oh, I'm in full agreement."

The baby let out a small cry.

"It isn't his feeding time, is it?" Clara looked up.

"Not yet," Julie assured her.

"Teddy-boy, Grandma's joy." Clara took the baby from Julie, patted his tiny back and sat down in the rocking chair

With infinite tenderness Daniel turned Julie into his arms, burying his face in the warm hollow of her throat. "I love you, Julie Van Deen." He looked deeply into her soft blue eyes.

"And I you, my husband."

"The hurts and doubts are gone forever. I've buried my yesterdays."

"And look with happy excitement toward our tomorrows," she whispered softly and smiled.

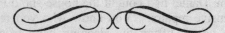

ADAM'S IMAGE

Debbie Macomber

He stood across the room, nursing his drink. Susan Mackenzie found her attention drawn to the tall, rather lanky man despite her first impression that he was strikingly unattractive. His face was too narrow, the chin square and abrupt; the dark brown eyes were friendly, but small. And his ears tended to stick out. But there was a kindness about him that she hadn't seen in a man for a long while.

Susan sat in a corner by herself. Cocktail parties were not her forte, but she had seen to the obligatory chitchat and now was free to sit and observe.

The stranger across the room was an onlooker too. Twice she had watched couples approach him. His smile had been warm and genuine, the sound of his laugh deep, rich and full. Just listening to him had made her want to smile. He gave whomever he was speaking to his full attention. A man who listened, another rarity.

She stood, taking her wineglass with her as she approached him.

"Susan Mackenzie." She held out her hand.

"Adam Gallagher." He shook it firmly.

"Are you a friend of Ralph's?" Susan asked. Ralph, their host, was celebrating the opening of his own literary agency.

"We attended college together." Adam smiled. "Are you in publishing?"

Susan nodded. "Associate editor. And you?"

"No." He shook his head. "I'm a doctor."

The profession fit perfectly with the man, his kindness, the gentle quality about him. He was a healer.

"Do you have a complaint?" he asked ruefully.

"Now that you mention it," she said, "my feet are killing me."

"New shoes?"

She nodded.

"Would you like to sit down?" he suggested.

What she wanted was to go home, but not if it meant missing the opportunity to talk to this intriguing male. She liked him, had liked him almost from the first moment she'd begun observing him. That was unusual.

They sat and talked for an hour. Adam wasn't shy, and somehow she found that surprising. He didn't possess her reasons for blending into the background. Susan's reticence came from a deep-seated shyness that she had struggled most of her life to overcome.

The more they talked, the more attractive Adam became. Less than an hour after she introduced herself, Susan no longer saw the too-square chin, or the large ears; she saw the man. And he was the most interesting one she had met in two years of living in New York.

Adam paused and glanced at his watch. "My goodness, I've been talking up a blue streak." A scowl touched his brow. "I don't usually do that." He stood. "Would you like a refill?"

"No, I'm fine. Thanks."

He examined his own empty glass. "What I'd really like is a cup of coffee. How about you?"

"I doubt that we'll find that around here."

"Sure we will, come on." His hand cupped her elbow as he directed her toward the back of the house, through the small groups that were milling around chatting. At the entrance to the kitchen, he held open the swinging door.

"Betsy will make us a cup of coffee."

A woman of about fifty was preparing a tray of hors d'oeuvres. She turned at the sound of someone intruding on her territory, the blue eyes stormy. But when she recognized Adam, the frown turned to a wide grin.

"Dr. Gallagher," she exclaimed, her voice filled with devotion. "I wondered if you'd come back to see ol' Betsy."

"I couldn't leave without saying hello to my favorite girl, could I?" He gave the older woman a bear hug.

"Oh, be away with you." Betsy laughed. "I suppose you're after a piece of my apple pie again."

"Not this time," Adam said, and moved slowly to Susan's side. He took her hand; the touch, although impersonal, produced a warmth within her.

"Susan and I would like a cup of that marvelous coffee you brew."

No more than a minute passed and they were served mugs of steaming coffee and thick slices of apple pie with hot cinnamon sauce. The pie was delicious.

Adam carried their plates to the sink when they'd finished, and kissed Betsy on the cheek. Lifting the glass coffeepot, he brought it to the table and refilled their cups.

Susan leaned back in the chair and held the mug with both hands.

"Here." Adam sat beside her, and lifted her feet onto his knees. "If you take these off, you'll be able to relax." Carefully he unbuckled the strap and slipped the sandal off her foot. Gently his fingers massaged the toes, the circular motion extending to the arch of her foot. The gentle rotating action was repeated on the other foot.

The ache all but disappeared as a tingling sensation ran up the back of her legs. Susan felt her throat tightening as she struggled not to purr. The featherlight touch was strangely intimate. She lowered her lashes because to look at him would reveal the havoc his touch was playing on her senses.

"Are you asleep?" The question was whispered.

"If I am, I don't want to wake up," she answered, then opened her eyes to watch his gaze move slowly over her.

"You're very beautiful." He'd stopped massaging her feet. "Those eyes are fantastic."

From any other man it would have sounded like a line. But not from Adam.

"Your hair is the same warm shade as your eyes. I imagine I'm not the first man who's wanted to run his fingers through it."

Their gazes met and held, and for an unbelievable moment Susan felt as if she'd never need to take another breath. It took every dictate of her will to keep from standing and pulling the combs from her hair to allow the long chocolate brown curtain to fall free. Her heart was pounding so loud she was sure he must hear it. His gaze lowered to her generous mouth. He didn't need to voice his thoughts; they were there for her to read.

A dish clanged against the counter, breaking the spell. Adam shifted uneasily. "Want some more coffee?"

Susan shook her head.

"I'll buckle these for you." Leaning over, he slipped one sandal onto her foot.

"You make me feel like Cinderella."

"I'm no Prince Charming." His cynical tone surprised her.

"Is something wrong?"

He paused, his mouth a thin line. "No. I'm sorry."

"Adam." Her fingertips gently stroked the angular line of his jaw. "Would you kiss me?"

He caught his breath audibly. "Now? Here?"

A smile tugged at her mouth as she nodded.

His eyes turned a deeper shade of brown as he stood, looking around him.

Susan's gaze followed his. Betsy was busy at the kitchen sink, her back to them. Susan wouldn't have cared if they'd been in the midst of all the guests; all she wanted was to discover what it would be like to taste his mouth.

"Outside." An arm around her waist led her out the back

door. Moonlight illuminated the cement patio. Adam slipped his arms around her and brought her against the muscular hardness of his chest. His hold tightened and his mouth moved closer.

Susan linked her arms around his neck and stood on tiptoe. Adam's eyes seemed to burn into hers. The tip of her tongue moistened suddenly dry lips, and with a muted groan, he lowered his mouth to hers.

The kiss was soft and gentle, as if she were as delicate as fine porcelain. Parting her lips in welcome, Susan yielded. A rush of intense pleasure washed over her and left her trembling. The kiss deepened as his hands roamed over her back, arching her closer, as if he wanted to fuse them together for eternity.

When Adam dragged his mouth from hers and buried it against the side of her neck, Susan felt cheated. This shouldn't end. She was on the brink of discovering in a few short minutes more of what it meant to be a woman than she had in all her twenty-four years.

She was conscious of Adam's body pressing against her and of his uneven breaths. Had he felt it too? Surely he must have...

She gave a small protesting moan as he pulled away. His hands moved to her upper arms.

"You are very kissable," he murmured. "But then, I imagine more than one man has told you that."

Several had, but Susan didn't want to think about anyone or anything except Adam. How could she possibly hope to explain that she felt more wonderful with him than she had with any man...?

"Your mouth is equally desirable." Leaning forward slightly, she softly pressed her lips over his.

His hands tightened as if to restrain her, but the tenseness quickly flowed from him. Instead of pushing her away, he gathered her to him, holding her in his embrace. One palm rested over his heart and Susan sighed as she felt the erratic beat. The flame that was blazing within her had touched him too. She couldn't remember feeling more content.

"Susan." Her name had become a gentle caress as he held her, his chin resting on the crown of her head. "We should be getting back," he said.

But neither moved, unwilling to break their embrace.

"Are you cold?" Adam asked as if suddenly conscious that the early-October night might be uncomfortable on her bare shoulders.

Susan laughed. "Cold? Are you joking?"

Silence stretched between them. The party would be breaking up soon, and although he continued to hold her, Susan could sense him mentally withdrawing. The notion that they would part tonight and she would never see him again tightened the muscles of her abdomen. The thought was intolerable. Yet Adam made no suggestion they meet.

"Can I see you again?" she asked. "Tomorrow?"

"I'm on duty at the hospital in the afternoon." He drew away, dark eyes narrowed on her face.

"Morning's fine. I'm an early riser." Normally she was anything but.

"I've got a soccer game. I coach a team for the Boys' Club." He drew in a deep breath. "Not tomorrow. Maybe sometime next week. I'll give you a call." The softness had left his face.

Stunned for a moment, Susan stared at him, disbelieving. His mood had changed so quickly. "You're giving me the brush-off, aren't you?" She had come on strong, a lot stronger than she did with others. Some men didn't like that.

"I'm not." The way he said it told her he was lying.

Susan took a step in retreat, studying him in the soft moonlight. She saw displeasure in Adam's features. His jaw was clenched and tight; a muscle twitched beside his eye.

"Don't worry, I get the message. Don't call me, I'll call you." She laughed tightly. "Now if you'll excuse me."

"Of course."

The back door closed. It felt heavy and hard. But so did her heart. Pausing, she glanced out the kitchen window. Adam remained exactly as she'd left him, his shoulders hunched, and she watched as he wiped a weary hand over his face. Some inner turmoil seemed to be troubling him.

"Mighty fine man."

Susan swiveled around. "Pardon?"

Betsy was wiping her hands. "I said Dr. Gallagher is a fine man."

"I'm sure he is." Susan meant that sincerely.

"Not much to look at though." The older woman chuckled, but her eyes seemed to appraise Susan. "That means a lot to some people. My Ben was a good-looker. Biggest mistake of my life, marrying that man. Caused me nothing but heartache."

"Looks aren't everything," Susan agreed. "Thanks for the coffee and pie, Betsy."

The woman's gaze followed her. "Good night, miss."

"DID YOU HAVE a good time last night?" A sleepy, disheveled Rosemary Thomas sauntered into the cozy living room and asked Susan early the next morning. Both worked for Silhouette, Rosemary in the contract department, and they shared a tiny one-bedroom apartment off east Eighty-eighth Street.

"As good as can be expected." Susan sat sideways on the sofa. She sipped from a steaming mug of coffee.

"Meet anyone?" Rosemary persisted.

Susan's dark eyes widened. "What makes you say that?"

Rosemary shrugged. "I don't know, you look different. Brooding, like you met Mr. Wonderful."

"I've given up on the dream of finding Mr. Wonderful."

"Do my ears deceive me?" said Rosemary. "How can a romance editor forsake Mr. Wonderful?"

"Mr. Wonderful's an illusion," Susan announced. "I'm looking for Mr. Nice Guy."

Rosemary sat in the worn chair covered in the same material as the sofa. "Doing anything this weekend?" she asked.

"No," Susan answered.

"I think I'll head out after breakfast. It's Mom's birthday Wednesday. She'll be disappointed if I don't spend some time with her. You're welcome to come."

With a quick shake of her head, Susan declined the invitation to visit her friend's family in New Jersey. "I've got some proposals I want to go over this weekend." Bringing work home from the office was essential. Working with as many as fifty authors made it impossible to find the time to read all the new material she wanted to at work. Constant interruptions were part of her job. But one of its most fulfilling aspects was the chance to spot and develop new writing talent.

WEDNESDAY afternoon, Susan did something that shocked her. She phoned the Boys' Club and discovered the youth soccer games were played at nine and ten-thirty on Saturday mornings in Central Park. If she felt like a fool then, she felt more of an idiot the next Saturday as she zipped up a baby blue warmup jacket and headed for the park.

"Why am I doing this?" she repeatedly asked herself. Brilliant fall colors cloaked the avenue. The day was glorious.

The soccer fields were on one end of the Great Lawn. As she approached them, Susan picked out Adam easily. Just watching him, even from this distance, did something to her heart. What was it about this man that had haunted her all week? What had happened that night at Ralph Jordan's party for him to withdraw from her so suddenly? In the beginning she was sure it was because she'd come on so strong. But there had been nothing that evening to indicate that. He had seemed as caught up in this attraction as she. And she had been attracted to Adam Gallagher physically, mentally and spiritually almost from the moment she'd first seen him.

The official's whistle blew, and for a moment Susan thought the game had ended. Instead the players ran off the field and Adam's boys huddled around him. Adam knelt on one knee in front of the group.

Halftime, she mused, watching from a position camouflaged by trees. The second half of the game was exciting, and Adam's team won. Susan couldn't restrain her sense of pride. Her intention had been to saunter past him casually and act shocked that they had run into one another.

Now she realized she couldn't do it. Turning, she stuck her hands in her pockets and headed toward the sidewalk. She took a deep breath of the autumn air.

"Susan." Someone was shouting her name.

She turned to see Adam running toward her.

If she'd hoped for a friendly greeting, she was in for a disappointment. His eyes were dark and brooding.

"What are you doing here?"

"Oh, hi. Adam, isn't it?" Susan hoped to give an impression of indifference. "I just happened to be enjoying a walk and stumbled onto the soccer game. You have a good team. Nice day, isn't it?"

"Beautiful." Adam smiled ruefully.

"Well, I won't keep you. I've got some errands to do," she said. "It was good seeing you again. Give Ralph my best." She offered him a weak smile and turned. *He's actually going to let me leave,* her mind screamed.

Without even knowing she would do anything so crazy, Susan collapsed onto a huge mound of leaves.

"Susan."

Never had she heard such emotion in the sound of her name.

The clamor of running footsteps followed. At precisely

the right moment, she turned and threw a huge handful of leaves into his face.

Adam looked stunned. Before he could recover, she stood and tossed more at him.

Susan was laughing harder than she had done in a long time.

Adam stared at her. "What did you do that for?"

"Because I couldn't stand for us to talk to one another like polite strangers," she yelled. Bending down, she scooped up more leaves, but one gentle push toppled her onto the soft pile. She was deluged with leaves as Adam dumped several armloads over her head.

In an effort to escape, she rolled onto her side, kicking up the leaves as she turned. Laughter hindered her movement, and a second later Adam had joined her on the ground, his hands pinning her to the earth.

Her breasts heaving with the effort to breathe evenly, she gazed into the powerful face that had haunted her all week. Amusement glittered from his dark eyes, and the corners of his mouth were quivering. Their looks met, and the world about them seemed to fade into oblivion. The leaves, the sun, the trees were gone, as were the sounds of the city. Adam brushed the hair from the side of her face. His touch was gentle, sweet. The laughter had left his face as his attention centered on her softly parted lips.

Susan inhaled deeply, anticipating the union of their mouths. He didn't want to kiss her; she could see it in the set of his jaw. But at the same time, he couldn't stop himself. The knowledge thrilled her, and instinctively her arms curved around his back.

The kiss renewed every sensation she had experienced the night they met. Somehow deep inside she'd been hoping it had been the wine or the moonlight. But this was real. So real and wonderful. Magic.

She hadn't realized she'd whispered the word until Adam raised his head. "Magic?" he repeated.

She smiled and nodded.

Adam released her and sat up. He linked his hands around bent knees and stared into the distance.

Susan sat in the same position. "Why?" she murmured softly. There wasn't any need to explain the question.

"I knew someone like you once," he began, but didn't turn to look at her. "Gail was as beautiful as you are."

"Pretty girls are a dime a dozen." She shrugged.

"She had the most incredibly thick auburn hair."

Susan hated her already. "Mine's brown." So he'd been hurt, she thought, probably jilted. None of it had anything to do with her. Unless...unless he had been pretending he was holding Gail, kissing Gail.

"Are you still in love with her?" she asked.

Adam looked taken aback. "I don't think so. No."

"Well, that's encouraging." She didn't mean to sound ill-mannered, but love's course hadn't been smooth for her either. She didn't know that it was for anyone.

She bounded to her feet, suddenly angry. The one thing Susan thoroughly detested was being confused with someone else, especially if she'd been his one true love. "It was nice seeing you again, Adam. As always, it was an adventure."

He stood too, brushing leaves from his pants.

"The name's Susan, in case you forget. That's S-U-S-A-N. And the hair's dark brown." She wove her fingers through its length. "And for that matter, I'm not all that beautiful. My nose is a little odd." Pivoting sharply, she strode out of the park. He didn't try to stop her. Somehow she knew he wouldn't.

*

SUSAN LIFTED her glasses and pinched the corners of her eyes with her thumb and index finger. This job was definitely taking its toll on her eyes. She coughed. Her health too. The little romp in the damp leaves last Saturday had resulted in a horrible cold.

That night, her violent sneezing caught Rosemary's attention. "You know what you need, don't you?"

If Susan heard about the wonders of vitamin C one more time she thought she'd scream. Her roommate had been on a health-food kick for weeks.

"What you need is to get those endorphins pumping through your body," her friend said forcefully.

Susan shook her head scornfully. "Endorphins? Have you been reading romance novels again?"

"I can't believe anyone can graduate from Cornell and not know what endorphins are."

Susan sneezed again. Her throat ached and her eyes were beginning to water. "All right, tell me all about it." She might as well capitulate. From the look in her eye, Rosemary would tell her anyway.

"Endorphins are a secretion your body produces that gives you a natural high, both physical and mental. So exercising will actually make you feel good. That's why I've started to walk to work."

For over a month Rosemary had trekked the two and a half miles to the Avenue of the Americas every weekday morning. Susan had scoffed, but her friend was as fit as an Olympic runner, while she felt steps away from missing a week's work.

She sat on the sofa. "I feel awful," she admitted.

"Scratchy sore throat? Eyes burning? Ears plugged?" Rosemary questioned softly.

Susan nodded. "I think my chest is tightening up too."

"I can help," Rosemary said. "But you have to trust me."

A half hour later Susan couldn't believe what was happening. Rosemary had her change into pajamas and housecoat. Then she'd hung a huge head of garlic around her neck and applied a mustard plaster to her chest.

"This better work, Rosemary. That's all I can say."

"Trust me," she declared, leading Susan into the bathroom.

"There's more?" she protested loudly.

"Sit," Rosemary ordered, and helped lower her onto the edge of the bathtub. She fetched a steaming bucket of water. Immediately the small room was filled with the scent of lemons and spice. At least it helped kill the garlic odor.

"Lean forward," Rosemary instructed. "Breathe in as much of this as possible." She draped a thick towel over Susan's head.

"How long do I have to sit like this?" The words sounded muffled even to her own ears.

"I don't know. Let me check the book again. Keep your head down until I get back," said Rosemary.

"Wonderful, just wonderful," Susan muttered, breathing in the citrus-scented steam.

Somewhere in the distance she heard a buzzer. It sounded as if it had come from the stove in the kitchen.

"Susan, it's for you."

She lifted her head and peered out. "What's for me?"

"The door."

"The door?" she repeated, and her heart leaped to her throat. Adam Gallagher was standing directly behind Rosemary.

"Hello, Susan. It's Adam, spelled A-D-A-M."

Immediately Susan lowered her head, hiding under the towel. "Rosemary," she shouted, "do something."

"I didn't know he was following me," Rosemary said. "I thought he'd sit down."

"I should have," said Adam, a smile in his voice. "But I confess to being curious about a certain smell that seemed to be coming from this room."

"Would you two mind leaving?" Susan screamed, and seethed silently. At the sound of the door closing, she ripped the garlic from her throat and let the towel fall to the floor.

Dear heaven, she'd never be able to look Adam in the eye again. How would she ever live this down?

As MUCH AS Susan hated to admit it, she felt much better the next morning. Rosemary had already left for work, but there was a note for Susan beside the coffeepot: "Hope you feel better. Adam wanted me to ask if you'd meet him tonight, six o'clock at Tastings for a drink. I would have said something last night, but I didn't think you'd talk to me. I don't blame you. Hope to see you later. Rosie."

Susan crumpled the note and tossed it into the garbage can. Every encounter she'd had with Dr. Adam Gallagher had been disastrous. She wouldn't go.

By the time she broke for lunch, Susan had decided she was behaving childishly. Of course she'd meet Adam.

At five-thirty, she cleared her desk, or as much of it as she could. There seemed to be a sense of never really being finished. If she didn't love the work and New York, her job could have depressed her. Instead she was challenged.

No, she wouldn't meet him. What was the use? Her thoughts were muddled. Her heart was telling her she should meet Adam. But the more practical part of her personality was issuing repeated warnings.

Without admitting to herself that she would or wouldn't accept the invitation, Susan strolled toward Tastings, a popular restaurant six blocks up the street. She preferred to think that she was leaving her options open. At any time she could turn around and head home.

Adam was arriving just as she got there. Walking toward her with a wide grin that was directed at her alone. And like a magnet drawn to steel, she returned his warm greeting with a smile of her own.

"Hello, Susan."

"Adam." She couldn't look away. He really was plain

looking. He was tall but muscular, and his wide shoulders narrowed to lean hips and long, long legs. Plain, but compelling in a way she couldn't describe.

"I see you're feeling better," he said with a smile.

Susan flushed. "Yes, much better. Thank you."

A low chuckle rumbled from his throat. "The wonders of modern medicine never cease to amaze me."

"Adam Gallagher, if you mention one word about last night, I'll leave."

A large hand cupped her elbow as a smile crinkled the corners of his eyes. "No more, I promise."

Tastings was a long and narrow room with emerald green tablecloths on the square tables. One wall contained a huge wood bar with upholstered stools. It was a popular place to meet for drinks. Although it was early evening, the room was nearly filled. Adam found an empty table and helped her out of her coat. A waitress took their order and soon returned with Susan's Cabernet Sauvignon and Adam's Beaujolais.

Adam cupped his glass. His shoulders were hunched forward slightly, and Susan asked, "Tired?"

He nodded. "But it's not the company I keep." His gaze rose to meet hers. "The stork got me out of bed this morning about four. A beautiful baby girl, but the mother had a difficult labor and I wanted to be with her. Her husband left her, and she was alone and needed someone. By the time I finished there, it was time to go to the office."

"We can make it another time if you'd rather," Susan offered.

"No." He reached across the table and squeezed her fingers. "In fact, I don't know about you, but I'm starved. I'm not dressed for anything fancy, but I know where we could find a decent meal."

Susan nodded, pleased at the invitation.

He took her to a small restaurant near Times Square that served charcoal-broiled hamburgers and fresh-baked bread.

The owner shook hands with Adam and personally escorted them to a booth.

Adam introduced Susan, and Ambrose Lockridge shook her hand. He wouldn't allow them to order from the menu, insisting he would personally cook the specialty of the house in their honor.

Ambrose delivered hamburgers that looked as tall as the Empire State Building. Melted cheese, sliced pickles, thick slices of tomato, lettuce and a sauce oozed from the sides of the buns. The meat patty alone must have weighed half a pound. One person couldn't possibly manage to eat the entire hamburger.

Susan did her best, downing almost half. Again she discovered how much she liked Adam. He talked for a long time, telling her about his office and the decision to go into family practice. Not until they finished their meal did he mention Saturday morning. "I feel I owe you an explanation."

Taking a sip from her coffee cup, Susan avoided looking at him. She didn't want to hear about Gail.

"You don't owe me anything, Adam," she said. "I got the picture from what you said Saturday."

"I'm sure you thought exactly the wrong thing," he contradicted. "I wasn't comparing you to Gail, although there are striking similarities."

"I doubt that." Susan took another sip of coffee.

"I like you, Susan."

He was saying so much more. Susan wished she knew exactly what. She set the cup down. "I like you too."

Again his gaze settled on her face. "You're a beautiful woman, and I'm not exactly a knight in shining armor."

"I'm not Lady Diana, either," she countered. With any other man her attractiveness would have been an asset. But not with Adam.

"You're prettier than royalty. Prettier than Gail."

Susan felt as if her heart would burst. "Did this...other woman hurt you so much that you can't trust again?"

"Gail," he said. "I loved her very much. But I was young and stupid."

Susan had never felt such intense dislike for someone. "What happened?" she asked.

"We met when I was in med school."

That long ago! Susan thought with a sense of frustration. Adam had to be thirty-four, maybe thirty-five. He had loved Gail all these years?

"There's not much to say except that we fell in love. I fell in love," he corrected. "Gail fell for dollar signs she was sure were in my future. I should have known a beautiful, popular girl like Gail couldn't really love someone like me."

Susan had to swallow back words so as not to interrupt him. It had been on the tip of her tongue to say she was half in love with him already.

"At the end of my first year we got engaged. A couple of months later my father became seriously ill and I decided to discontinue my studies and help out at home until Dad was better. Gail opposed my leaving school. We had a bitter argument.

"Anyway," Adam continued, "I did go home, and my father died a couple of weeks later. By the time I returned to school, Gail was engaged to another medical student."

"And you still care about her?"

"No. But a man doesn't easily forget his first love."

They'd been lovers. The thought was unbearable.

"How can Gail and I possibly be alike?" asked Susan.

"In addition to being beautiful, you both have the tendency to go after what you want."

Susan released an inward groan. She knew it! They had gotten off to a bad start. If Adam only knew how extraordinary such behavior was for her. Never, she promised herself, would she instigate anything with him again.

"I'm not like her, Adam. But you'll have to discover that yourself." She reached for her purse. "I should be going. Thanks for the drink and dinner," she murmured.

Adam paused to place some money on the table before following her outside. She heard him call something to Ambrose.

A hand on her shoulder halted her progress as she moved to wave down a taxi. "Just a minute." Adam said. "I've offended you, haven't I? That wasn't my intention."

Susan already knew that. Adam would never knowingly hurt anyone. "I'm sure it wasn't," she replied.

"When you're in my arms, Susan, I can think of little else."

Well, she certainly hoped so! She looked down the street. Where were the taxis when she needed one?

The pressure of his hands turned her around. His eyes were smiling into hers. Slowly he lowered his mouth to claim hers in a gentle but surprisingly ardent kiss.

Susan melted into his arms as he wrapped her in his embrace. A soft, involuntary moan came when he lifted his head, but he quickly lowered it again, parting her lips with a plundering kiss that sent the world in a tailspin.

Susan buried her face in his light jacket and sighed unevenly. Adam's mouth was pressed against the top of her head.

A taxi pulled to the curb. "You looking for a ride?"

"Yes," Adam answered for her and held the door open. "Good night, Susan."

She pressed her fingers to her lips and waved a goodbye. Not until she was almost home did Susan realize that Adam had not mentioned seeing her again.

SUSAN OFFERED Jack Persico an apologetic smile. The evening had been a waste. What was the matter with her? Couldn't she have fun anymore? Why should her life hinge on whether she heard from Adam again? She hadn't, and for over two weeks now, she'd lived and breathed anticipation.

"I had a nice time. Thanks, Jack," she murmured.

"Little liar," he said. "What's wrong? Problems at the office?"

Shaking her head, she turned and inserted her key into the lock. "I hope you aren't offended if I don't invite you in, but I really am tired."

"I understand," he told her gently, and in a strange way Susan was sure he did. He gave her a knowing smile and kissed her lightly. "I'll give you a call later."

"Thanks, Jack." She let herself into the silent apartment. Rosemary had gone out after all, she mused. Friday night and Susan had turned down two invitations, hoping to hear from Adam. When she didn't, she accepted Jack's casual offer for a movie. Releasing a low, uneven breath, she hung up her coat.

Just as she closed the closet door, Rosemary came out of the bathroom, her face covered with a green goo.

"Oh, you're back. How was the movie?"

"Great. Any phone calls?"

"One. He didn't leave his name."

Susan's heartbeat nearly tripped over itself. Adam! "Was there a message?"

"No, he said he'd call back later."

"When did he call?"

"About an hour ago," Rosemary mumbled as the facial plaster began to slip. "But I don't think it was your doctor friend. This guy's voice was different."

"Oh," she whispered. "What's that on your face?"

"Avocados." Rosemary returned to the bathroom.

THE CLOCK RADIO went off early the next morning. Susan fumbled with the switch that killed the music. One eye fluttered open to note the time—seven fifty-five. Perhaps that had been Adam phoning last night. Then it'd be entirely proper for her to contact him in return. And since an early-morning walk in Central Park would be good for her health, there was no better time than Saturday morning. If she just happened to run into Adam coaching his soccer team, then that would be the perfect time to ask.

Slipping out of bed, she grabbed jeans and a sweater and walked into the bathroom. With luck she could be out the door before Rosemary knew she was gone.

Forty-five minutes later, fortified with several cups of strong coffee, Susan let herself out. One look at the threatening dark sky and she cringed. Only for Adam; there wasn't another reason on earth she'd be out this early on a Saturday morning.

Hoping to look as casual as possible, she strolled to the field and stood on the sideline. Her toe played with the chalk line. When she glanced up, her eyes met Adam's. She knew hers were a little apprehensive, but her doubts quickly faded at the welcome in his.

He shouted something to one of the boys, who ran forward and took his place as he trotted to her side.

"Hi."

"Morning." She glanced away, fearing he'd read her eagerness.

"I was hoping you'd come."

He was hoping she'd come! For two miserable weeks she'd heard nothing from him. She shot him an angry glare.

Surprise flickered over his face. "Is something wrong?"

"Nothing," she lied. "I got a phone call last night. Rosemary said she thought it might have been you."

"No," he said casually, "it wasn't me."

Inhaling deeply, she hoped to calm herself and fight off the attack of indignation. "It seemed like such a nice morning for a walk. I didn't mean to intrude."

"You're not," he assured her quickly, and exhaled a slow breath. "Are you always this beautiful in the morning?"

Beautiful! She'd barely worn any makeup, just a light application of lip gloss. Her hair was brushed away from her face and held in place with two barrettes. Struggling for a witty reply, she murmured, "You should see me before I've downed two cups of coffee."

"I'd like that very much."

The words were issued so softly that Susan wasn't sure he'd said anything. But the way her heart somersaulted into her throat assured her she hadn't imagined it. But now his gaze was directed onto the field.

"We're going to need lots of encouragement today. We're playing the first-place team."

"Terrific," she said, beaming. "I'll have you know I was a high-school cheerleader. Let's win this game."

Chuckling, Adam ran back onto the field.

The game was clearly a defensive one, and neither team had scored by halftime.

Like an anxious parent, Adam moved up and down the sidelines. Susan was convinced he'd forgotten she was there until one boy weaved the ball through the defenders and kicked it past the goalie, scoring for the first time. Before she knew what was happening, Adam's arms shot around her waist and she was lifted from the ground and swung around. Happiness gleamed from his eyes, and it was all Susan could do not to throw her arms around his neck and kiss him.

The final score was one to nothing, and the boys left the field triumphantly waving their hands high above their heads and shouting their glee.

"Congratulations, coach," Susan said with a warm smile when Adam joined her.

"That's thanks to you cheering," he said with a happy laugh. A hand on her shoulder brought her close. "Have you had anything to eat? I'm starved."

"Me too."

"What would you like? The sky's the limit."

"Anything I like?" she asked, her voice low and seductive. "For openers," she said, "I'd like to know why you haven't called me. Following an acceptable excuse, I want you to find a secluded corner and kiss me before I do something rash. And lastly, I'd like the assurance another two weeks aren't going to pass before I'm forced into making an excuse to see you."

Something unreadable flickered in his eyes, and his mouth thinned into a hard line. Susan groaned inwardly, knowing that she had displeased him again. When would she stop making a fool of herself? Fiery color stained her cheeks.

Dropping her gaze, she stepped aside. "On second thought, a hot dog with mustard would do."

"But not for me," he murmured thickly. Fingers pressing the back of her waist, he directed her to a small stand of trees. Before she could say anything, he took her in his arms. With his hands looped easily around her trim waist, his eyes, serious and dark, met hers. As if in slow motion, he lowered his mouth to hers. An eternity passed before his lips found hers in a kiss that told her everything she needed to know.

As she linked her arms around his neck, her breath became ragged. One kiss and her senses were inflamed. "Two weeks," she moaned. "Why did you make me wait that long?"

"I don't know," he whispered against her hair and then his mouth crashed down a second time. The intensity stole her breath, and her knees threatened to buckle.

"Now for that hot dog," he whispered, and brushed his chin and jaw across the creamy smoothness of her cheek. "There's a place not far from here we can walk to if you don't mind."

"I don't," she assured him. Not when he had his arm around her; not when she felt as if she were walking on air.

As they strolled out of the park they met a vendor with a red cart selling giant pretzels. "Want one?" Adam asked. "They come with mustard," he added.

"Sure." Susan was surprised that they were still warm. "Hey, these are good."

"You mean you've never had one of these?"

"To be honest, I've lived in New York two years and you wouldn't believe the things I haven't done." They continued strolling down Fifth Avenue with no clear destination. "There's one thing I've wanted to do. I mean, we don't have these things in Oregon."

"What?" He threw her a curious gaze.

"Subways. You're talking to a girl born and raised in Tillamook, Oregon. I thought I'd hit the big time at Ithaca."

"You attended Cornell?"

"Why are you so surprised? I'm not an airhead."

"I know that." He took her hand and squeezed it. "Come on, you'll be safe."

An entrance to the underground station was three blocks east. Adam paid for their tokens while Susan stared at the green walls littered with graffiti.

A roaring sound filled the tunnel as the huge metal monster soared into view. Susan took an unconscious step closer to Adam. The roar dissipated into a swishing hiss and came to a stop. Steel doors glided open and people filed out. Susan and Adam waited until there was a clear path before hurrying inside. There was no seating available, so Susan kept her balance by clasping a steel pole. Adam's arm was wrapped around her waist.

He had never held her this close for so long, and she couldn't help but marvel at the power he had over her senses. Everything about the day held a glorious promise.

"We get off here," he told her as the train halted a second time.

"What did you think?" he asked, once they reached the street.

Susan shrugged. "I'm not sure. I do know I'm going to appreciate those surly cabdrivers a little more next time."

They'd walked several blocks before she asked, "Are you going to tell me where we're going or not?"

"You'll see."

Adam directed her into a multistory building on the next block, led her into the elevator and pushed the button indicating the tenth floor.

She ventured a guess. "Your apartment?"

He feigned shock. "We hardly know one another."

"Your office?"

"The girl's a marvel," he issued softly. His mouth curved into a tantalizing smile. "There's someone I want you to meet. But before I go to the hospital I've got to change clothes, and here is closer than my apartment. You don't mind waiting?"

"Of course not, but, Adam..." She hesitated. "I'm not really dressed to be meeting people."

"No one's going to look past that gorgeous face to notice." Placing a hand on both shoulders, he brought her close. "I don't make many promises, but that's one I have no qualms about." He kissed her lightly.

He brought her into his private office, then left to change in an examination room. She paused to read the framed degrees and certificates. Of more interest was a bulletin board in the reception room with pictures of babies he'd delivered and several thank-you notes from children. A proud smile softly curved up the edges of her mouth.

"I told you that wouldn't take long," he said from behind her. He was dressed in a thick Irish cable-knit sweater and dark slacks.

Smiling, she held her arm out to him. "Now I look like something the cat dragged in. I wish you'd said something. I hate to meet anyone looking like this."

An arm around her shoulders firmly guided her out of the office. He paused to lock the door, placing a plain brown bag under his arm as he did so.

"To be honest, I don't think Joey will notice."

"Joey?"

"A leukemia patient of mine. He's going home today, after a long stay at the hospital. Poor fellow's been through quite a bit, and I wanted to stop in and see him before he's released. Interested?"

From the look in his eye Susan realized this was someone Adam cared about deeply. "You bet." No doubt Joey worshiped his doctor. "If I ever get sick, can I make an appointment?" The question was asked in a teasing tone, but with an underlying note of seriousness.

The hesitation was enough to make Susan edgy.

"Of course," he said at last.

The hospital was only three short blocks from his office. Adam was cornered almost at once by a nurse, who engaged him in a series of questions.

Ten minutes later he directed Susan to the nine-year-old's room.

"Hi, Joey."

"Dr. Gallagher." The youth smiled, sitting up in bed. He was dressed in *Star Wars* pajamas, and a watchman's cap adorned his bald head. Blue eyes sparkled with mischief.

"This is my friend, Susan Mackenzie," Adam introduced, curving an arm around her shoulders.

"Hi, Susan." Joey grinned at Adam. "She's real pretty."

"Congratulations, Joey. Dr. Gallagher tells me you're going to be released today."

"Honest?" Excitement vibrated through the boy.

"Seems that way," Adam admitted.

"Yippee," Joey shouted, and threw his cap in the air.

"Remember what we talked about before you had the chemotherapy?" Adam's eyes turned serious.

"I remember," the boy mumbled, glancing away. "I know I wasn't as good as I should have been, but I tried real hard."

"I know you did. So I contacted a friend of mine. He wanted me to give you this." Opening the bag, Adam took out a baseball and handed it to Joey.

"Dave Winfield signed this?"

"I think he might have put your name on it too."

"Wow." The one word was barely above a whisper.

"The rest of the Yankees asked me to give you this." Adam produced a leather mitt covered with autographs.

"Everyone on the whole team?" Joey asked in awe.

"It seems they don't often hear about boys as brave as you."

Joey threw his arms around Adam's neck. "You've got to be the best doctor in the whole world."

SOMETIME LATER Susan sat across from Adam at a small Italian restaurant.

"How'd you manage the autographed baseball and mitt?"

"Don't ask. I owe so many people favors for that one, I may be giving free exams until the year 2000."

"You don't know Dave Winfield?"

"Heavens no." He chuckled.

"You really love that little boy, don't you?"

"I do. There aren't many people I admire more."

"Is he going to make it?"

"Yes." The lone word was issued forcefully, as if the strength of Adam's will would be enough to heal him. "What would you like to order?"

Susan realized he didn't want her to question him about the boy. "The lasagna," she said, and Adam ordered two of the same.

Everything was delicious, but when their dishes were cleared away, Susan glanced at her watch and sighed.

"What's wrong?" Adam asked.

"I've got to get home. I didn't even tell Rosemary I was going to be gone. We're supposed to attend a party this afternoon." Replacing her cup in the saucer, she glanced at Adam. He seemed to be lost in his own thoughts. She glanced down.

"Susan." Her name was spoken softly. "There's another game next Saturday. Would you like to come?"

"Adam Gallagher," she cried. "I could kiss you."

*

THE ALARM rang early Saturday morning, and Susan threw back the covers. A quick glance out the bedroom window revealed heavy clouds and a good possibility of rain. Instead of taking her leather jacket, she pulled on a beige raincoat and matching cloche. In twenty-four years she couldn't remember having been happier, and it was all because she was on her way to Adam.

By the time she entered the park, a light sprinkle was dotting the ground. Brisk steps carried her to the soccer fields. But there was no one else around. Had the game been canceled? Looking around, she noted a tall male figure walking toward her. He waved and she returned the gesture.

"Morning," she greeted cheerfully. "What happened?" Tiny waves of pleasure pulsed through her at the raw, virile sight he presented. He wore a tweed jacket and dark slacks, and Susan couldn't remember a time he looked more enticingly masculine.

"The other team forfeited the game."

"Oh." She tried to disguise her disappointment.

Adam placed a hand along the side of her neck and tilted her head back with the subtle pressure of one finger.

Susan's breath became shallow. Anticipating his kiss, she

parted her mouth willingly and slipped her arms around his neck. The kiss lingered as if they were both unwilling for the intimacy to end. When he buried his face against the slim column of her neck, Susan moaned, not wanting him to stop. One kiss and the whole crazy world took a tailspin.

Susan dropped her hands just in time to see several runners jog past. "They jog in packs now?"

"Do I detect a sarcastic note?" Adam asked fighting a smile. "Don't be so hard on us."

"Us?"

"Sure, I'm a runner. I thought you knew."

"No," she said. "When do you run?"

"Weekdays right here in the park. I usually follow the same route as everyone else. Two and a half miles is all I have time for, but I love it."

Susan's mind was buzzing. Perhaps Rosemary wasn't so crazy after all. Maybe it was time she joined the physical fitness craze.

"You look a million miles away."

"Oh, sorry." She snapped out of her private thoughts.

"I guess I forgot to tell you today's game was the last one of the season."

Disappointment washed over her. "Yes, I guess you did. Do you coach anything else?"

He flashed her a brief smile. "Only soccer. I don't have time for anything else."

Was he saying he didn't have time for her either?

"Are you going to treat me to a decent breakfast?"

"I imagine that could be arranged."

"FIRST THING we're going to do is take you to the health-food store. Fred will set you up on a vitamin program." Rosemary's eyes gleamed with enthusiasm.

"I want to start running. Not once did I mention taking vitamins."

Rosemary sighed. "You've got to learn to trust me, Susan. Without the proper vitamin fortification, you could be sick within a week.''

"How much is this going to cost?" Susan demanded. She had already spent fifty dollars for a turquoise running suit.

"Does your health have a price?"

"This month, yes," she returned forcefully.

"Okay, okay. We'll start with the bare essentials." Rosemary was in her glory, believing Susan to be her first convert.

When the first alarm rang early Monday morning, Susan rolled over, assured of another hour of sleep.

"Susan," Rosemary's voice broke into her dream. "Time to get up."

"No, it's not," she mumbled. "If you're going to become physically fit, the best way to start is with walking."

Twenty minutes later, Susan stared at Rosemary, who had completed one hundred and fifty sit-ups to her own fifteen.

"How do you feel?" Rosemary shouted, hands on her hips as she lifted her knees while running in place.

"Like I should quit while I'm ahead."

"That's probably not a bad idea. Don't make the mistake of doing too much at once."

"How long before I'll be ready to jog?"

"Depends on how far you want to go."

She shrugged. "I don't know, two miles, two and a half."

"That'll take weeks."

"Weeks?" Susan cried. She couldn't wait that long. True to character, Adam hadn't set a time to see her again. "I've got to be able to hit the streets faster than that."

"I don't suppose this has anything to do with Adam?"

"What makes you ask?"

Wiping her face with a hand towel, Rosemary said, "I

know you. I've seen men come and go. But I've never seen you act like this.''

"I've never felt this strong about anyone else. And I learned last week that Adam's a runner.''

A look of understanding flashed over Rosemary's face. "Ah, now I get the picture.''

A week later, Susan was almost desperate. It'd been ten days since she'd last seen Adam, and she hadn't heard a word from him. But Rosemary had devised a workout program that left her exhausted. Every night she crawled into bed and fell into an easy slumber.

Within six days Susan was matching Rosemary in sit-ups and jumping jacks. Although she wasn't thrilled about the two-and-a-half-mile walk to work, she faithfully made the trek each morning.

On Wednesday, she woke at five-thirty, long before the alarm. Wouldn't Adam ever phone? Hadn't he guessed how much he meant to her?

Without questioning the wisdom of her actions, she laid back the covers and quietly slipped out of bed. She was out the door before Rosemary knew she was gone.

Although the morning was crisp and the sky dark, several runners were already in the park. She had no idea what time Adam ran, but with his office hours and hospital rounds, it had to be around six. She would wait around by the picnic area until he came into view and casually join him.

Fifteen minutes later, Susan stood shivering and miserable, convinced that Adam wasn't coming. And how would she ever manage to give the impression she'd "accidentally" run into him?

"Susan." Her name was shouted from the distance and she had to squint to see the source.

"Hi," she called, and waved, forcing herself to smile.

"I didn't know you ran." He slowed his pace to match hers.

"Yes," she mumbled, already feeling breathless. "Since I hadn't heard from you, I thought I'd join you once around the reservoir and see how you've been."

"Great, and you?"

"Wonderful," she lied. Just once, couldn't he tell her he'd been thinking of her? Her lungs were beginning to hurt, and she struggled to maintain the pace. Talking and breathing were almost impossible.

"How many miles do you run a week?" Adam said.

"Ten." She managed to get out the one word.

"Have you ever averaged your minutes per mile?"

"No." She concentrated on placing one foot in front of the other. She'd finish the course if it killed her. At just the moment Susan was convinced she was either going to faint, vomit or die, Adam stopped.

"Wow, that felt good."

Susan didn't respond. Instead she collapsed.

Adam joined her on the grass. "You okay?"

She didn't have the breath to assure him. Nodding her head was all she could do.

"I imagine my pace is a bit faster than yours."

She struggled to sit up. If he wouldn't say it, she would. "I missed you."

"I was going to call," he murmured.

"Why didn't you?" she whispered.

"You're an extremely attractive woman." There was a ragged edge to his voice.

"That's an excuse?"

"Susan," he said, then paused. "I'm a plain-looking man. People are going to take a look at us and see beauty and the beast. I don't think…"

"Stop it, stop it right now! Don't you ever say that to me again." Raising herself up, she jabbed a finger at his chest. "You are the most attractive, wonderful, fun person I know, and if I ever hear you talk like that about yourself or me again, I'll…scream," she said.

"You're managing to do a fair job of that now." He glanced around self-consciously.

"I know what I'll do," she cried. "I'll scar myself and then maybe you won't look at me like I'm Miss Perfect...or Gail. That was her name, wasn't it? Then maybe you'll treat me like a normal woman—as everyone else does."

A muscle jerked in his jaw, and Susan knew she had gone too far. He didn't like her to mention Gail.

"Have you ever stopped to think that maybe I didn't want to see you?" he demanded in a low growl. The look in his eyes was almost savage.

The words hurt more than if he'd slammed his fist into her stomach. For a stunned second she didn't breathe. Tears filled her eyes and she lowered her gaze.

"No, I guess I hadn't." She whispered the words in a husky, pain-filled murmur. Wearily she stood, her back to him. "I'm sorry, I won't bother you again." By the time she made it to the outskirts of the park, her vision had become a watery blur.

Pausing outside her apartment door, she wiped the tears from her face then let herself in.

"Susan," Rosemary cried. "Where have you been? I was worried." She stopped abruptly. "Susan..."

"Go to work without me today, will you?" Susan asked. "Tell Karen I'm sick. Maybe I'll be in later...."

"Sure. Are you going to be all right?"

"No." She tried to laugh. "But you go on. I'll live."

Rosemary left a few minutes later and Susan sank onto the couch.

Someone banged on her door. The sound reverberated around the silent room and her head shot up.

"Yes." She unlocked the door and her gaze collided with Adam's.

"Susan, I'm sorry." He didn't bother with a greeting. "I didn't mean what I said." After a brief hesitation he reached out and touched her shoulder.

Wordlessly, Susan walked into his arms and buried her face in his chest.

"Why?" The sound of her voice was muffled by the strength of his hold.

Two large hands cupped her face as his gaze probed hers. Susan noted a curious pain that tinged his eyes.

"You're so beautiful."

For the first time in her life, being attractive was a detriment. "Adam, please," she said. "I'm not."

"Enough for anyone to question what someone like you is doing with me."

"That's nonsense." Raising her own hand, she cupped his and pressed a kiss into his palm.

A sound came from deep in his throat as his mouth descended to hers, plundering her ready lips with a kiss that was fierce and hungry. Gradually the pressure lessened to a gentle possession as his mouth moved lazily over hers. The yearnings he created within her left Susan trembling.

"When I'm with you," he began, "I think I'm the luckiest man in the world. I treasure every minute and die every time we say goodbye."

Susan couldn't believe what she was hearing. "But why don't you ever call me afterward?"

"That's the way I feel when we're together," he admitted dryly. "Later I realize you've probably got plenty of men wanting to date you."

"I don't," she murmured. "Oh, Adam."

"I wish I had a dime for every time I picked up the phone to call you or all the times I've found myself standing outside your apartment building. Then I stop and realize you'd be crazy to be interested in me."

"I admit it then," she told him. "I'm crazy, because I'm interested in you, Adam Gallagher. Do you need more convincing?"

His soft chuckle mussed her hair. "That'll probably hold me until I get downstairs. I'm not the most secure person when it comes to romantic involvements. I don't know if that's a result of Gail or just being homely.''

''I wish you'd stop saying that,'' she said. ''You are not ugly! But I don't know what to do or say to convince you.''

''When you're in my arms, I don't need anything else. It comes after a long day at the office and I find that I want to share my day with you.'' His grip tightened as his mouth moved roughly over her hair. ''Do you want to meet again tomorrow morning?''

''You mean—'' she swallowed tightly ''—to run?''

''Sure.''

Susan wasn't about to refuse.

''Only this time let's complete the full loop. We only went a mile today.''

*

THE FOLLOWING Monday morning, Susan was at the park expecting to meet Adam for their usual run. They had been meeting daily for almost a week. When he didn't show up, Susan assumed he was extra busy or had forgotten. When he wasn't there Tuesday or Wednesday, she felt hurt and disappointed. Was he playing games with her again? For the rest of the week she didn't go to the park. But when the weekend arrived, she couldn't stand it any longer.

Against her better judgment, she called him.

The phone rang five times. ''Yes,'' he snapped.

''It's Susan.'' Her resolve wavered.

''I've been meaning to phone. I've had a hectic week.'' His voice softened somewhat.

''I thought you probably had.''

Silence.

''You're closing me out again, aren't you?''

''No. I've just been busy, that's all.''

''Too busy to run? You love to jog.''

"Maybe next week. Listen, Susan, I've got something going on here. I'll call you next week."

True to his word, he did phone the following week, but the conversation was short and stilted. Susan was certain he'd given up running because he didn't want to meet her, so she told him that her schedule had been changed and she wouldn't be able to jog anymore.

Another week passed without hearing from him. Whatever was troubling Adam had to be settled in his own way. Susan didn't know what more she could do. Adam couldn't hold her and kiss her as he had, then turn away so abruptly.

He continued to phone, usually when she least expected it. He didn't ask her out, or suggest that they meet, and Susan didn't prod.

At Christmas she spent hours searching for a special card that would say exactly how she felt, deciding in the end that she'd never find one. She ended up mailing the same one that she had sent to all her family and friends.

Adam mailed her a card with his name scribbled at the bottom. There was no written message.

A few days before Christmas he phoned.

"I just wanted to wish you a Merry Christmas."

"You too, Adam." She paused.

"Are you going home for the holidays?"

"Yes, I'm flying out the twenty-third and will be back the twenty-sixth." She couldn't afford it, but her parents had paid part of the airfare.

"You're not staying long, are you?"

"I can't spare the time from the office."

An awkward silence followed.

"Are you jogging these days?"

"All the time," she lied cheerfully, anything to keep the conversation going. "I...was thinking about going this morning, in fact."

"I won't keep you then. Have a nice holiday, Susan."

For a long time after the line was disconnected, she held

on to the receiver. She hadn't seen him since before Thanksgiving and was starving for the sight of him. Maybe he'd been hinting that he'd be at the park.

Shivering, Susan briskly walked the two-and-a-half-mile course, desperately clinging to the hope of seeing Adam. When he hadn't shown by the time she'd finished the full circle, tears of frustration and disappointment filled her eyes. Quickly she wiped them aside....

Dejected, she returned to the apartment and took a warm bath.

"KAREN WOULD like to see you," the receptionist, Dana Milton, told Susan when she walked into the office the second Monday in January. Christmas with her family had been wonderful, and Susan had returned to New York feeling relaxed and refreshed.

It was as well, since the impulsive Rosemary had eloped over the holidays with Fred from the health-food store. Susan would now be on her own in the apartment.

Later in the month she was scheduled to fly to Texas and speak at a writers' conference. That was probably what Karen wanted to talk to her about right now.

It wasn't. The first thing that came to mind as Susan went back to her office was that she'd need new business cards. She was now a full editor.

The first person she called was Adam. She hadn't talked to him since before Christmas.

"He'll be right with you," the receptionist told her.

"Susan, are you all right?" She'd not called his office before.

"Yes. I know I shouldn't call you like this, but I had some good news, and you were the first person I wanted to tell. I got a promotion. I'm a full-fledged editor now."

"Congratulations. I'm sure you deserve it." There was genuine pleasure in his voice.

"I won't keep you. I know this is an awful time to phone, but I was so excited I wanted to tell someone."

"I'm glad you did."

An hour after their conversation, a dozen beautiful red roses were delivered to her office. The sender's card bore only one word: "Adam."

WITH THE promotion came new responsibilities, and Susan threw herself into the task eagerly. But when she hadn't heard from Adam in several weeks, she nervously dialed his phone number. He answered on the third ring. "Hello."

"Hello, Adam. I haven't heard from you in a long time. Did you get my card?"

"It arrived last week. There was no need to thank me."

"Of course there was. But the reason I phoned was to let you know there's a small party next Friday night to celebrate my promotion."

He hesitated. "I'll have to check my calendar."

"Go ahead, I can wait."

"It looks like I've got hospital duty that night."

Disappointment washed over her. "I'll talk to Rosemary. I'm sure we can change it to Saturday night."

"I don't want you to do that."

"But I'd like you to be there."

"I told you, I'm busy," he said gruffly.

"Adam," she pleaded, angry with herself. "Please."

"Susan, *no.*"

Never had any word sounded more hurtful or cruel.

THE MORNING of February second, Susan made an appointment with Adam's receptionist. A few days later she sat nervously in one of his examination rooms, praying this was the right thing to do. Once again she was swallowing her pride and coming to him.

"Susan?" The disapproval in his voice did little to calm

her. But a gleam softened the hard look in his eyes. "You've cut your hair."

She'd forgotten he hadn't seen it. "It's not as short as it looks. I had it styled is all. Do you like it?"

He ignored the question. "What's the problem?" He remained on the opposite side of the room as if he wished to put as much distance between them as possible.

"Remember you said I could come see you if I was sick?"

"I remember." He didn't look pleased about it.

"I'm having a small pain," she continued, "on the left side of my chest, about the center."

"Your heart?" he questioned sarcastically. "Let me listen." He walked to the table where she was perched. Lifting up the back of her sweater, he placed the cold stethoscope on her sensitive flesh. "Take two breaths."

Susan complied. This wasn't going well. What had she expected? It was all she could do not to reach out to him, touch him. He looked tired, as if he was putting in long hours, but then so was she—immersing herself in work to forget.

"Everything sounds fine," he said flatly as he moved to the desk and pulled out a pad.

"Adam," she whispered. "I've waited three months to see you. At first you phoned me. Now you don't even do that. Adam, I thought by this time you would have worked things out. I need you. I'm miserable."

He ripped the sheet from the pad. "Have your druggist fill this."

"Are you listening to me at all?"

His eyes refused to meet hers. "If you continue to have problems, I'd suggest you see a specialist." His hand clenched the doorknob, and Susan noted that his knuckles were white.

"Don't do this to us, please." She hung her head, the soft curls falling forward to shield her.

"That prescription should take care of any problems you have. Goodbye, Susan."

She didn't even bother to read it, knowing it was for placebos. Grabbing her purse, she hurried out of the office.

Her cab jerked in and out of traffic, speeding up only to have the driver slam on his brakes a minute later. Susan hardly noticed until he yelled at her to hold on. She looked up to see a bus racing out of control, heading directly for the passenger side of the cab. Susan screamed.

The terror in her own voice was the only thing she heard as metal slammed against metal and she was thrown violently against the door.

DEEP, piercing pain filtered into the dark world in which Susan lay. Her head throbbed so hard that she raised a tentative hand to feel. Her fingers encountered a gauze wrapping. She tried to open her eyes, but one refused. The other opened just enough for her to recognize that she must be in a hospital.

A raised voice could be heard across the room. "I want a plastic surgeon brought in."

"I don't think she'll need—"

"I don't care what you think, I want one *now*. Is that understood?"

"Yes, Doctor."

Adam. Adam's voice was the angry one. Susan had never heard him talk that way to anyone. He moved to her side.

"So you're awake." The gentle quality she loved about him was back. "How do you feel?"

For a moment her mouth refused to obey. "Don't ask."

"I'll have the nurse give you something for the pain. You've been in an accident," he said softly. "One eye is swollen shut. The pain in your chest is from cracked ribs."

"My head?"

"You've got a whopper of a concussion."

"My face?" Her voice quivered.

"Luckily you put your hands up, which prevented your face from being cut any more than it was. There are several scratches. Nothing major."

A weariness flooded her, waves of fatigue rippling through her. Susan fought it as long as she could. Finally she succumbed to the overwhelming force as Adam whispered something about talking to her later.

When she woke again, the room was filled with light. She turned her head when a tall nurse opened the door.

"Morning, I thought you'd be awake by now." The white-capped nurse moved to the side of the bed and stuck a thermometer in Susan's mouth.

"When will Dr. Gallagher be in?" Susan asked.

"Dr. Gallagher?" she repeated. A frown marred her wide forehead as she removed Susan's chart. "You've been assigned to Dr. Manson."

Susan didn't need to ask, she already knew. Adam had requested to be relieved of her case. It shouldn't have surprised her, when he'd rejected her so many times.

"What do I look like?" Susan had to know.

"Let's put it this way—" the nurse chuckled "—I wouldn't want to see the other guy. But you'll improve. Don't worry."

Dr. Manson was a short man with thinning gray hair and twinkling blue eyes. Susan liked him immediately.

"Good morning."

She smiled. "Morning. When can I go home?"

"We were worried last night about internal injuries, but you seem to be doing fine. I imagine tomorrow we can release you if you like."

"I like," she stated emphatically.

"Don't do too much today. Get out of bed if you want. I'll check with you tomorrow morning."

"Thank you, Doctor."

Breakfast arrived and Susan managed to down some applesauce and a small bowl of Jell-O. Afterward she was so weak she lay back and, before she knew it, was sound asleep.

A noise in the room woke her. When she opened her eyes, Adam was standing beside her bed.

"Dr. Manson says you can go home tomorrow. I'll take half the day off and pick you up about noon."

Susan jerked her head around, shocked at his offer, then winced at the pain that shot through her head. "You were in the emergency room last night, weren't you?"

Adam nodded. "They called me."

"But how? I didn't give anyone your name."

He glanced away. "Apparently the prescription I gave you was clenched in your fist. The ambulance driver found it."

"Adam," she whispered imploringly. "Is my face bad? No one wants to tell me anything."

Again she noted how a nerve twitched in his jaw, but his eyes softened. "You've got a few cuts, but they'll heal quickly. Your eye's swollen, but quite a bit less than yesterday." He hesitated. "You're still the most beautiful woman I know. Within a month no one will know you were ever hurt."

"A month," she groaned.

"Honey, believe me, when I first saw you, I was afraid it was much worse."

Honey! The affectionate term rolled off his tongue as if he'd said it a thousand times. His lips lightly brushed her cheek.

"I'll see you later," he promised.

Susan leaned against the pillow and sighed. Immediately her ribs protested, and she released a quivering breath until the pain subsided.

After dinner Adam returned, helping her out of bed and walking at her side as they strolled the hallway several times. One hand was linked with Adam's while the other pushed the portable I.V. pole. Two beautiful bouquets had arrived that afternoon. One was from Adam and another from her co-workers at Silhouette.

"How long will it be before I can go back to work?" she quizzed as they headed back to her room.

"I think a week should do it."

"A week," she cried. "I can't miss that much time." Already her mind was racing toward a writers' conference she was scheduled to speak at in Florida in the middle of March.

"Sure you can," he contradicted. "After the first couple of days, I don't see why you couldn't go in for a few hours in the mornings. But not more than that," he warned.

SUSAN LAY for a long time thinking after Adam had kissed her good-night. A light kiss against her forehead. Just the day before, he had pushed her from his life. The accident was the only reason he was back. But for how long?

He stopped in briefly early the next morning with the reminder that she should be ready to leave about noon, and Dr. Manson gave his smiling approval shortly after. "So, you're Adam Gallagher's girl. I must admit I've never seen him lose his cool the way he did after they brought you into the emergency room."

At Susan's shocked look, Manson continued. "Most doctors agree it's better not to treat family members, or those we love. The difficulty is in keeping ourselves detached enough not to react emotionally. It only took me two seconds to see Adam cared deeply for you."

Susan wanted to argue that she was sure he was mistaken. But was he? Did Adam truly love her? If so, what could have prompted him to act as he had these last months?

During the ride home, Adam worked hard to lighten the mood and tear down the tension between them. Joking, he set her on the sofa, and fluffed up the pillows.

Susan tried to throw herself into his happy mood but

failed miserably. When he insisted on cooking their dinner, she watched with amazement as he set the table and brought out an expensive bottle of wine.

As much as Susan wanted and needed him, she couldn't let this continue. "Adam," she whispered, "the accident wasn't your fault."

"I know that."

"Then why are you doing this? I don't know how to react when you're kind to me. I'm afraid." To her horror, large tears filled her eyes.

"Damn it, Susan. Don't cry. I can't stand to see you cry."

"Then just leave." She pointed a finger at the front door.

Adam stared at her, finally grabbing his jacket.

"Don't you dare leave me," she shouted.

He got as far as the front door, his hand on the knob. His back was to her.

"I need you," she whispered.

When he turned, a tumult of emotions played over his strong face. Of its own volition, her hand reached out to him and he hurried to her side, falling to his knees and wrapping his arms around her. Even in his urgency he was conscious of her ribs and the pain his hold could inflict.

"Susan, dear God." He murmured her name over and over again. "I saw you in that room, blood everywhere, and I died a thousand deaths. If I lost you…"

Her hands roamed his back as she buried her face in his chest. "Oh, Adam," she cried, tears streaming down her face. "I've missed you so much. You sent me away and I wanted to die."

A tense groan was muffled as he found her mouth and savored again and again the softness of her lips.

Her hand lovingly explored the line of his jaw before curving into his thick dark hair. The kiss hardened, demanding and relentless, drawing from Susan her heart, and touching the softness of her soul.

When he pulled away, his breathing was hoarse and uneven. "Susan, we've got to stop," he groaned.

"I know," she agreed, and unbuttoned his shirt, desperate for the feel of his bare skin. When her fingers encountered the cloud of dark hair, Susan became incapable of coherent thought. The potent masculine feel of him enveloped her senses until they cried out at fever pitch.

When Adam's hands opened her blouse and cupped her unrestrained breasts, he gently kneaded their fullness and she grew weak with desire. Lost in a mindless whirlpool, Susan groaned softly, as he kissed the swelling curve.

He pressed her back against the couch, and Susan drew in a sharp breath as pain pierced her ribs.

Adam hesitated, then pulled away. Still within the circle of his embrace, she could feel his aching regret.

"I'm sorry, love," he whispered. "Those ribs must be hurting like hell."

"Not as much as..." She paused, biting off the words. He already knew how much sending her away had hurt.

"Are you ready for a glass of wine?" His jaw was set in a determined line as he battled his need and desire. Gently he tugged her arms from his neck. He kissed her fingertips and then the bridge of her nose before helping her fasten her blouse. Standing, he moved into the kitchen and returned with two glasses of wine, handing her one.

Forcing herself to smile, Susan looked up. "What's for dinner? I'm starved."

"Crepes stuffed with shrimp and fresh mushrooms."

"Adam! You can cook like that?"

"Not quite, but I do an excellent job of placing something in the oven and setting the timer."

"Oh, Adam," she said happily. "We have so much in common."

THEY PLAYED a game of Monopoly after dinner. Adam won, but Susan's interest wasn't on the board. Adam waited until she'd changed into her pajamas before kissing her good night. The kiss was almost brotherly.

"Miser," she complained.

"Troublemaker," he countered, kissing her soundly. But he didn't allow it to deepen into passion.

Locking the door after him, Susan leaned against the solid frame and swallowed a happy lump.

Adam was hers.

THAT EVENING was the first of many they spent together. Adam couldn't have been more gentle or loving. He kissed and touched her often. He made excuses to be with her. But he never allowed their lovemaking to rage out of control.

When Susan was able to return to work, he met her two and sometimes three nights a week. Occasionally they dined out, other times cooking for themselves, "setting the timer." Susan had never been happier. But late at night, alone, she couldn't push the doubts aside. How much longer would this last before Adam pulled away?

Three weeks after the accident and it was difficult to tell that anything had happened. Her face had healed beautifully, as Adam repeatedly told her.

Humming happily one night, she set the table, anticipating Adam's arrival. She placed a candle in the middle of the fresh linen cloth and popped a tuna casserole into the oven.

Adam knocked, and when she let him in, carelessly tossed his coat over a chair. Surprised at the restrained anger that seemed to exude from him, Susan didn't comment.

She kissed him on the cheek. "Have a bad day?"

"No worse than usual."

"I tried my hand at a tuna casserole."

He stared at the table. "What's the candle for?"

"I thought it might add a little romance to our meal."

"Romance," he spat. "You live and breathe that garbage, don't you?"

"If you don't like the candle, I'll take it away."

"I hate tuna," he shouted at her unreasonably. "If you'd bothered to ask, you might have known that."

"I'm sorry, I…I guess I should have."

"Do you have to apologize for every little thing? Don't you ever get tired of groveling?"

Susan breathed in sharply in an effort to control her temper. Wordlessly, she walked across the room, took Adam's jacket off the chair and handed it to him.

"It's obvious you've had a rotten day. I'm sorry about that. But I think it would be better for both of us if you left now. We'll have dinner another night." She held open the door.

"There won't be another night," he informed her casually. "The whole situation between us should never have happened. I knew the minute I saw you at Ralph's that you spelled trouble." He jerked his arm into the jacket. "This is it, Susan."

Did he expect her to cry and beg? She wouldn't, not anymore.

His shirt was stretched across his broad chest, and Susan directed her gaze to the rippling muscles rather than meet his eyes. Her pulse drummed to an erratic tempo, and she cursed the telltale tremble in her voice.

"Goodbye, Adam," she whispered softly.

Two miserable days later Susan flew to Florida for the writers' conference. She arrived home late Friday afternoon.

Saturday morning, rather than face the day staring at the walls alone, Susan rose early and walked to the office to catch up with the workload on her desk. Letting herself into her small office, the first thing she noticed was a bouquet of flowers. The attached card read: "I'm sorry. Meet me at Tastings Thursday. Love, Adam."

Thursday! The flowers must have arrived when she was away. What must he be thinking? Grabbing her coat, she flew out of the office. Once on the street, she waved madly at a taxi and breathlessly relayed Adam's address.

She almost threw the fare at the astonished driver as she leaped out and raced inside to take the stairs two at a time until she arrived at the fourth floor.

She was leaning against the wall taking in giant breaths when Adam casually opened the door.

"Adam." She hugged him fiercely.

"Susan, are you all right?"

"Yes…" she gasped. "Adam, I was in Florida."

He sat her down in his living room and went to the kitchen.

"Here." He handed her a glass of water.

She set the water aside, and with eyes sparkling with happiness, she placed her hands on his shoulders. "I've missed you so much."

"You idiot," he groaned, and hugged her. "There was no need to half kill yourself to get to me. I already knew you were in Florida. When you didn't show, I called your office."

Her happy gaze met his as he kissed her hungrily.

"Were you miserable?" she asked him.

"Yes," he replied on a forceful note.

"I love it," she cried cheerfully, but her heart repeated that it was Adam she really loved.

He took her to the Palm Court at the Plaza Hotel, and they lunched on luscious salads. Not until the meal was finished did Susan notice the pinched look about Adam's mouth.

"I've been talking fifty miles an hour and hardly giving you time to say a word."

Wearily he rubbed his face. "It's been one of those weeks. I've been miserable without you, Susan."

He needed her, but he wouldn't admit as much. Something deep and dark was troubling him. He couldn't hide it from her; she knew him too well. Perhaps that bothered him more.

"Adam?" she questioned softly. "What's wrong?"

"Did I mention that Joey Williams was back in the hospital?" He said it so casually that for a moment she didn't recognize the significance.

"No, you didn't." So that was it. Joey. The little boy Adam loved. "How...how's he doing?"

"Not good," he answered at last.

SUSAN DIDN'T hear from Adam until late Tuesday night of the following week.

"Hi, honey, how's your week going?"

"Fine, and you?"

"Great." The word was emitted in a flippant tone, and Susan wanted to shout at him that it wasn't necessary for him to lie to her.

"Any news?" She didn't need to clarify about whom.

"Nothing," he responded.

They met for dinner early the next week. Susan was several minutes late and found Adam already seated and studying the menu when she arrived.

"Sorry, but I got held up in traffic," she said as she slid into the seat opposite him and shrugged off her coat.

Adam looked up. "Are you ready to order?"

"Order?" she asked. "I've barely caught my breath. Adam, you wouldn't believe the day I've had. First an agent who was making the most unreasonable demands. And just before I left an author called wanting to go over the editorial changes I'd made. By phone, mind you."

He offered her a poor facsimile of a smile.

"I'm sorry, Adam," she said sincerely. "I didn't even ask about your day."

"Nothing unusual. Mine certainly can't compete with a popular romance editor's day."

Susan decided to ignore that. "Ralph Jordan called today. He's giving another party. Are we going?"

"We?" He raised one thick brow.

"Adam, what is wrong with you? You haven't said a civil word since I arrived."

"Not for lack of trying, I assure you." His face was buried in the menu. "With you babbling inanities, it's difficult to speak at all."

Susan expelled a slow, measured breath. "Is it Joey?"

He slammed the menu on the table. "Joey's home. Are you satisfied?" He was nearly shouting, his voice biting and bitter.

Susan closed her eyes to a rush of pain. She never would have believed Adam could talk to her that way. "I think I've heard enough." Scooting out of the booth, she hurriedly put on her coat. "When you've settled whatever's troubling you, then give me a call. I'll be waiting."

He started to say something, but Susan didn't wait to listen. Instead she hurried out of the restaurant and hailed a taxi before he had the opportunity to follow.

Another week passed before she heard from Adam again. He called to apologize, but he didn't suggest they meet and she didn't ask. Susan couldn't recall a more frustrating time.

Late one night, Susan lay in bed staring at the ceiling. There were only the darkness and the doubts. How could a man who was gentle and kind one minute turn into a snarling, unreasonable bear the next? Maybe she was totally wrong about him. Maybe the time had come…

The doorbell interrupted her thoughts.

Susan sat up and threw back her bedcovers. It was well past midnight. Who could it possibly be at this time of night? In her robe, she turned on the light switch in the living room.

The bell sounded again.

Peeking out the small hole in her door, Susan saw no one. "Who is it?" she called.

"Adam."

Susan unlocked the door.

He hesitated, searching her face. "I woke you."

"No," she told him. "I wasn't asleep. Come in."

He paused. "A cup of coffee would help."

"I'll put some on right away." Her eyes didn't leave him as he came into the apartment and slowly lowered himself onto the sofa. He looked terrible.

Moving quickly, she poured water into the teakettle. As she worked, Susan glanced into the room at Adam. He was leaning forward, elbows on his knees, face buried in his palms.

She moved to his side, kneeling in front of him. "Adam," she whispered, all the love in her heart shining through her eyes. "What is it? Won't you tell me?"

Although he looked at her, Susan was sure he was hardly aware she was there. "Joey Williams died tonight."

A soft protesting moan came from deep within her throat. "Oh, Adam," she whispered, "I'm so sorry." Sliding her arms around his stomach, she rested her face on his chest and started to cry. "You loved him so much." Sobs shook her.

Adam tried to push her away, but she wouldn't let him. He held himself stiff and unyielding until something seemed to snap within him.

He shuddered against her and released a deep, mournful cry like that of an animal caught in a trap, facing death. Fiercely he hauled her into his arms, hugging her so close that for a moment Susan was afraid he would crush her. Huge sobs racked his body as he buried his face in her neck and wept.

"All the years I studied and there wasn't a damn thing I could do. Never have I felt so damn helpless."

"You did everything you could," she whispered.

"Not enough, not near enough."

She couldn't understand anything more he said, his words muffled in her hair and by his tears. As the shuddering sobs subsided, she heard the whistle from the kettle.

Briefly Adam raised his head, noting the source of the distraction. Reluctantly he released her.

Susan walked to the kitchen, poured them each a steaming cup and returned to Adam. After a few sips of coffee, she placed her cup aside. Adam curved an arm around her shoulder, bringing her close. Soon he was asleep.

Carefully, she slipped from his embrace. He was exhausted, mentally and physically. When his head dropped to one side, she brought out a pillow and blanket from her bedroom. After removing his shoes, she lifted his feet onto the sofa and covered him.

Even in sleep, his look remained troubled. Susan watched him for a long time. He had come to her in his grief, and that meant more to her than the finest gifts. His trust and love were beyond price.

Flipping the switch to the lamp cast the room into darkness. Gently she bent down, lovingly brushed the thick hair from his forehead and kissed him.

When she woke the next morning Adam was gone. A scribbled note left on the kitchen table briefly thanked her and stated the date and time of the funeral. Susan didn't see him until that day. She slipped into the pew beside him and listened to the service, her hand tightly clenched in his.

Afterward the Williams family came over to Adam. Mrs. Williams hugged him.

"We owe you more than words can ever express," she said. "Thank you for making it possible for Joey to come home those last days." She smiled weakly at Susan.

"You must be Miss Mackenzie. Joey mentioned how pretty you are." She inclined her head toward Adam. "Hold on to this man," she whispered. "There aren't many as wonderful as Dr. Gallagher."

"I know that," Susan agreed.

"In the end he hardly left Joey's side. Lord knows when he slept. Our family will never forget him."

Susan nodded because the lump in her throat had grown so large it was impossible to speak.

*

"HAVE YOU got everything?" Adam lifted her suitcase.

"I think so." Susan surveyed her bedroom.

"I'm ready." Adam was driving her to the airport. After dinner she would be flying to Boston for a five-day promotional tour with several authors. Susan always enjoyed working with the publicity department, but she almost regretted having agreed to go. Something was happening with Adam, and she had no idea what.

"That look is in your eyes again," she told him as they sat in a cozy restaurant not far from the airport.

Even his kisses had been different lately, almost polite yet wonderful and gentle. She didn't know how to explain it. But now wasn't the time to discuss it.

When it came time to board her flight, Susan couldn't fault his kiss.

"I'm going to miss you." His voice was a caress, husky and warm.

"Good, because you know how I feel." Adam had never verbalized the words, but neither had she.

"Yes, I do."

She heard the taut pain in his voice.

"Yes, I do," he repeated, as he lowered his mouth to savor the softness of hers. The kiss was slow and exploring, his tongue outlining her lips, coaxing her mouth open. Gladly Susan succumbed to the sweet tide of longing that swept through her.

TIME AWAY from New York helped put her relationship with Adam into perspective, but it didn't offer the answer to the doubts that plagued her.

When the plane touched down at Kennedy, she eagerly anticipated their meeting.

He waved when he saw her, and Susan had to restrain herself from running into his arms. Adam looked wonderful. The color was back in his face; his eyes were warm and excited.

"Welcome home." He looped an arm around her waist, took her hand baggage and kissed her cheek.

"You look marvelous."

"I am. How was the trip?"

"Great," she said, "but it's good to be home."

"It's good to have you back. I've got some fantastic news."

"What?" She stopped walking.

"I've accepted a position in Seattle, at the Fred Hutchinson Cancer Research Center. I'm moving next week."

"Seattle, Washington?" The shock hit her full force.

"It's the opportunity of a lifetime," Adam continued, undaunted by her obvious surprise.

"Congratulations," she murmured.

"Honey, I've got a hundred and one things that need to be done. I've got to get back to my office right away. You understand, don't you?"

"Oh, sure. Of course I do." Fixing a smile on her face, she followed him to the baggage claim area, barely aware of where they were going.

When he carried her suitcases into the apartment, she stepped aside, a determined lift to her chin. He kissed her at the door. A brotherly kiss.

"Be happy for me."

"I'm thrilled," she lied. *I'm dying,* said her heart. "Go," she commanded. "I understand."

She understood all too well. Adam was running from New York. Running from the memories of the little boy he couldn't save. But most of all he was running from her love.

She barely slept. Just when she felt herself drifting off, the pain would return and she'd jerk awake.

Because she couldn't tolerate the thought of staying in the apartment on a Saturday morning, she dressed and walked to the park.

"Are you going to let him do this?" her voice asked. *Yes,* her heart answered.

Hating herself for being weak, she phoned him when she got back to the apartment.

"Hello." He sounded preoccupied, busy.

"Morning," she said. "Have you had breakfast?"

"No time. I'm sorting through my things, deciding what I want to take and what I'm going to store."

"Let me help you. I'll bring some croissants."

The pause was only momentary. "Sure."

"I'll help you pack books and stuff."

"There's no need," Adam answered unevenly.

I'm not letting you go that easily, her mind shouted.

The flaky croissants were still warm, but neither Susan nor Adam seemed to have much appetite. With a shaky smile, she pushed up the sleeves of her sweatshirt.

"I'm ready. Where would you like me to start?"

Boxes littered the living room. Most of the furniture was pushed to one side. Bookcases stood against one wall.

"Go ahead and pack up those."

He left her alone, and went to work in his den. Susan recognized that the move was intentional.

After a half hour of silence she called to him.

"Do you want a cup of coffee?"

"Sounds great. I could do with a break."

She poured them each a cup and sat on the plush carpet drinking hers. Adam continued going through his desk drawers.

"There's a chance I'll be in Seattle sometime in June."

She didn't add that was when her vacation was scheduled, but let him think it was business related.

"Wonderful." He didn't sound as if he meant it.

"My parents live in Oregon."

He looked up. "I'd forgotten that."

Of course he had. Washington State was as far away from her as he could get, and without knowing it he'd placed himself in her home territory.

"But I think I should warn you, my schedule is very tight."

Susan didn't know how much more of this she could take. He was saying that if she did come, he'd make excuses not to see her. A sad smile touched her face.

"What's so funny?" Adam asked.

"My thoughts, I guess."

The natural question would have been to ask her what she was thinking, but Adam didn't.

"I'll finish packing the books," she said, and stood.

Two boxes were already filled and Susan scooted them aside. She pulled a third cardboard case across the carpet, then carefully slid out the bottom row of books. As she did, several Christmas cards fell onto the floor. One was flowery and romantic: "TO THE WOMAN I LOVE." Another was humorous: Susan had read it that Christmas while looking for a special card for Adam.

Sharply she sucked in her breath. Four cards had spilled onto the carpet, each one fresh and unsigned. Adam had bought these cards for her. He'd deny it. But she knew. Because she had done the same thing.

Tears stung the back of her eyes.

"Susan, would you mind...." Adam came into the room and paused when he saw the cards in her hands. "Throw that stuff away. They're just some old cards."

"They're unsigned." One tear fell.

"Yes, well, just throw them away."

Another tear joined the first, followed by several more. "I don't understand you, Adam Gallagher."

He put a hand to the side of his head. "Damn it. You know how I feel about tears."

Susan hurled the cards at him. "You have no idea, do you? I practically killed myself just for the pleasure of running with you!" she shouted. "I was cheerfully jogging miles and miles just to be near you. I swallowed my pride so many times I nearly gagged on it." Sobbing uncontrollably, she stormed from one room to another, finally locating some tissues.

Stunned, Adam stood in the hallway.

"You know what your problem is?" She pointed a finger at him. "Adam Gallagher, you're a coward. You won't say it, so I will. I love you. I'll love you all my life. Move to Washington! Have a good life! But I swear I'm going to haunt you. When you look into another woman's eyes it'll be my face you'll see. When you run in the mornings it'll be my footsteps you'll hear behind you. And...when you look into some little boy's face, you'll see the son you wouldn't give me."

Tears were streaming down her cheeks now. Wiping them aside, she looked at him one last time. He stood proud, defensive, stubborn...and insecure. "Goodbye, Adam." The words were issued softly, belying the inner turmoil. Taking her jacket, she stepped out of his apartment and out of his life.

Before she was aware of her destination, Susan found herself in Central Park. Her eyes were dry now.

She paused at the bench where they'd met in the mornings. Those few short days were the happiest of her life. Dejected and miserable, she sat, leaned against the back of the bench, stretched out her legs and crossed them at the ankles.

She'd done it again—made a fool of herself in front of

Adam. Fool or no fool, how could he leave her when she loved him so much?

Someone sat at the other end of the bench. Susan took it to be a stranger until he assumed the same position as she, crossing his feet at the ankles. Those shoes were lovingly familiar. Adam's shoes.

"I have to go away," he said in a controlled voice. "I'm so much in love with you that I can't hide it anymore."

She didn't move, the words paralyzing her.

"When we first met I couldn't believe someone as beautiful as you could be interested in me."

The argument was old. She was sick of it.

"Later, when I learned you were a romance editor," he continued, "I knew it would never work."

"Why?" The one word came out high and uneven.

"Because I can never be like the men in those books. The man every woman dreams about, the kind of man you deserve. I'm not rich or handsome. I'm a weak man. The night Joey died, I proved that to you. A man crying. I'll never be the strong and silent type."

"What makes you think I want that?" Still she didn't turn.

"It would be impossible for you to read and not compare me with the heroes in those books. Maybe not at first, but eventually, and I'd fall short. It's not only that," he murmured. "You work with beautiful people and unreal situations. I deal with reality."

"I love you, Adam," she told him. "You, Dr. Adam Gallagher. I'm flesh and blood and capable of distinguishing between fantasy and reality."

"You were right when you said I'm a coward. I was in the park watching you last Christmas. Hiding."

"Hiding? When?" For the first time she turned to look at him.

"I purposely mentioned something about running, hoping you'd come to the park. Yet when you did, I stood in the distance, afraid that when I saw you again, I wouldn't be able to hide my love.''

She released a shuddering breath. ''You know, Adam, I was the one who introduced myself to you. I asked you to kiss me that first time. I followed you, made excuses to see you. I even had to be the one to tell you I was in love first. But so help me, if I end up proposing, I'll never forgive you.''

''Will this help?'' He took something out of his pocket and handed it to her.

Susan sat up shocked. A diamond engagement ring from Tiffany's. ''When? How?''

''I got the ring after the accident. I knew then I couldn't live without you.''

''Why has it taken you so long?'' she asked.

Adam slipped the ring on her finger. A smile of immense pleasure turned up the edges of his mouth. ''I was just waiting for the right moment.''

''Oh, Adam!'' She smiled and threw herself into his arms.

ROOMFUL OF ROSES

Diana Palmer

It was the most wonderful kind of spring day—warm after the recent rain, with butterflies gliding around a puddle beside the porch of the weathered old country store in southern Creek County. Wynn Ascot went up the cracked concrete steps onto the dusty porch and through the screen door. She shook back her long black hair as she walked into the store.

Mrs. Baker looked up.

"Loafing, huh?" the white-haired woman teased.

Wynn grinned.

The older woman pursed her lips. "You do a story about my boy Henry and I'll keep your guilty secret. He caught a fifteen-pound bass this morning over at James Lewis's pond," Mrs. Baker said proudly.

"You tell him to bring it by my office about two o'clock today and I'll get a picture of it for the paper," Wynn agreed. "Now, how about a soda? I'm parched!"

With a sigh, Wynn took her pop and sank down beside the wooden fruit bin into a comfortably swaybacked cane-bottom straight chair.

Mrs. Baker leaned on the counter. "How's Katy Maude?" she asked.

"Aunt Katy Maude is up in the north Georgia mountains visiting her sister Cattie." The young woman grinned. "The two of them have been threatening to ride an inner tube down the Chattahoochee this summer."

Mrs. Baker burst out laughing. "I'll just bet Katy would do it on a dare! Say, when are you and Andy getting married? Will McCabe come back to give you away?" Mrs. Baker asked.

Hearing his name was enough to cause volcanic sensations in Wynn. McCabe Foxe held the administrative keys to her father's legacy, doling out her allowance and taking care of her investments until she was either twenty-five or married. At her next birthday, she'd be twenty-four. But before then, she'd be married to Andy, and McCabe would fade away into the past where he belonged. Thank God, she added silently.

"I don't think so," she replied finally, smiling at Mrs. Baker. "He's down in Central America right now, covering that last skirmish for the wire services. And getting fodder for his next adventure novel, no doubt," she added with a trace of bitterness.

"Isn't that something?" The elderly woman sighed, her eyes suddenly dreamy. "Imagine, a famous author who lived just a couple of houses away from you for all those years. Right up until he went into wire-service reporting with your father."

Thinking about that made Wynn uncomfortable. She didn't like the memories of those days.

"Good thing your father let McCabe handle the money," Mrs. Sanders remarked. "Your mother left quite an estate, and you were still in your teens when your dad died."

Wynn finished her soft drink and placed the empty bottle on the counter. "Well, I'd better get back to the salt mines, I reckon. It's press day and if I know Edward, he'll be calling all over the county any minute to find out where I'm hiding. See you later." She made a run for the door, her skirt flying.

Wynn started the small car and was roaring away toward Redvale. Thinking about McCabe had upset her. Wynn had stopped watching the newscasts because she couldn't bear to see what was happening in Central America. She couldn't bear the thought that McCabe might be badly hurt.

It shouldn't have mattered, of course. They had never gotten along. She leaned back hard against the seat, her foot easing down on the accelerator. Arrogant, hardheaded man—she still couldn't believe that her father had legally had McCabe appointed executor of his will and Wynn's estate. It seemed ridiculous somehow, when Katy Maude would have been the logical person to put in charge, since she'd had responsibility for Wynn since her childhood, while Jesse Ascot was off covering news.

When she got back to the Redvale *Courier*'s office, Edward Keene looked up, aiming a glare at Wynn.

"Do you know what day it is? Do you realize that I'm making this paper up alone and trying to help Judy proof copy and set ads..."

"I got photos," she said, holding up the camera with a grin. "A house fire and that new bypass bridge they just finished in Union City. That gives you pix for the front page."

He nodded. "Okay, with what I've already got, that'll fill 'er up."

"I'll take it back to Jess in the darkroom," she said, and started into the outer office.

"Uh, after you do that, come into my office for a minute, will you?" Edward hesitated.

Wynn glanced at him, puzzled. He looked strange for an instant. She shrugged and rushed to the back with the film. It was press day, she told herself. Everybody looked strange then.

She handed the film to Jess with a grin at the harassed look that immediately appeared on his thin, aging face. "Here I am with three rush jobs, one to get out by two o'clock, I haven't made the first negative..." He kept right on muttering, and she dashed back into the newspaper office and closed the door.

Edward was sitting behind the heavily loaded desk. He pulled off his glasses and whipped out a spotless white handkerchief to clean them with.

"Well, sit down," he said impatiently.

"What is it?" she asked, getting scared. He looked... really strange.

He cleared his throat. "Why don't you keep up on what's happening in Central America? Then you'd know and I wouldn't have to stumble all over myself."

Her blood actually ran cold. She gripped the arms of the chair. "McCabe," she gasped.

"He's alive," he said. He tossed an issue of the Atlanta morning daily over to her.

She looked away from the banner headline to the accompanying story. "WAR CORRESPONDENT INJURED." There was a small, very dark photo of McCabe and she strained her eyes to see if he'd changed much over the long years, but she couldn't even make out his features. She read the copy. McCabe had been hurt while covering a story, and there was some speculation as to whether the incident was connected to the deaths of two French correspondents that had been reported earlier that week. According to the story, McCabe had been roughed up and had a torn ligament in one leg and a trace of concussion, but he was alive.

"It doesn't say where he is now," she murmured.

"Uh, I was afraid you'd wonder about that. Be kind of hard to miss him, of course," he mumbled, "when you walk in your front door. Big man..."

"He's at my house?" she burst out. "What's he doing at my house!"

"Recuperating," he assured her. Edward looked at her over his glasses. "After all, he's your guardian."

"Guardian! My tormentor, my inquisitor, my worst enemy, and you've put him under my own roof!" she wailed.

"He's hurt," Edward reminded her. "Poor wounded soldier, and you'd turn him out in the cold!"

Her full lips pouted at him. "You don't know McCabe like I do," she argued.

"He wants to meet your fiancé," he continued. "He's concerned about your future."

"He wants to dictate it, that's why," she growled, standing. "Well, he won't get away with it. He's not going to wrap me around his thumb!"

"Where are you going?" he called.

"Off to war," she called back. "I'm taking my lunch hour late," she told him. "I'll be back in an hour."

Edward threw up his hands. "We're already an hour behind schedule and she'll only be gone an hour."

But Wynn wasn't listening. She was running for her car, with sparks flying from her green eyes. If McCabe thought he'd been through a war, he hadn't seen anything yet!

WYNN COULD sense McCabe even as she opened the unlocked door of the white frame cottage. She stormed in, her hair flying as she turned to go into the living room. She stopped short just inside the doorway and caught her breath.

All the years rolled away. McCabe looked just as Wynn remembered him, big and bronzed and blond—larger than life. His craggy face looked battle-worn, and the light eyes that were neither gray nor blue but a mixture of the two narrowed as they roamed boldly over her slender body.

She stared helplessly, trying to reconcile her memories with the man before her.

"You're older," she said in a tone that was unconsciously soft.

He nodded. "So are you, honey."

Casual endearments were as much a part of him as his square-tipped fingers, but the word caused an odd sensation in Wynn. She didn't understand why, and she didn't like it.

"Just months away from my inheritance," she reminded him with a smile. "When Andy and I marry, I'm a free woman."

"Andrew Slone," he muttered, leaning back in the chair with a sigh. "How in hell did you get landed with him?"

She gasped. "I love him!"

He ground out a cigarette in the ashtray on the table beside his chair. "You'd stagnate married to a man with his hang-ups." He met her eyes squarely. "I'm going to stop you from making the mistake of your young life. I grew up with Andrew, for God's sake. He's a year older than I am!"

"He's just thirty-six, hardly a candidate for a nursing home!"

She stopped herself abruptly. "You don't have any right to burst in here and start grilling me…and what are you doing here, anyway?"

"Don't get hysterical," he said soothingly. "I let the lease on my apartment expire and the only quarters I have at the moment are in Central America." His eyebrows arched. "You wouldn't want me to go back there to heal?"

She averted her eyes before he could read the very real fear in them. She looked at the big leg resting on the hassock. The papers had said something about a torn ligament, but the shape of a thick bandage was outlined against one powerful thigh under the khaki fabric. A bandage.

Her eyes went slowly back up to his. "That's no torn ligament," she said hesitantly.

His shaggy head leaned back. "Hard to fool another journalist, isn't it, Wynn?"

Her own face paled. "You've been shot."

He nodded. "Bingo."

She could feel her heart going wild, her knees threatening to buckle. "You *were* with those journalists who were killed, weren't you, McCabe?" she asked with quiet certainty.

His darkening eyes fell to his leg. "I got away by the skin of my teeth and spent the night in a chicken house. I nearly bled to death before I was able to get back to town."

Her heart was hurting now. She felt oddly sick. She stared at him, memorizing every hard line of his face. It had been a compulsion, even years ago, to look at him. She enjoyed that even when she imagined she hated him. It was an effort to drag her eyes away.

"You're in pain," she said suddenly.

He laughed mirthlessly. "Honey, I've hardly been out of it for the past week, and that's God's own truth."

"How long will it take for it to heal?"

"Another month or so," he said with obvious distaste. "I really do need a place to stay," he said.

She glanced at him warily. "Andy's going to go right through the ceiling."

"Let me handle Andy," he said generously. "Man to man, you know."

That didn't quite ring true, but perhaps she'd misjudged McCabe. She hoped so.

"Won't you be bored to death staying in Redvale for a whole month?" she asked.

"If I didn't have anything to do, I might," he agreed. "I don't have another book due for six months, and I was between assignments, so I took a job here in town."

She stared at him with dawning horror. "What job?"

"Didn't Ed tell you?" he asked pleasantly. "I'm going to edit the paper for the next month while he goes on vacation."

Wynn felt as if she'd been kicked in the stomach.

"I quit," she said. "I can't live with you and work with you for a solid month and stay sane!"

He watched her with an odd, quiet smile. "What's the matter, honey, afraid you won't be able to resist me?"

She went scarlet. Before she could think up something bad enough, insulting enough, to say to him, the phone rang. She grabbed up the receiver.

"Andy!" she gasped, glaring at McCabe. Her hand twisted the cord nervously.

"Ed said you'd gone home," her fiancé said suspiciously. "Wynona, have you gone crazy? You simply can't let McCabe stay there!"

"Now, Andy," she said soothingly, trying to ignore McCabe's smug grin.

"I remember McCabe. Can I help feeling threatened?"

"I'm engaged to you," she reminded him, furious at McCabe's open eavesdropping.

"Invite him to supper," McCabe said sotto voce. "I'll cook. Invite him over. About six."

She felt as if she were walking obligingly into a shark's mouth.

SHE WENT BACK to work with a frown between her wide-spaced green eyes. It deepened when she saw Ed.

"You didn't mention that you were taking a vacation," she said with grinning ferocity.

"Have a heart," he groaned. "I just hope he'll give himself time enough to heal before he goes back down there."

She felt the blood leaving her face. She stared blankly at the half-made-up page in front of her.

The hectic pace kept her from thinking about McCabe any more until quitting time. The phones rang off the hook, people walked in and out, there were additions and deletions and changes in ads and copy until Wynn swore she'd walk out the door and never come back. She threatened that every Tuesday. So did Ed. So did Judy. So did Kelly and Jess. It was a standing joke, but nobody laughed at it on Tuesday.

She dragged herself in the door at a few minutes past five, weary and disheveled.

"Is that you, Wynn?" McCabe called from the kitchen.

"It's me." Her heart jumped at the sound of his deep voice.

Ten minutes later, she went into the kitchen and McCabe stopped with a spoon in midair above the stove and just stared.

The backless dress she'd put on was emerald-green jersey. It clung softly to her when she walked.

She said, "I'll make the salad dressing."

"Not in that dress you won't," McCabe said curtly. He moved, leaning heavily on his cane, and was behind her before she knew it. One big warm hand caught her waist firmly and held her away from the counter. "It would be a crime to ruin it."

Her body tingled wildly under his hard fingers, as if she'd waited all her life for him to touch it and bring it to life. She felt herself tremble and hoped he wouldn't feel it.

She moved jerkily away from him. "I...I'll get an apron," she faltered.

McCabe didn't say a word. She glanced at him nervously as she fumbled with jars and bowls and spoons. She looked into his eyes and ached all the way down to her toes.

Before she could move, or run, the doorbell rang sharply. She turned and walked like a zombie to the front door.

Andy's brown hair was rumpled, as if he'd been running his hands through it, and his dark eyes were troubled. Wynn sighed and led him back toward the dining room.

Andy made an irritated sound. "Does he really cook?"

"Of course I do, Andy," McCabe said from the kitchen doorway, leaning heavily on his cane. "Beef bourguignonne."

Andy gaped at him. "Beef bourguignonne?"

"Sit down and I'll bring it in," McCabe told them.

But Wynn was horrified at the thought. "You sit down," she said coldly, glaring at him. "I don't want stew all over my floors. How in the world do you expect to manage a tureen of that plus your cane?" She went into the kitchen, still muttering.

By the time she had everything organized, there was an odd silence in the dining room. She shot a glare at McCabe.

Supper was a quiet affair. She nibbled at her beef bourguignonne—which was truly excellent, wine-red and thick and full of melty bits of beef and vegetables—and salad, and wondered why Andy was so quiet.

"We had a bad car wreck to cover today," she mentioned, trying to break the cold silence. "Some out-of-state people—"

"For heaven's sake, not while I'm eating!" Andy burst out, making a face at her.

McCabe's eyebrows went up sharply. He leaned back with his coffee in hand and pursed his lips. "Did I ever tell you about the food I had in South America when I was covering the conflict down there a few years back? I went deep into the Amazon with some soldiers and we camped with a primitive tribe in the jungle. We had snake and lizard and some kind of toasted bugs—"

"Excuse me," Andy gasped, leaping to his feet with a napkin held tightly over his mouth. He ran toward the bathroom and slammed the door.

"McCabe!" Wynn burst out, banging the table with her hand.

He held her eyes and frowned. Then he leaned forward. "You've got a smudge, just here." His big warm hand pressed against her cheek while his thumb ran roughly back and forth across her lips.

Her lips parted as she looked into his darkening eyes. She caught his hand and started to pull it away, but he brought her palm up to his mouth and caressed it softly, tenderly, while his eyes held hers.

She was actually leaning toward him across the scant inches that separated them when the sudden sharp click of the bathroom door opening sent her jerking back into her own chair.

Andy returned, looking pale.

"Feeling better?" McCabe asked pleasantly.

Andy glowered at him. "No, thanks to you."

"Reporters do bring the job home, Andy," the taller man commented. "There are going to be times when Wynn will need to tell you about things she's seen, to save her sanity."

Andy turned to speak to Wynn, and his eyes went homing to her swollen mouth, devoid of lipstick and looking as if it had been hotly and thoroughly kissed. He drew in a harsh breath.

Wynn put a hand to her mouth. "Andy, it wasn't what you're thinking," she said shortly.

"Sure." Andy stood up, almost knocking over his chair. "He's only been here a day, for heaven's sake!"

"I'm a fast worker," McCabe said with a wicked smile.

Andy gave Wynn a killing glance. He whirled and slammed out of the house. A minute later, the roar of his car filled the silence.

"You troublemaker," Wynn accused hotly. "What was the point of that lie?"

"It wasn't a lie," he said calmly. "You'd have let me kiss you."

She stood up. She gathered the dirty dishes, but as she started by him, he caught her around the waist and turned her, pressing his open mouth to her backbone. His lips brushed between her shoulder blades down to her waist. His hand moved slowly, insidiously, to the flatness of her stomach and back up in a warm, lazy circle. Her hand went to catch it, to stop it, and lingered helplessly on the curling hair that covered the back of it.

He let her go all at once and she moved away from him as if she'd been scalded.

She lifted the stack of dishes. It tottered precariously in her hands and she marched into the kitchen stiff-legged, viciously kicking the swinging door closed behind her.

She finished washing up and went back into the living room. Sorting words and explanations in her mind, she marched into the room ready to do battle. McCabe was sitting in his easy chair.

"The wreck bothered you, didn't it?" he asked, studying her over the rim of his coffee cup. "Why?"

She shrugged. "There was a child involved. Two years old. He was killed."

"Who else?"

"The baby's father." She looked at him. "The baby's mother is in a coma. If she lives, think what a horrible awakening she's going to have. I wouldn't want to live, I don't think." Tears welled in her eyes.

He sighed heavily. "Wynn, you have to learn to report the news without becoming part of it. And if you can't handle what you see, it's time to quit."

Her eyes ran over his craggy face. "Can you still handle it, even after what you've seen?"

He smiled carelessly. "Barely. I can take care of myself."

She glanced up. "Sure you can. Look what good shape you came home in!"

He chuckled softly. "So I slipped up. Everybody's entitled to one mistake. I owed your father my life once or twice," he said. "He pulled me out of some hairy situations. I'm only sorry I couldn't do the same for him, the one time it mattered."

"He admired you," she said.

"It was mutual. That's why I agreed to this crazy scheme of his, to oversee your inheritance." His eyes wandered over her slowly. "But I'm just beginning to understand his reasoning."

Her breath sighed out wildly and her hands clenched at her sides. "McCabe…"

His head went back and he studied her arrogantly, intently. "It's just as well I stayed away so long, Wynn."

She hardly understood what he was saying. She was too embarrassed. "It's been a long day. Good night, McCabe."

He watched her go down the hall with a purely predatory gaze. And slowly, calculatingly, he smiled.

*

WYNN HARDLY slept. All night, she kept feeling the touch of McCabe's hard mouth on her back until her skin felt unbearably sensitive. When morning came, she was feeling dragged-out and irritable.

She dressed in faded denim jeans and a T-shirt, because it was Wednesday and they'd all be working in the back to mail out papers.

McCabe was already dressed and in the kitchen. He turned as she walked in.

"Andy called."

She lifted her head. He looked odd. "When?"

"About six."

She glanced at her watch. "Over an hour ago? You didn't wake me."

"I asked Andy if he wanted me to hand you the phone," he murmured.

It took a minute for that to sink in. Her eyes scanned his face and she began to flush. "You didn't!" She got to her feet in one smooth motion. "McCabe, you didn't!"

"I did." He sipped his coffee calmly and raised an eyebrow at her. "He is suspicious, isn't he? He jumped immediately to the conclusion that you were in the bed with me."

She lifted a saucer and slammed it down on the table, shattering it into a dozen pieces.

JESS STAMPED the papers that went out to local post offices, while Wynn put the single-wraps that went outside the local area into prestamped lightweight brown bags. McCabe handled the phone and the front office while the rest of them sacked and lifted and tied bundles and loaded the truck that carried the papers the five miles to the post office. By the end of the day Wynn was black down the front from newsprint and her face was smeared with it.

She was just about to leave the office when Judy motioned her to the telephone.

"Hello," she said dully.

"Wynn?" Andy asked, his tone conciliatory. "Would you like to have dinner with me tonight?"

She brightened. "I'd love to. And despite what McCabe might have told you, I sleep alone," she added curtly.

"He just rattled me," came the embarrassed reply. "I can't keep my wits around him."

You're not the only one, she thought, but didn't say it.

THEY HAD dinner out and went to see a comedy at a local theater before they drove back to Redvale, apparently in perfect accord for the time being.

Andy walked Wynn to the porch, and was just giving her his usual gentle good-night kiss when the door opened and McCabe appeared.

"What do you mean, bringing Wynn back home at this hour?" McCabe asked curtly, checking his watch. "You keep her out this late again, Andy, and you'll regret it."

And before Andy could decide what to say, McCabe had jerked Wynn into the room and slammed the door.

"Where were you?" he asked curtly.

"Eating supper," she stammered. "And seeing a play." She tossed down her purse and glared at him, getting some of her wind back. "What business is it of yours? And how dare you give my fiancé the third degree!"

"My, how your eyes do sparkle when you get mad," he murmured approvingly. "Missing your good-night kiss, honey?" He chuckled, moving closer.

"Don't you dare!" she exclaimed as he reached for her. She pushed at his broad chest, but he only tugged her closer.

His cheek moved against hers as his lips smoothed over soft skin, down into the neck of her dress. "You smell of gardenia. Sultry and sweet and womanly." His nose rubbed softly against hers and the feel of him was beginning to do the wildest kinds of things to her pulse. She felt her breasts flattening under the crush of his chest, felt the warm abrasive brush of his jaw. Her hands touched his cheeks hesitantly before they moved up into the cool thickness of his blond hair.

His mouth coaxed hers open with a tantalizing pressure that made her wild with need. She arched up against him, surging with hungers she'd suppressed all her life, until this moment.

He jerked up, his eyes glittering as they met hers, and he smiled slowly. "You're passionate, Wynn. Andy isn't. And that's what's eating you up. Because I can match you, and he can't."

She got away and stood glaring at him, her eyes wild, her hair a glorious tangle, her very posture expressing fury.

"Andy respects me," she panted.

"I respect you, too. I respect you enough to want all of you."

"Stop!" she burst out. She almost threw something at him. But she couldn't think of anything big enough to make a dent in his monumental arrogance, so she turned and stormed into her bedroom and slammed the door violently.

THE NEXT night, they were no sooner home from work than the phone rang. McCabe picked it up, listened, glared at it and handed it to Wynn.

"It's Romeo," he growled. "Don't tie up the line, if you don't mind. I've got a call coming through from New York."

He hobbled off.

"You didn't get into any trouble last night, did you?" Andy asked. "I meant to call sooner, but I got tied up."

"I'm fine," she replied.

"Good. McCabe looked... I wish you'd get him out of the house, Wynn."

"Why don't you come and do it for me?" she asked with venomous sweetness.

He cleared his throat. "I've got to do some paperwork," he said. "How about dinner Friday?"

"Sure."

"See you soon, darling," he said. "Goodbye."

McCabe glared at her when she joined him in the kitchen.

"My, my, you do have long conversations with your loved one, don't you?" he asked.

Her nostrils flared. "You did ask me to keep it brief. That phone call you're expecting," she said uneasily. "It wouldn't be from your wire service?"

He glanced down at her, frowning. "Wynn, I'm still on the payroll," he said quietly.

"You don't have to explain it to me," she said tautly.

He tilted her face up to his. "Don't I?" He searched her face for a long moment. "I'm here for a rest, and to help you get sorted out. Then I'll go where they send me."

Her eyes searched his. "You write adventure novels, too," she reminded him coolly. "You've made the best-seller list several times."

"And someday I'll write novels for the rest of my life, and I'll enjoy that, too. But, Wynn," he murmured, cupping her face in his hands, "I'm still too young and too restless to settle down. I don't want any ties. You're tangling me up in a web I don't like," he murmured absently.

"I didn't ask you to come here," she managed.

"Yes, I know. But I needed something," he said. His hands shifted onto her rib cage. "I think I needed to know that it would matter, if I died," he said unexpectedly, lifting his eyes to catch the surprise in hers. "Do you know what Ed told me, Wynn? He said that you wouldn't even watch newscasts about Central America."

She swallowed down a surge of nervous energy.

"Were you afraid for me, Wynn?" His hands on her waist contracted.

"I've known you for a long time," she muttered, raising her gaze to his chiseled mouth. "Of course it matters."

"Why don't you go into politics?" he asked. "You're so damned good at avoiding the issue, you'd be a natural."

"I'm not avoiding anything." She pushed at his chest. "Oh, McCabe, stop confusing me!"

"Then stop avoiding the issue," he murmured. "Stop throwing Andy between us."

She lifted her head to protest, but before she could get the words out, the phone rang again. She made a beeline for her bedroom, leaning back exhausted against the door. McCabe was tearing her safe world apart, and she didn't have the faintest idea how to stop him.

AFTER A HECTIC week, Andy took Wynn to dinner. McCabe hadn't said anything when Andy came to pick her up, aside from a curt nod and a glare for Wynn.

"Well, at least he's stopped grinning at me like a Cheshire cat," Andy remarked during the ride home. "Didn't you see the glare he gave me when I put my arm around you? As if you were his personal property! I tell you, Wynn, you've got to get him out of that house. People are starting to talk all over town about it."

"Andy, you know what kind of condition he's in!" she exclaimed.

"He manages to get to the office every day, though, doesn't he?" Andy asked.

"That doesn't mean he's capable in other areas," she said hotly.

"How do you know?" he asked suspiciously. "Have you tried?"

It was a good thing they were pulling into her driveway, because she'd have jumped out onto the highway rather than put up with another second of his suspicions.

"How can you say such a thing?"

"Well, there's more than one position for people to make love in."

She swallowed. "As it happens, you're absolutely right about McCabe and me," she said, feeling the words burst out of her in indignation and anguish. "We're lovers. I sleep with him every night. He's wonderful in bed, Andy, really wonderful."

He blanched and his hand lifted. He slapped her. Slowly she took the ring from her finger and dropped it on the floorboard. Then she opened the door and got out, leaving him alone in the car.

The house was quiet. She went to the liquor cabinet and poured a generous measure of bourbon into a glass, added ice and water, and proceeded to get soused.

She was halfway through her second glass when McCabe made an appearance. He was limping badly.

She lifted the glass in an exaggerated toast. "Ahhhh." She sighed. "Isn't liquor great? I wonder why I never drank before?"

He moved closer. Then he saw the livid red mark on her cheek and his eyes exploded with anger.

"Did he hit you?" he asked coldly.

"Yes, he hit me," she muttered. "And it's all your fault, McCabe. All your fault." She felt morose and reckless, all at once. "You're my lover, did you know?" she asked with a laugh.

Her eyes ran over his broad bronzed chest with the thick wedge of hair that ran down it to his belt buckle. "You have the most marvelous body," she said, as the liquor dragged the truth out of her.

"Wynn, you're drunk."

"I sure am, darling. Isn't that what you called me the other night before you kissed me? I didn't tell Andy you kissed me, McCabe."

"I'm glad about that, at least," he muttered.

"No, I just told him we were lovers," she continued, and laughed at the shock that widened his eyes. "Well, it was what he wanted to hear. I even gave him back the ring." She put down the glass and leaned back. "Why don't you come to bed with me, McCabe." Her hand went to her blouse and she unbuttoned the buttons and unclipped her bra.

"I'll even take off my clothes...." she was offering.

He caught her, pushing her roughly back while he clipped the bra back in place, his face oddly strained, his eyes dark and glittering. He took her arm and pulled her toward the hall.

"Get in there," he said harshly, "and put on your gown while I make some black coffee."

He thrust her into her room, snapped on the light and hobbled painfully back to get his cane.

With an uncaring sigh, she stripped off her clothes and dragged on an old cotton gown. She felt wonderful.

"I'm not engaged anymore," she sang, collapsing on the bed on her back as McCabe returned, his face like thunder.

He sat down beside her, grimacing with the movement, and handed her the coffee. "Drink it."

She lifted her eyes to McCabe's bare chest and felt herself going warm all over.

"I never liked Andy without a shirt," she said absently. "You're..." She blinked, trying to find a word to describe it. "Sexy," she said triumphantly, lifting her eyes.

Whatever she expected to see in his face, it wasn't pain. But he was almost white with it, and the sight was more sobering than the coffee.

"Your leg," she said softly. "Oh, McCabe, your poor leg. And I didn't even think, and you were walking without your cane!"

"My leg is all right," he said coldly.

There was a curious silence around them, and it forced her eyes up to his. They were glittering under his thick lashes. Almost as if he couldn't help it, his hand went toward her gown where ten pearl buttons fastened it from collarbone to waist. He looked down at his own big callused hands and watched as his fingers unlooped the first, then the second, the third...

Unconsciously her body lifted, an involuntary kind of pleading.

Very gently he took her shoulders and drew her up against his broad bare chest, closing his arms around her. Her cheek slid softly against his as he drew her even closer until her bareness was warming his. He didn't say a word. He just held her, rocking her slowly, sweetly, against the warmth of him.

A long moment later, he drew back. He looked down at the soft bareness of her body one last time before he helped her back into the gown.

His nose nuzzled hers, his lips brushed softly over hers, biting at them until her mouth opened hotly. Her nails moved restlessly against his chest and he moaned sharply.

But all at once he sat up. "No," he said.

She swallowed, her body aching.

"You've had a shock tonight," he said, watching her, "and too damned much liquor to know what you're doing."

"You weren't drunk," she stated.

He shook his head. "No, I wasn't." He brushed her face with his fingers, studying every inch of it. "Why did you think I was in pain?"

"Your face was white," she said. "And you looked...so agonized."

"Haven't you ever seen a man eaten up with desire before?" he asked matter-of-factly.

She turned beet red and dropped her eyes to his chest. "No," she admitted after a minute. When she looked up, he was only smiling.

His eyes darkened. "I wanted you tonight, Wynn," he

said. "I wanted you obsessively, and because of that I'm going to get on a plane tomorrow and fly up to New York for the weekend. I'm going to put some space between us until we cool off."

"I won't seduce you," she said bitterly.

"You could," he said, watching her. "You could seduce me just by walking into the room and touching me."

That shocked her, and he nodded when he saw the betraying wideness of her eyes.

"So, that being the case, I feel like a brief vacation." He got up and moved slowly away from the bed toward the door. "I can't think of a time in my life when I've been so aroused so fast. I'd almost forgotten that I was a man." He stared across the room at her. "I keep wondering how it would be with you," he said huskily. "Your body and mine with nothing between us, and the cool night air washing over us while we made love...."

"Go away!" she whispered.

"I am," he reminded her. "And now you know why."

SHE MISSED McCabe. She always had, ever since he'd left Redvale all those years ago, even though she hadn't admitted it. She'd missed him, worried about him, brooded over him.

She wandered around, lingering helplessly in McCabe's room. Her eyes wandered over the bed he slept in, and glared at the battered suitcase he'd left behind with its multicolor stickers from all the countries he'd visited. And every time she remembered how it had felt to hold him and be kissed by him, she wanted to wail. It was going to make it so much worse when he left.

Late Sunday night McCabe walked in, leaning heavily on the cane. He looked worn and tired. "I feel as if I've had part of my thigh sawed off." He sat down heavily in the chair, rubbing his leg. "Wynn, could you make me a cup of coffee?'' he asked wearily. ''And do you have an aspirin in the house?''

''I'll get them,'' she said.

Minutes later, when the aspirin was working and he'd finished his second cup of coffee, he studied her.

''I did a lot of thinking while I was gone,'' he said quietly.

''About what?''

He laughed shortly. ''You know perfectly well about what.'' He shifted, grimacing as he shifted his legs. ''About reorganizing your life for you.''

She glanced at him warily. ''Does that mean you're going to stop interfering?''

''Oh, not at all, darling,'' he drawled, smiling at her confusion. ''As a matter of fact, I've decided that I was right in the first place. You need Andy like a hole in the head. A man who'll knock a woman around is lower than a snake's belly.''

''I provoked him by telling him I was sleeping with you.''

''I wouldn't have hit you.''

''No,'' she agreed. ''Probably you would have kissed me, the way you did Friday night.''

He searched her face, and the room was suddenly alive with tension and remembered passion. ''That backfired on me, didn't it?'' he murmured. ''I never meant to get so involved.''

She felt herself go hot. Her lips parted. ''I...I have my own life here and I like it. I don't want to...complicate it.''

''You don't want to sleep with me,'' he interpreted. ''Why?''

Her eyes fell. ''Because I couldn't survive it.''

''At the moment, I'm doubtful if I could, either,'' he said, touching his thigh with a harsh laugh. ''But with the right encouragement...''

She blushed to her hairline and stood up. "I need to get some sleep. Mondays are rough."

He got to his feet and stood in her way as she started past him. "I missed you," he said shortly. "I didn't like that—missing someone."

"Join the club," she said with a nervous laugh.

She went into her room and closed the door before she weakened and threw herself onto his big body and begged him to love her.

*

MONDAY WAS always frantic, the last full day to gather news and ads, since the press deadline was at noon on Tuesday. Wynn covered a visit from the lieutenant governor of the state, who was in Redvale to see firsthand the necessity for the mayor's proposed water-system expansion. By the time she'd driven to the airport, followed him around with the camera and taken pictures and then got back to the office to write the story, the piece had already taken all morning.

"I want this ready by the deadline too," McCabe said curtly, tossing a page of copy at her.

She glanced at it and frowned. "This is a suicide," she told him. "Ed doesn't run suicides."

"Ed isn't here. It's news. Print it."

"This is a small town," she shot back, rising to battle. "You're only here to recuperate, but I live here twenty-four hours a day, and so do Ed and the rest of the staff. You may be a big-time journalist, and the manner of a man's death may not mean that much to you, but here it's a matter of honor. Did you even notice his last name?" she added, gesturing toward the copy. "His family is one of the oldest and finest in the community. When we needed a city park, they donated land. When the Burnes family was burned out, they gave them a home until they could find a new one. Those are special people, McCabe, and I can't see trading on their tragedy to fill a hole on your front page.'' She got up from the desk. ''If you want to run it, go ahead, but you rewrite it and please add your byline. And if you do run it you can have my resignation.''

He was watching her with narrowed eyes. ''You're too soft, Wynn. You care too much.''

''Isn't that better than being dead inside?'' she returned hotly. ''You've been in international journalism too long,'' she said quietly. ''You've forgotten how it is in small towns. I meant it. If you print this—'' she picked up the story ''—I'll go right out the door. And tomorrow's Tuesday.''

He drew in a deep breath. ''That's blackmail.'' He lifted his chin arrogantly. ''But if you feel that strongly about it, I'll back down this once.'' He emphasized the last two words. ''In the meantime, you remember that I'm editing this paper, and I'll do it my way.''

''Yes, McCabe,'' she said with a sweet, demure smile.

Later that afternoon, there was a bank robbery. Wynn heard it come over the police scanner.

She was putting her pad and pen into her purse when McCabe walked in.

''Where are you off to?'' he asked.

''There's a bank robbery in progress at Farmer's Bank,'' she burst out. ''I'm on my way.''

''Oh no, you're not!'' he growled, taking the camera away from her. ''Sit down.''

''McCabe!''

''Sit down, I said!'' he barked harshly, forcing her down into the chair. ''Bank robbers carry guns, you little fool!'' He looked oddly pale. ''You sit there and listen on the scanner. You can go down and get pix of them carrying him off to jail when the police make an arrest. But you don't leave this office while it's going down, do you understand?''

His face was set into rigid lines, and for the first time since he'd been back, she saw the man underneath the careless, easygoing mask. She saw right through to the steel that had carried him through all the years in the front lines.

"Do you know how big a hole a pistol makes? I was shot at point-blank range with a pistol," he told her flatly. "And except for a friend in the junta who knocked the guard's arm and then helped me escape, it would have been through the head. I was being executed for trying to save those other journalists."

She burst into tears as the impact of what he'd confessed hit her.

"Now, you know," he said with a cold smile. "So don't get adventurous." And he turned and went back out, closing the office door behind him.

She hardly heard the scanner at all. She couldn't seem to stop crying. McCabe was being executed, executed, executed... If not for that soldier, he'd be dead now. And when he was healed, he was going to climb on a plane and fly straight back to that other world, that bloody world. And she knew she'd never survive the fear again. It was one thing to worry about a man she'd hero-worshiped, quite another to worry about a man she loved.

Ten minutes later, Kelly burst into the room, all eyes. "I just heard about the robbery on my scanner," he said excitedly. "They've made an arrest. Can I go...would you mind? I'll get good pix, honest I will."

Wynn handed him the camera like a zombie. And he was gone like a shot.

SHE WENT TO sleep early that night, emotionally exhausted, and found herself sitting straight up in bed hours later as a wild, harsh cry woke her. It was coming from McCabe's room.

She burst in without even knocking and found him thrashing like a madman on the crisp white sheets.

"McCabe," she said, shaking him.

She shook him again, harder, and he jerked upright. He caught his breath sharply and there was a strange glitter in his eyes.

"Oh, God," he ground out, shaking. "Someday I'm afraid I won't wake up in time…"

She drew his shaggy head down on her shoulder. "It's all right," she said softly.

He held her, shaking and damp with sweat, his heart thundering. "That was one hell of a nightmare."

Her hands soothed him. "McCabe, tell me about it."

"No." He held her tight.

"You're not invulnerable," she replied. "There's no shame in fear."

"I suppose that most people with a pistol against their temples would feel fear," he agreed. "I dream about it all the time, except that when I dream, there's no friendly soldier there to save me."

She caught one of his big hands in hers and held it, savoring its callused warmth.

So he told her about the fighting and the slaughter. About the children lying dead in the streets and the native journalists who were put to death if they dared to print anything unfavorable to the regime. And then, slowly, reluctantly, about the death of his friends and how it had been when the soldiers took him out of the small, stifling rock building with the dirt floor, and one of their number had put a pistol to his head.

She stood up, disengaging her hand. "Why do it at all?" she demanded.

"Because someone has to!" he shot at her. "I love my work, Wynn. I always have. And I told you, I don't need ties."

"So you did. But I do," she said defiantly. "You just go back to your jungles and get yourself killed. I'll marry Andy and sleep with him and have his babies."

"I'll kill him first!" he said passionately.

She jumped at the violence in his voice.

"I'm too old," he began hotly, "to be remodeled or renovated. I am not changing professions and I am not marrying you."

"I haven't asked you to," she said reasonably.

"You'll find someone...a man who'll be able to give you what you want."

Did he know, she thought with terror, did he realize that she loved him? She finally met his gaze, uncertainty and apprehension in her eyes, and he searched them slowly.

"I'm not domesticated," he said in a husky voice.

"I haven't said a word," she reminded him. "You do what you like, McCabe. Now that you mention it," she added, wanting to goad him, "I've always wondered what it would be like to work for the wire services."

His face actually paled. "Oh, no, you don't."

"I'm over twenty-one," she reminded him. "The Middle East would be interesting to me. I could see the pyramids. What a wonderful idea!"

"No way, Wynn. I'll stop you!"

"How?" she asked calmly.

He blinked, as if the question caught him off guard, and just stared at her.

She could hear him cursing roundly as she started down the hall to her own room, and she smiled. Let him chew on that possibility for a while and see how he liked it!

THE NEXT morning McCabe looked like a volcano about to erupt.

"You are not going to join the wire-service staff," he told her without any attempt at civility.

Her eyebrows rose. "I'm not?"

He lifted his head and stared at her for a long moment.

She pushed her chair away from the table. "There's no time for discussion. It's press day." She groaned. "Maybe

I'll just quit right now and save myself the bother of doing it around two o'clock like I usually do."

And by late afternoon he was agreeing with her. There wasn't enough time. But somehow they finished up and put the pages into the flat box, and Kelly rushed out the door with them on his way to the printer.

"I quit!" McCabe said shortly, rubbing his thigh with a big weary hand.

"Too late," Wynn told him. "You have to quit by two, or nobody listens to you."

He looked down at her, his eyes warm and quiet and searching.

"We'd better get home," she said. "We have to cover a city-council meeting tonight. They're going to discuss the water system."

They had a quick supper and went straight to city hall, and Wynn was frankly amused at the stares they got. Everyone knew McCabe was her house guest, but most of the people she dealt with hadn't seen him in years. The impact he had on the townspeople was fascinating.

Harry Lawson shook hands with him before the meeting was called to order.

"If you've already put the paper to bed, you may have to tear up your front page after this meeting," he confided. "I got a terrific piece of news late this afternoon."

Wynn's eyes widened. "He got the money he was counting on from the governor."

McCabe glanced down at her as they eased into chairs near the front of the crowded room.

"You really are interested in this water-system expansion project, aren't you?"

"Yes, I am." She looked up. "Everybody thinks we can't ever run out of water. But we can, McCabe. The water table is already dropping, and the increased demand from municipalities and industry and agriculture is beginning to catch up with supply."

He stared at her. "We've got two major rivers feeding our water supply."

"I think you ought to read that water study in my files," she told him. "Every drop of water in them both will have been allocated within ten years."

"My God!"

McCabe turned back toward the podium, where the mayor was calling the meeting to order. His eyes were interested for the first time, and he began taking notes and asking questions.

The mayor's news was that the governor had allowed Redvale ten thousand dollars. When the time came for a vote, the city council went unanimously for the project.

"What were you talking to Harry about after the meeting?" Wynn asked McCabe as she headed the car toward home.

"Water," he confessed with a sideways grin. "I told him I'd be glad to do some public-relations work for him gratis if he needed it. It might make a good feature story for one of the national magazines."

"You're super," she said quietly.

"I'm glad you think so. No, don't go home. Let's go get the front page. I'll have to tear it up to make room for this story. I'm beginning to see that there are quite a few big challenges even in small towns."

It was midnight when they got home. It was a good thing the printer was an accommodating gentleman, Wynn thought with a smile. But then, he was an old newspaperman himself, and understood.

Wynn had already started to her room when McCabe called her name and hobbled up to her. He drew her against him. His hands linked behind her back at her waist and he lowered his forehead to rest against her own. "Wynn, you didn't really mean what you said about going back to Andy, did you?" he asked, as if it really mattered.

"No," she whispered shakily, wanting nothing more

than to lie in his arms and do all the things she'd dreamed of doing with him.

His lips parted and his breath came roughly. "I want to lie with you," he breathed against her mouth. "I want to lie with you and on you and under you, Wynn." His big hands slid up and down her back.

She shook her head. "I couldn't bear it," she whispered. She lowered her eyes to his chest. "I can't."

"Yes you can!" he burst out. His hands caught the back of her head and held it while his mouth lowered onto hers and he kissed her until she moaned and clung.

"Wynn," he whispered, anguished, as his hands moved to her breasts and cupped them softly, warmly. "Oh, Wynn, Wynn, I've never wanted anyone so much!"

"I want you, too," she managed. "But do you really think that I could take that kind of intimacy with you in my stride, and pass it off as a pleasant interlude?"

He frowned slightly.

"In my world, intimacy is between man and wife, and it means something. And before you make some cutting remark, no, I don't expect you to offer me marriage for a few hours of fooling around."

He looked as if she'd hit him. His eyes searched hers. "I want to lie down with you and love you," he said softly. "Is that such a shameful thing?"

Her eyes closed and tears stung them. "No," she whispered. "But I couldn't bear having nothing but the memory of it, after you leave."

His hands stilled on her waist and she heard his breath go ragged. "What are you telling me?"

"I can't be intimate with you and then watch you walk out of my life. It would tear me apart. It's bad enough already!" She slumped, letting all the tension out in one unsteady breath as her eyes closed. "I love you," she whispered.

He didn't speak. He seemed to stop breathing. The hands

on the nape of her neck stilled and she felt his body tauten where it touched hers.

She hadn't realized how she'd been hoping that he'd be happy about her confession, that he'd tell her he felt the same and ask her to marry him and the future would be rosy and bright. But he didn't speak. And she felt rejection more sharply than any she'd felt in her life.

She drew away from him. He was watching her. Just watching her. And she was afraid to look up and see what might be in his eyes, because she couldn't bear pity.

"You needn't worry, I'm not going to threaten to throw myself under a train or anything," she said, moving to open her bedroom door. "I just thought it might make things easier if you understand the situation. I'm...very vulnerable with you. So stop making passes, will you?" she added on an unsteady laugh. "Because it's all a game to you. But it isn't to me."

She turned away, but his hand caught her arm and gently turned her back.

"Wynn," he said softly, "it's no game."

And before she could protest, he lifted her face to his and kissed her. It was slow and fierce, but achingly tender.

"Does this feel like fun and games?" he whispered over her lips. "Do I feel like a man who's playing?"

He lifted his head, and she could see the turmoil in his face that she'd already felt in the tremor of his body.

"We'll get married," he said in a voice she hardly recognized. "Just as soon as I can get a license."

Her lips parted. "No."

"Yes." He bent and kissed her again, slowly, lazily, smiling when he felt her body lift to meet his.

"You...you'll just hate yourself," she whispered, "when the newness wears off, when you've had me." Her eyes were tortured. "I'd rather we just slept together...."

He shook his head. "I can't take you in my stride, either, Wynn. So we'll get married, and we'll see how it goes."

"And you'll rush right back off to Central America at the first opportunity," she said.

"I've already told you that I don't intend giving it up," he said curtly. "It's my life."

"Yes, I can see that," she said, her voice sad and bitter. "I won't marry you, McCabe. I won't stay here and try to work, worrying about whether or not you're going to die in some jungle."

"You want it all your own way, I suppose," he replied, his eyes glittering and blatantly unloverlike. He moved away from her to light a cigarette. "You want me to stay in Redvale and write books and forget all about it. Is that how the song goes?"

"Chorus and verse," she returned. "I am not having babies alone. What will I tell the children? Yes, you have a daddy, here's his picture, and you'll actually get to see him between wars!"

He was looking more thunderous by the second. "You're being unreasonable, Wynn, and you know it."

She nodded, her green eyes blazing. "So what are you offering me, McCabe? A few nights rolling around in bed with you once or twice a year?" She studied his tanned face under its disheveled blond hair, and loved him until it hurt. "No deal, McCabe, I won't marry you, and I won't sleep with you. Andy may not be for me, but eventually I'll find someone else I can love enough to marry. A man who's willing to give as much as he takes."

He looked dangerous for an instant, his eyes charcoal gray and savage. "What are you giving?" he taunted. "Just your body and a profession of love?"

"The body is standard issue," she said. "If you just want one for a night or two, may I suggest that you drive up to the city with a few fifty-dollar bills and stand on a street corner downtown?" She moved into her room. "My profession of love was a nasty mistake. You can forget I ever said it. As cheaply as you're treating it, it must not be worth much after all.'' And she closed the door on his shocked face and locked it.

McCABE WAS sipping coffee at the breakfast table when she went in. ''I poured you a cup when I heard you stirring,'' he said coolly. ''It should still be hot.'' He pushed it toward her as she sat down. ''I'm going to finish out this week and go back to work.''

She was expecting it, but it hurt just the same. Why did her eyes have to fill up with tears now?

''Did you hear me?'' he ground out.

She tried to speak, but couldn't, so she nodded.

''No argument?'' His eyes glittered.

She shook her head jerkily.

She took a sip of coffee, but her hand was trembling so that she had to put the cup down again.

''Wynn, don't do this!'' he said in a voice that was anguished. He got up from his chair and reached for her suddenly, dragging her up into his arms and holding her close enough to bruise her. His cheek scraped her skin, his mouth searching blindly for hers. He found it with a muffled groan and he kissed her and kissed her, tasting tears and feeling uncertain about where they came from.

''McCabe,'' she sobbed against his warm mouth. Her arms tightened around his neck as she kissed him back. ''I don't care if you leave,'' she whispered, her green eyes swimming in tears. ''I don't care!''

''Yes, I can see that,'' he said unsteadily. He held her face in his big warm hands. ''Don't cry,'' he said softly. ''You don't know how it hurts me to watch you.''

She dabbed at her eyes with the backs of her hands. ''I'm sorry I've made things hard for you,'' she said softly. ''I won't interfere in your life anymore. I'll take what you can give and I won't ask for the moon. Okay?'' She looked up at him with such love and trust in her green eyes that he groaned.

"You make me feel like the worst heel God ever made," he ground out. "But I can't quit, Wynn, not...just yet. In a few years, maybe I can settle for small-town politics and writing books. But...not yet. I wish I could. I wish I could give you everything you want, the moon, the stars...a roomful of roses."

"All right," she said, capitulating totally.

"No argument?" he asked suspiciously.

She shook her head with a quiet, sad smile. "I love you," she said simply. Then her lower lip trembled and spoiled the whole effect.

His teeth ground together and he sighed, drawing her close. "Wynn, marry me. I can't live without you now. I've faced that squarely."

She felt the same way, but he already knew that. She moved closer.

He kissed her warmly, slowly, rocking her softly against him from side to side in a wildly erotic rhythm.

"I said the first time I kissed you that you were passionate," he murmured, lifting his head to look into her eyes. "But I didn't know the half of it, did I, darling? Sweet and wild in my arms, as abandoned a lover as any man could want."

"We...aren't lovers," she whispered.

"Not yet," he murmured, bending to kiss her tenderly.

She felt him shudder and her eyes widened. "Oh, McCabe," she whispered, awed. Her fingers touched his face, tenderly for all the fierce emotion she felt. "I'll let you."

He swallowed, and his eyes dropped to her lips. "I want to," he said. "But I don't think I want to spoil things."

Her misty eyes questioned him and he laughed self-consciously and brushed the disheveled dark hair away from her face.

"It's different, somehow," he said slowly. "I want you in white satin walking down the aisle. I want the whole world to know that you didn't toss your principles down the drain and go promiscuous even when the rest of the world did.'' He frowned slightly, watching her. "And I want it in a church, even if we just have a small ceremony. I want everything proper and aboveboard,'' he added on a sigh.

She loved him more at that moment than she ever had. She nuzzled her face into his shoulder. "Will you wear my ring, too?''

"If you like.''

"Of course I like,'' she muttered, sliding her head back to glare up at him. "I don't want other women thinking you're available. My gosh, competition is fierce these days.''

"As if you'd have to worry about that,'' he mused. He watched her, relaxed, delighted. "Aren't we supposed to go to work today?'' he asked lazily.

She gasped, running to find a clock. "It's nine-thirty!'' she exclaimed. "We're late.''

"My, my,'' he murmured, grinning at her blush. "What a pity we aren't already married.... Speaking of that, we'll get the license and the blood tests this morning, and next week we can put the wedding in the paper. We'll get Jess and Judy to be witnesses, Kelly can give you away. We'll let old preacher Barnes marry us in the Presbyterian church...." He glanced at Wynn, who was feeling shell-shocked by the speed with which he was planning. "You're still Presbyterian?'' And when she nodded in a dazed way, he continued, "And we can be married Saturday. Okay?''

She was still nodding, feeling her whole life pass before her eyes.

"Come on, before you freeze in that position,'' he said, taking her arm. "We've got a lot of loose ends to tie up. Move, darling.''

She followed him out the door. Those few days went by in an incredible rush. It was Friday afternoon, the blood tests were over, the license was in McCabe's pocket, the ceremony was set for ten o'clock the next morning, and Wynn was staring at a wall in the office trying to imagine being married to McCabe. He'd gone off to a civic-club luncheon and hadn't returned, but he'd been muttering something about going with the mayor to a budget meeting, so he was probably going to be late. She smiled. One more night alone in her bed, and then...

The sudden trill of the telephone caught her off guard, and she picked it up.

"Redvale Courier. Wynn Ascot speaking."

"Just the girl," said one of the women she knew from the drugstore. "Listen, do you know what's going on over at the cotton gin? Old Mike Hamm said he heard they'd cornered an escaped murderer over there."

There was something muffled, then the woman's voice again. "That was Ben, with the fire department—I ran out and caught him as he went by the door. He said it's two escaped murderers from the prison in Reidsville. One of them had family south of here. The police stopped the stolen car and Randy Turner's been shot."

"Randy!" He was a young man with a wife and baby who'd been with the police department only six months. "How is he?"

"Bad. They don't know if he'll live. Ben thought he heard them say they'd made an arrest. Thank God, can you imagine—"

"I'd better get over there, if I want my pix," Wynn interrupted. "Thanks for the tip! That's one I owe you!"

"Anytime."

Wynn grabbed up her camera and stuck a pad and pen in her purse. "Be back soon," she called to Judy. "They've just arrested a couple of escaped murderers at the gin!"

"Be careful!" Judy called after her.

"I'm always careful," she called back.

She knew a back way to the gin, so she took it, weaving

down an alley toward the metal building, which was deserted now that peanuts and soybeans were the main crop instead of cotton.

Her skirts flew as she turned the corner...and found herself suddenly, sickeningly, in front of a leveled pistol, held by one of two badly dressed men coming straight down the alley toward her.

*

BOTH MEN were flushed and sweating wildly, and she could smell their fear. Or was it her own?

The shorter man thrust her hand behind her, angrily dislodging the camera and purse from her shoulder and slamming them to the ground. "Now, hold still, lady!" he growled.

"Hey, fuzz!" the taller man yelled as the three of them pressed against the corner of the building where the alley led to the street.

The police chief stood up behind his car. Wynn recognized Bill Davis.

"We picked up a passenger," the tall man yelled. "A lady. With a big camera."

"Wynn!" Bill burst out.

The tall man raised his voice. "Now, you just do like I say and she won't get hurt. I want a helicopter. And a pilot to fly us anywhere I say."

There was a pause and voices rumbling. "I can't get a chopper in less than two hours!" Davis called back. "But there's a light aircraft at the airport, the pilot's right here. He says he'll take you up."

The two men looked at each other. "They'll bring in more fuzz and pretty soon they might decide to rush us. We got no choice!" the tall one said.

The taller man relaxed a little, but the gun pressed harder against her throat.

"Maybe we could take her with us," the shorter one said. "Yeah, Jack, we can take her along!"

Jack nodded.

"Okay, fuzz, we'll take the plane," the one convict yelled at the policemen. "But the broad comes with us."

"I understand," Bill Davis said calmly. He yelled to his men to put away their weapons.

And then the longest walk of Wynn's life began. The pistol barrel was cold and hard in the small of her back, and she was trembling.

The men were nervous, wildly nervous, and she understood. The threat of being shot and killed was enough to make anyone shake.

The men jerked her out onto the sidewalk, and the first person Wynn saw, standing rigidly beside Bill Davis, was McCabe! He was leaning heavily on the cane.

"This is the pilot," Davis said, nodding at McCabe. "He'll fly you out."

McCabe limped forward on the cane. His eyes were on the two men and they didn't waver as he came close. McCabe stopped just in front of Wynn. "You just let the lady go, and I'll be your hostage. Okay?"

The two escapees looked at each other nervously.

"He's crippled," the one called Jack muttered. "Hell, it'll be easier just watching one of them. We'll take him."

The other one loosened his grip and finally released Wynn altogether. But she didn't move. What if they shot McCabe, for God's sake?

The convict leveled the pistol at McCabe.

McCabe gave it a hard stare, and Wynn imagined he was remembering another time, another place.

"He ain't gonna try nothing," the taller man said with a sarcastic grin. "Are you, big man? You're just a cripple."

"That's been said about one time too many," McCabe growled in a dangerously soft voice. And before anyone realized what that tone meant, he moved. Quickly, as if his leg were in mint condition, he shot forward, grabbing the smaller man's arm to jerk him forward. McCabe's massive fist connected with a crunch. The man cried out and sank to the ground, leaving the pistol behind in McCabe's hand. He swung backward without even looking, slamming the pistol barrel straight into the face of the second convict and sending him reeling into the arms of the police. It happened so fast that Wynn's eyes blinked incredulously. And the look on McCabe's impassive face was as calm as milk in a bowl, until he turned his head and she got a look at his eyes.

The police chief's men got the groggy convicts to their feet and marched them off to patrol cars.

The chief took off his hat and wiped his sweaty brow. "That was a terrible chance you took, McCabe!"

"Before you explode, look at this." McCabe broke open the chamber of the police special the convict had carried and showed it to Davis.

"Empty!" the policeman burst out.

McCabe told him, "When the little guy pointed it at me, the look in the man's eyes told me he was bluffing. That was all I needed."

Davis studied him. "What if the gun had been loaded?"

"I'd be dead," he said simply. He was staring at Wynn, his eyes blazing, glittering. "Are you all right?" he asked in a deep, husky tone.

She swallowed and nodded. "I'm all right," she said weakly, and managed a smile. "Sorry I got in the way, Bill. I thought they said you'd made an arrest."

"Never trust a rumor. Don't you know that?" He patted Wynn on the back. "Stick to reporting and leave catching crooks to us, will you, Wynn?"

"Sure, Bill," she said shakily.

McCabe took Wynn's arm and escorted her back down the alley. He was grim and unsmiling.

He took Wynn into the office and pulled her into his arms. The arms holding her trembled, his body trembled.

"Oh, God," he ground out huskily. "I've never been so afraid in all my life!"

She smoothed the hair at the nape of his strong neck. "It's all right, darling," she whispered softly. "I'm fine, really I am."

"I could have lost you."

"But you didn't," she said softly. "And a miss is as good as a mile, isn't it?"

"No, it damned well isn't!" He took in a sharp breath and lifted his head. His face was paper white, his eyes filled with raw emotion. "That's it. You're quitting. You're going to go home and have babies and raise roses! But you're not going to work here."

Her eyes widened. "It's my job!"

"It was," he said coldly. "Not anymore."

"You won't give up your job, why should I?"

He stood there staring at her, and all the expression drained out of his face. Every last bit of it. "This is how you felt when I told you how I got shot, isn't it?" he asked slowly, with dawning realization. "This...sickening coldness is just exactly what you felt."

She nodded. "Just exactly."

He took a deep breath and studied her pale face.

"Well—" he sighed heavily "—I guess I'd better get some information on the water situation in south Georgia. Harry's going to need a lot of help to get the message across to the voters when they call a referendum on the countywide water system this fall."

Tears sprang up like green fountains in her eyes and she stared at him uncomprehendingly.

"You'll have to be patient at first, of course," he continued, unabashed. "If I start wearing bush shirts and carrying a machete in the backyard, you'll have to pretend it's perfectly normal."

THEY SPENT their wedding night in a luxurious motel on a Florida beach, McCabe having coaxed Ed back home early for the occasion of their wedding.

She lay in his arms on the balcony and watched the whitecaps hit the moonlit beach.

She smiled as his mouth found hers in the dim light. He lifted her up and tugged her back into the room, pausing to turn down the double bed. He pulled off his clothes while she gaped at him, chuckling when he was through and she was still frozen in position.

He came close, removing her blouse and the rest of her outfit until she felt the cool ocean breeze on her bareness with an incredible sense of freedom.

She caught her breath on a wild, husky little moan as she felt for the first time in her life the silky roughness of a man's bare flesh against every inch of her own.

"McCabe," she moaned.

"You need to learn some new words," he whispered in her ear as his hands made new, exciting discoveries about her. "Before morning, you'll have a great vocabulary."

He was a patient lover. And he knew where to touch, how to arouse. She found herself obeying his soft, tender whispers without a single protest as he led her deeper and deeper into a morass of sensuality that surpassed even her wild imaginings. She went with him every step of the way, his willing companion in a journey of exploration that ended all too soon.

She nestled close in his arms, still shaking with mingled pleasure.

"Oh, McCabe, I love you so much. I'm just so glad that you're not going to be risking your life anymore."

"That goes double for me, darling," he said flatly. "I wouldn't want to live if I had to do it without you."

She caught her breath at the genuine emotion in his deep voice.

"I love you, Wynn."

She let him pull her down into the maelstrom with him. He was hers. And she was his. Totally.

A long time later, they ordered coffee and pie from room service and sat together on the balcony.

"McCabe, about your job," she began uneasily. "Will you be able to settle for what Redvale can offer?"

"I've thought about that a lot," he said. "And I think I can, Wynn. As long as you don't mind traveling with me once in a while. I want to climb the ruins at Machu Picchu and on Crete and see the pyramids. I'd like to go around the world without being obligated to report what I see. Would you like that?"

"Yes, I would," she said.

He kissed her nose. "Will you miss reporting a lot?"

"No more than you will, I guess," she admitted.

"Wynn, Ed made me a proposition," he said after a minute. "He offered me the paper."

She sat up, holding her breath. "And?"

He studied her. "How would you like to run it with me?"

"Oh, McCabe!" she burst out, laughing, loving him. "McCabe, what a nice wedding present!"

He drew her close and kissed her. "I'm still working on the roomful of roses." He eased her back down into his arms. "Now, this is how I thought we'd start out," he began. And she nuzzled closer as she listened. She lifted her hand to his face, and her wedding ring caught the moonlight. It was no more radiant than Wynn's eyes, with the glow of fulfillment blazing softly in its depths.

WOMAN HATER

Diana Palmer

When Gerald Christopher first suggested going to his family ranch in Montana to rest his recently diagnosed ulcer, Nicole White had reservations. He was the boss, of course, but she liked the pleasant routine of life in Chicago, where she'd spent the past two years working as a secretary for the Christopher Corporation.

Nicole's family had been one of the old moneyed ones of Kentucky. Her father, in fact, was still a horse-racing magnate. But two years ago, after her mother's death—her father had been with his latest mistress at the time—Nicole had renounced her share of the family fortune. And once her new fiancé, Chase James, had found out that she'd been foolish enough to give up her family money, he'd asked for his ring back. His immediate defection to one of Nicole's rich and eligible girlfriends had shattered her young life. At the age of twenty, Nicole had left the elegant brick mansion of her childhood in Lexington, Kentucky, to live the frugal life as a secretary in Chicago.

It all seemed a long time ago now, a part of her life that was like some slowly fading photograph of a reality she no longer belonged to....

"You'll like it there, Nicky," Gerald Christopher said dreamily, staring out the window.

"But your brother and his family—won't they mind having your secretary to house and feed?" she asked, her pale green eyes hesitant in a plain but interesting oval face, surrounded by naturally curling short dark hair. She knew he had a brother, and he'd mentioned a woman named Mary, whom she'd assumed was his sister-in-law.

"Winthrop doesn't have a family," he said, smiling as

he turned toward her. He was a terrific boss, and Nicky adored him. In a purely businesslike way, of course.

"Your brother came to the office once, didn't he?" she ventured, recalling vaguely a tall, very cold sort of man she'd barely glimpsed on an unusually hectic day.

"Yes," he said. "Winthrop owns a small share in the corporation, and I have an equally small share in the ranch. He's primarily a cattleman, and I'm a businessman, so we each have what we like most. As long as we keep out of his way, we won't have any trouble."

That sounded ominous. "A month is a long time," she said slowly.

"Come on, Nicky, a month in the country would do you good. The ranch is way up in the Rockies, near the Todd place." He paused, glancing at her with an odd expression. "You remember Sadie, don't you?"

"Yes. She was very nice." Mr. Christopher had dated Sadie and had been devastated when she left several months ago to take care of her invalid mother. Nicole wondered if her boss had more than just health reasons for wanting to work at the ranch. "All right, I'll go," she agreed. "But you're sure your brother won't mind?"

He looked vaguely disturbed for a second. Then he smiled. "Of course I'm sure."

Becky, who worked for one of the vice presidents, breezed into the office after Mr. Christopher had left.

"What's this I hear about a vacation you're taking with the big boss?" she teased.

"I have visions of being eaten by a puma or carried off by a moose," Nicole joked.

"You might be carried off by Winthrop." Becky grinned. "He's a wild man, from what we hear. He used to be a ladies' man, and he traveled in those ritzy circles. But since the accident three years ago, he's pretty much given up his playboy status and turned to the great outdoors."

Nicole frowned. "What accident?"

"Deanne Sharp—of the Aspen Sharps, and Winthrop's fiancée at the time—was driving and they crashed. He almost lost his leg, and during his recovery, she walked out on him. I hear she's on husband number three now, and has millions," Becky said. "An experience like that could make a man bitter, you know."

Nicole drew in a slow breath. "A real woman hater."

"Now, that's the truth." Becky laughed. "So make sure you take lots of warm clothing. That way you won't get frozen—by the weather or Winthrop."

A WEEK LATER, Nicole and Mr. Christopher flew out to Montana in the corporation jet. The gray jersey dress she wore for the flight, along with a minimum of makeup, made her look sweet and young and totally unlike a glamorous socialite. She stared out at passing clouds, a little anxious about the welcome she was going to get when they got off the plane.

"Mr. Christopher, your brother does know I'm coming?" she asked him when they were about to land.

His dark eyebrows arched. "Of course. Don't worry, everything's going to be fine."

Sure it was. She knew that the instant they got off the plane.

She recognized Winthrop Christopher at once. He was a big man. Broad shouldered and lean hipped with a battered black Stetson twisted into an arrogant slant over one dark eye. He hadn't shaved, and the white line of a scar curved from one cheek into the stubble on his square chin with its faint dimple. His black eyes gleamed with a cold light, and the look he was giving Nicole would have curdled fresh milk.

"Hello, Winthrop," Gerald said, shaking his brother's hand. He glanced at Nicole with a smile, which the older brother didn't return. He was too busy glaring at her, his dark eyes making an unpleasant inventory of what he saw. "Winthrop," Gerald continued quickly, "this is my secretary, Nicole White."

"How do you do, Mr. Christopher," Nicole said politely.

Winthrop's dark eyes narrowed. His thin, chiseled lips pursed thoughtfully, but there was no smile to ease the hardness of that rugged face. His voice was deep and curt. "You're young."

"I'm twenty-two," she said.

"Young." He turned abruptly, with a care that no physically fit man would have had to take. "I'll get the luggage." He started toward the plane, favoring one leg, and Nicole hesitated, her eyes speaking her thoughts. He gave her a look that stopped her from moving or speaking. With a violent flush, she turned away and followed Gerald.

"Not what you expected, Miss White?" Winthrop chided much later as he gunned the truck up what seemed like a mountainside.

"It's very mountainous," she began.

"That it is." He wheeled around another curve, and she got a sickening view of the valley below. Nicole, who had no head at all for heights, began to feel sick.

"Are you all right, Nicky?" Gerald asked with concern.

"I'm fine." She swallowed. Not for the world would she let Winthrop see what his careless wheeling was accomplishing.

Another few miles, and they began to descend. The valley that opened before them took her breath away. "Heaven," she breathed, smiling at maples gone scarlet and gold, delicate aspens and fluffy cottonwoods and the wide swath of a river cutting through it all.

Winthrop's eyebrows levered up a fraction as he slowed the truck to give her a better view. At the end of the road, a huge sprawling two-story house seemed part of its environs.

"Lovely, isn't it?" Gerald sighed. "It's been this way

for forty years or more, since our mother planted those maples around the house when our father built it.''

''I thought they looked as if someone had planted them.'' Nicole laughed.

''Amazing, that you were able to pick it out so easily,'' Winthrop mused, glancing coldly at her.

''Oh, Nicky grew up on a farm, way over in Kentucky.'' Gerald grinned, tweaking her hair.

''Good thing they plant trees in perfect order in Kentucky, and teach native sons and daughters to recognize the difference between a planted tree and a naturally seeded tree,'' Winthrop said without looking at her. ''I guess there are people who assume God planted them in rows.''

That was a dig, and Nicole wondered what the big man would do if she leaned over and bit him. It was incredible how easily this man got through her defenses.

''Did I write you about the Eastern sportsmen I'm expecting?'' Winthrop asked Gerald unexpectedly.

''I remember.'' Gerald nodded.

Winthrop frowned as he glanced at Nicole, but he didn't say anything. Her name, her last name, rang a bell, but he couldn't remember why. No matter, he thought; he'd remember eventually.

A big, elderly woman came ambling out onto the front porch to meet them. She had high cheekbones and a straight nose.

''That's Mary,'' Winthrop said, introducing her. ''She's been here since I was a boy. She keeps house and cooks. Her husband, Mack, is my horse wrangler.''

''Nice girl,'' Mary muttered, watching Nicole closely as the three newcomers came up onto the porch. ''Plain face but honest. Which one of you is going to marry her?'' she demanded, looking from Gerald to Winthrop with a mischievous smile.

''I'm Mr. Christopher's secretary, Nicole White,'' she

said quickly, and forced a smile as she extended her hand. "Sorry to disappoint you, but I'm only here to work."

"And that is a disappointment." The woman sighed. "Come. I will settle you."

"Mary is Sioux," Winthrop told Nicole. "And plain-spoken. Too plainspoken, at times," he added, glaring at Mary's broad back.

Mary whirled with amazing speed and made some strong gestures with her hand. Winthrop's eyes gleamed. He made some back. Mary huffed and went up the long, smooth staircase.

"What did you do?" Nicole asked, amazed.

Winthrop looked down at her from his great height, his eyes faintly hostile but temporarily indulgent. "The Plains Indians spoke different languages. They had to have some way to communicate so they did it with signs."

"It's fascinating," she said, and meant it.

"If you ask Mary, she might teach you a little." Winthrop smiled with cool arrogance. In other words, that look said, don't expect any such favors from me.

She ran upstairs, careful not to look at him. Winthrop Christopher wasn't going to pull his punches, apparently. Nicole was only sorry that she couldn't dislike him as forcefully as he seemed to dislike her. Quite the contrary; he disturbed her as no man ever had, scarred face, limp and all.

*

THE ROOM Mary led Nicole into was delightful. It had pink accents against a background of creamy white, complete with a canopied bed and ornate mirror.

"Are you sure I was meant to go in here?" Nicole asked hesitantly.

"Mr. Winthrop said so." Mary winked at Nicole without smiling. "With his hands, you see."

Nicole shook her head. "He seems very…" She turned, shrugging as she tried to find words.

"His path has not been an easy one," Mary told her, those dark eyes sizing her up.

Nicole searched the smooth old face quietly. "He hides," she said perceptively.

Mary smiled. "You see deep."

"I won't hurt him," came the quiet reply.

"I see deep, too," Mary mused. "He won't let you close enough to do harm. But watch yourself. He might take out old wounds on you."

"I'm a survivor," Nicole said, laughing. "I'll manage. But thank you for the warning."

Mary only nodded and left.

Nicole put on a pair of faded jeans and went downstairs. There was no one around, so she went outside and found a comfortable seat on the porch swing. She closed her eyes as the breeze washed around her. Heaven.

"I see you've found the swing."

She jerked upright as Winthrop came out onto the porch. He'd taken time to shave, and his face was dark and smooth now, with the hairline white scar more visible without the stubble of a beard to hide it. Her pale green eyes wandered over him. He looked lean and fit and a little dangerous, despite the faint limp when he moved toward her.

He dropped into a big rocking chair and crossed his long legs. "It's still pretty wild here in the valley. That's why we attract so many bored Eastern sportsmen. They come here to hunt and pretend to 'rough it.' " He glanced down at her. "I hate rich people."

"I'm not rich," she said, and it was the truth. "But I thought you were."

"Did you?" he asked deliberately, and the mockery in his face was daunting. "Was that why you came with Gerald?"

He moved away from her without another word, almost

colliding with Gerald, who was coming out of the house as he was entering it.

"Sorry, Winthrop," Gerald murmured, curious about the expression on his brother's face. "I was looking for Nicky."

"I'm out here, Mr. Christopher!" she called.

"I'm Gerald here," he said shortly, joining her with a resigned glance over his shoulder as the door slammed behind Winthrop. She moved over to make room for him on the swing, and struggled to regain her lost poise.

"I'm sorry Winthrop's so inhospitable." Gerald glanced at Nicole's quiet face. "You aren't afraid of him, are you?"

"I'm not afraid of him," she said. And she meant it. "You must miss all this in Chicago," she said, looking up at her boss.

He stared at a house far on a hill in the distance, his eyes narrowed and unexpectedly sad. "Sadie Todd lives over there," he said absently, "with her invalid mother. We'll have to go and visit her while we're here."

"I'd like very much to go and see her," she said.

He smiled down at her. "You're a nice person, Nicole." He got up. "I'm going to make a few phone calls. Just sit and enjoy the view, if you like."

"Yes, sir," she promised.

He went inside, and she lounged in the swing until Mary called her to have a sandwich. Then Nicole went out the back door and wandered down to the river, just to look around. She sat down on a huge rock beside the river and tore at a twig, listening to the watery bubble of the river working its way downstream.

"Daydreaming?"

She turned to find Winthrop Christopher sitting astride a big black stallion, watching her.

"I like the river," she explained. "We have one in Chicago, of course, but it's not the same."

"I know. I've been to Chicago. Even to the office." His eyes narrowed. "You don't remember me, do you?"

She did, but it wouldn't do to let him know that. "It's always hectic. I don't pay a lot of attention to visitors, I'm afraid, Mr. Christopher."

"Winthrop," he corrected. "I'm not that much older than you. Eleven years or so. I'm thirty-four."

"How old is your brother?" she asked, curious.

He lifted his chin. "Thirty."

"Sometimes he seems older," she mused. "You inherited the ranch, didn't you?"

He stared at her for a minute, then nodded. "My father knew I'd hold it as long as I lived, no matter what. You'll find that Gerald isn't terribly sentimental. He'd just as soon have a photograph as the object itself."

"I'll bet you saved bobby pins and bits of ribbon when you were a teenager," she said daringly.

He blinked, then laughed, but it wasn't a pleasant sound. "I had my weak moments when I was younger," he agreed. "Not anymore, though, Kentucky girl. I'm steel right through."

She wouldn't have touched that line. She turned, glancing at the distant ribbon the river made running into towering, majestic peaks. Winthrop shifted restlessly. "Where's Gerald?"

"Back at the house, I suppose," she said. "He had some important phone calls to make."

"Want a ride back?" Winthrop offered, then seemed to withdraw, as if he regretted the words even as he was speaking them.

"You look as if you'd rather sacrifice the horse than let me on him." She grinned, daring him to mock her. "Anyway—" she shuddered with more sarcasm than he could know, because she'd practically grown up on horses "—I'd probably fall off. It looks very high."

"It is. But I won't let you fall." He kicked his foot out

of the stirrup and held down a long arm, giving in to an impulse even he didn't understand. He wanted her closer. He wanted to hold her.

Nicole hadn't realized how intimate it was going to be. His hard arm went around her middle and pulled her back against a body that was warm and strong and smelled of leather and spice. She felt her heart run away, and that arm under her breast would feel it, she knew.

"Nervous?" Winthrop asked at her ear, and laughed softly, without any real humor.

"Yes, I'm nervous," she said. "You're dangerous."

His eyebrows arched. "You're plainspoken, aren't you?" he asked, gathering her even closer.

"I try to be," she said. She held on to the pommel, her eyes on his long fingers. "You have beautiful hands, for a man," she remarked.

"I don't like flattery."

"Suit yourself, you ugly old artifact," she shot right back.

It had been a long time since anything had made Winthrop laugh. He felt the sound bubbling up his chest, like thunder, and then overflowing. He couldn't hold it back this time, and the rush of it was incomprehensible to him.

The lean arm contracted, and for an instant Nicole felt him in an embrace that made her go hot all over. What would it be like, she wondered wildly, if he turned her and wrapped her up in his embrace and put that hard, cruel mouth over hers...?

"AMAZING, that we worked together for two years and know nothing about each other." Gerald sighed, shaking his head as he and Nicole sat sipping coffee in the living room after supper.

She smiled at him. "You're very nice to work for, though. You don't yell, like some of your vice presidents do."

He laughed. "I try not to. Winthrop, now," he said, watching her face as he spoke, "never yells. He has a voice like an icy wind when he loses his temper, which isn't often."

"He doesn't want me here, you know."

Gerald's shoulders rose and fell. "He's buried himself up here for three solid years. Don't let him hurt you, Nicky."

She colored delicately. "You think he might?"

"I think you attract him," he said bluntly. "And I have a feeling that you aren't immune to him, either."

Hours later, when Nicole went up to bed, she could picture Winthrop behind her closed eyes, and the image made her sigh with mingled emotions. She wanted him in ways that she'd never dreamed she could want a man and she didn't quite know how to cope with the new and frightening sensations.

She was almost asleep when she heard slow steps coming past her door. She knew from the sound that it was Winthrop, and her heart beat faster as he passed her room.

*

THE NEXT MORNING Nicole had finished her two hours in the study, taking dictation from Gerald, and now she was lazing around the corral looking for Winthrop's thoroughbred horses. The stallion was there, but she didn't see the mare anywhere.

A noise from inside the barn caught her attention. She darted into the dim warmth of the big barn, down the neat corridor between the stalls. "Winthrop?" she called quickly.

"In here."

She followed his voice to the end stall. The mare was down on her side, making snuffling sounds, and Winthrop was bending over her, his sleeves rolled up, bareheaded, scowling.

"Something's wrong," she said, glancing at him.

"Brilliant observation," he muttered, probing at the mare's distended belly with tender, sure hands. "This is her first foal and it's a breech."

Nicole eased into the stall, and gently approached the mare, talking softly to her with every step. While Winthrop watched, she slid down to her knees, watching the silky brown eyes all the while. Slowly she eased under the proud head and coaxed it onto her knees. She drew her fingers gently over the velvety muzzle, talking softly to the mare, gentling her.

"She'll let you help her now," she told Winthrop softly, never taking her eyes from the mare's.

"Yes," he said, watching her curiously for a few seconds before he bent to his task. Minutes later, guided by patient hands, hind fetlocks appeared, followed rapidly by the rest of the newborn animal. Winthrop laughed softly, triumphantly, as the tiny new life slid into the hay.

"A colt," he announced.

Nicole smiled at him over the mare, amazed to find genuine warmth in his dark eyes. "And a very healthy one, too," she agreed. Her eyes searched his softly, and then she felt herself beginning to tremble at the intensity of his level gaze. She got slowly to her feet.

"The stallion has a superior conformation," she said absently. "So does the mare. He might be a champion."

"The stallion is by Calhammond, out of Dame Savoy," he said, frowning as he moved away to wash his hands. "How did you know?"

"Kentucky is racehorse country." She laughed, sidestepping the question. "I used to beg for work around thoroughbreds, and one of the trainers took pity on me. One of the biggest racing farms in Lexington was near where I lived—Rockhampton Farms." Rockhampton was her grandfather's name; her mother's people had owned the stables for three generations.

"I've heard of it," Winthrop told her after a minute. He turned, staring hard at her with dark, curious eyes. Her name was White. Wasn't that the name of the jet-setting sportsman from Kentucky who was coming with the Eastern hunting party? "The owner of Rockhampton is a White," he said in a direct attack, watching closely for reaction. "Any kin of yours?"

She held on to her wits with a steely hand. She even smiled. "Do I look like an heiress?"

"You don't dress like one," he commented with narrowed eyes. "And I guess you wouldn't be working for Gerald if you had that kind of money," he said finally, relaxing a little.

"I couldn't have managed that alone," he added quietly. "I'm obliged for the help."

"You don't like me, do you?" she asked a moment later. "Hating me and making my life miserable for the next few weeks isn't going to erase your scars. So can't we be sporting enemies? And I'll promise not to seduce you in the hay," she added, her green eyes twinkling.

"What do you know about seduction, Red Riding Hood?" he asked with blithe humor, and she got a tiny glimpse of the man he'd been before the accident.

"Not much, actually," she said pleasantly, "but that's probably in your favor. Just imagine if I were experienced and sophisticated and out to sink my claws into you!"

Her earnestly teasing expression made him feel as if he were sipping potent wine. He had a hard time drawing his eyes away from her soft mouth and back up to her laughing eyes.

"I don't play games with virgins, honey," he said unexpectedly, catching her chin with a lean, steely hand. "I've forgotten more about lovemaking in my time than you've ever learned, but I'm not low enough to take out my hurt on you."

He was so close that she could feel the strong warmth of him. Her heart ran wild. This was new and wildly exciting, and she wanted more. She took an involuntary step toward him. One slender hand went hesitantly to his chest and pressed against it, feeling the shock of warm muscle. She felt him tense, even before his hand came up to remove hers with abrupt impatience.

"Don't do that." He ground out the words, glaring at her. "I don't want your hands on me."

Her own forwardness shocked her more than his irritable statement. She turned away, feeling a rush of tears that she couldn't let him see.

"I'd better get back to the house," she said quickly. "I'm glad the mare's okay." She said it all in a mad rush before she ran out of the barn as if her shoes were on fire.

He watched her go with mingled emotions. Anger. Irritation. Hunger. Frustration. He couldn't sort them out, so he didn't bother.

The next few days settled into a pleasant routine. Nicole spent her free time exploring outdoors or watching Mary in the kitchen. Winthrop was pleasant enough, but he kept things cool, although from time to time she found those dark, quiet eyes watching her in a way that excited her beyond bearing.

One morning she heard cattle bawling and excited male voices, and she succumbed to the need to see Winthrop. He was on his horse, helping to drive cattle into a holding pen where they were being vetted. Warmth coursed through her and she forced herself to watch.

Winthrop climbed off the horse to help catch a calf. He was rubbing his leg, and the limp was even more pronounced when he turned, leading his horse by the reins. He saw Nicole at the fence, and he stood very still for an instant. She could feel his anger even at that distance, and she made a discreet and quick withdrawal, walking quickly into the forest that encircled the house. She stopped, catching her breath. He was right behind her, still leading the horse. As he walked, he favored his right leg.

"Running away?" he taunted. "Why?"

"I don't know," she said quietly.

He lifted his dark head. "Did you want to see if the cripple could still throw a calf?"

She went forward without thinking and put her soft hand over his mouth. She said softly, "You're not a cripple."

The feel of her fingers shocked him. He stood over her, breathing roughly, his eyes dark with pain and anger as they searched hers. "I don't want you here," he said quietly, his eyes narrow, piercing.

"Yes, I know." She touched his cheek, tracing the long scar down his jaw, into the dimple in his chin. It was incredible how secure she felt with him, and not the least bit afraid. He was very close. She could feel the muscles ripple when he moved, feel him breathing, feel the warmth of him in the chill air.

His fingers slid into her hair, feeling the curls as he moved his hands to her nape and turned her head up with firm gentleness.

"It's been one hell of a long time since I kissed a woman," he said half under his breath, looking down at her coldly. "I'm not a boy, and I've gone hungry in recent years. You could start something that would ruin both our lives."

She looked up at him, unafraid, her eyes soft with understanding and compassion. "I'm not afraid of you," she said softly.

"I could make you afraid, Nicole."

His voice was velvety soft and deep. She wanted his mouth, and her lips parted in subtle invitation. Never in her life had she felt anything as sweet as this.

He looked down at her soft mouth, and something in him

snapped. He bent quickly, covering it with his hard lips. She was a child, playing at sensuality, and he wanted to make it so rough that she'd stop tormenting him with emotions he never wanted to feel again....

She yielded completely, no thought of fighting him. His mouth was hard and warm. He made no allowances for her youth, and despite her small experience, this was her first real taste of passion. She sighed hungrily, letting him draw her completely against the powerful hard length of his body, letting him crush her against it. Her mouth yielded eagerly to his insistent lips, tasting his tongue as it pushed into her mouth, penetrating her in a silence that blazed with kindling sensations.

He made a sound deep in his throat and lifted his head, his eyes black and blazing as they probed her dazed ones.

"Aren't you going to fight me?" he taunted with a faint, mocking smile as his mouth poised over hers.

"No." She reached up, sliding her arms around his neck. Her mouth was soft, parted and waiting, tempting his.

"Nicky..."

It was a groan, her name on his lips. But this time, he didn't try to hurt her. This time, he was achingly gentle. His hard mouth slowed and softened on hers, and he kissed her with a subdued passion that aroused all her protective instincts. She closed her arms tight around his neck and opened her mouth for him, drawing it over his as she was learning he liked it. Her tongue teased at his full lower lip and he made a sound that corresponded with the tautening of his body.

"I'm sorry," she whispered against his lips. "I don't...know much about this. I'm sorry if I did it wrong."

He lifted his head again. He was breathing roughly, and his eyes had a haunted look. "You really are a virgin, aren't you?" he murmured with a tenderness he wasn't aware of. "Why were you watching me?" he asked.

"I needed to," she whispered shakily. "It frightens me."

"It shouldn't." His mouth touched her forehead in a kiss as gentle as the arms that held her. "I won't hurt you again."

She nuzzled her face against him. "It's very exciting, being kissed like that," she whispered shyly.

He smiled. "Is it?" He tilted her chin up and searched her eyes. "Then let's do it again," he whispered into her open mouth.

It was wilder this time, hotter, more unbearably sweet. She gave him her mouth and melted into the hard contours of his body with a soft moan. It wasn't until she felt the tautening, felt the sudden urgency in the mouth devouring hers, that she realized things were getting out of control. She put her hands against his wildly thudding chest and pulled her lips away from his. "No," she said shakily.

He bit at her lower lip, his head spinning. "No?"

"I've never…and I can't. I'm sorry," she whispered.

He was breathing roughly, but he didn't seem to be angry. He brushed his mouth over her eyes, closing her eyelids. "What are you so afraid of?" he asked quietly. "It was just a kiss. I didn't even try to touch you in any way that would have offended you."

"It isn't fear," she whispered. How could she explain to him the intensity of her feelings, the aching tenderness she was beginning to feel for him?

"Are you afraid of intimacy?" he asked very quietly.

"I'm afraid of getting involved. Just as afraid as you are," she added.

"Why?"

She touched his face gently, running her fingers slowly along his hard cheek. "I got thrown over by my fiancé," she confessed. "He decided he wanted a rich girl, and I wasn't…" She almost added "anymore" but she caught the word in time.

"You didn't sleep with him," he said, gazing at her intently.

"I wanted the first time to mean something." Intimacy had become as careless as handshakes to her parents, and Nicole had determined that it would be treated more reverently in her own life.

There was more to it than that, Winthrop knew, but Nicole wasn't volunteering any more information. He studied her quietly, thinking how much like him she was. It was insane to be so pleased that she was still innocent. It excited him, as sophisticated women never had.

"I could eat a moose," he said conversationally. "Why don't we rush back to the house and raid the freezer?"

She laughed at him. His humor had surprised her. "Are you walking or riding?"

He grimaced. "I guess I'm riding," he muttered. "Damned leg hurts like hell."

She had a feeling he wouldn't have admitted that to anyone but her. It was the best kind of compliment.

"What happened to your leg?" she asked softly.

"Bone damage and torn ligaments," he said simply. "The surgeons repaired it as best they could, but I'll always limp. And when I overdo, I'll always hurt."

She pursed her lips, feeling mischievous, and almost asked an outrageous question. Then she blushed wildly and turned away.

He guessed the question and burst out laughing. "No," he murmured. "It doesn't cramp my style in bed."

She gasped, glaring at him. "I never—"

"You might as well have written it in twelve-inch letters on canvas," he retorted.

Her mouth opened and then closed while she thought up searing retorts, none of which came to mind.

"I'll qualify that," he said after a long exchange of eyes. "I don't think it will cramp my style. I haven't been with a woman since it happened."

Her breath caught, but she didn't look away. It was such

an intimate thing to know about him, and she struggled to
think of a suitable reply.

"That wasn't fair, was it?" he asked with a slow smile.
"And I can't tell you for the life of me why I wanted you
to know that. But I did. How about dinner tomorrow night?
I'll drive you into Butte."

"If Gerald doesn't need me, I'd love to," she said.

"Okay." He glanced at Nicole, shocked by the surge of
jealousy he felt at her remark about Gerald. He was afraid
that there was something between this woman and his
brother, and his own sense of honor and family wouldn't
allow him to trespass on Gerald's territory. He wanted her
to be heart-whole. He wanted that desperately. Could she
have kissed him that way and still belong to Gerald?

"SADIE INVITED US for dinner Friday night," Gerald said
later that evening as he and Nicole worked in the study.
"Is that convenient for you?"

"That's fine," Nicole said. "Winthrop asked if I'd go
into Butte with him tomorrow night. To a restaurant."

Gerald pursed his lips. "So Winthrop's out to take my
girl away from me, is he? I'm not sure if I like that."

It was an old joke between them. She laughed, and he
was smiling. But the man out in the hall didn't see that.
Winthrop was within reach of the doorknob, but his lean
hand faltered.

"He's not likely to take me away from you, so you can
stop worrying," she said, tongue in cheek. "You're quite
unmatchable."

"And Winthrop is too much a gentleman to steal from
people, so I can relax."

Winthrop turned and walked out the front door.

The next morning Gerald found a note waiting for him
when they sat down to breakfast. He read it over, obviously
puzzled.

"Winthrop," he said, waving the slip of paper, "has

gone to Omaha. Something about a cattle deal. He said he's sorry about this evening, but he'll have to take a rain check on your dinner date."

"That's all right," she said, hiding her disappointment. "I'm sure he couldn't help it."

"With Winthrop gone, would you rather spend tonight at Sadie's?" Gerald asked with old-world politeness.

She smiled. "You're a nice man. Would you mind?"

"Heavens, no," he murmured.

They went that night to have dinner with Sadie and her mother, and Nicole accepted Sadie's invitation to stay the night. After dinner, Nicole visited with Mrs. Todd while Sadie and Gerald did the dishes. Later when Nicole went to say good-night, she found Gerald and Sadie in an embrace that spoke volumes, and the way they were kissing said everything. She tiptoed back and shut Mrs. Todd's door.

"Did you say good-night?" the elderly woman asked Nicole.

"No. They're having a discussion. I expect it will be some time before we hear from them." She smiled and settled back to watch the movie.

LATE THE NEXT MORNING Nicole heard the sound of a vehicle coming up the drive. "Thanks for letting me stay," she told Sadie. "I had a wonderful time."

"I'm glad you came," her hostess mused. "Mother hasn't enjoyed herself much since her stroke. And now I know you aren't making eyes at my Gerald."

Nicole's eyebrows arched in surprise. "You didn't think that?"

"Of course I did," Sadie replied, amused. "So did everybody else."

Nicole wondered then about Winthrop's strange behavior, and if he could have thought the same thing. She looked up as a knock sounded on the door, and Sadie went to open it. It wasn't Gerald standing outside—it was Winthrop.

"Where's Gerald?" Nicole asked hesitantly.

Winthrop positively glared at her. "He's at home coping with some office disaster."

Nicole glared back. He was wearing jeans with a chambray shirt and he looked very Western—deliciously sexy. He was telling Sadie something about a party.

Nicole snapped back to the present. "A party?"

"Gerald thinks you're getting bored," Winthrop told her. "There'll be a band and all the neighbors will come. You too, Sadie. It'll be Friday night, around six. I'll drive Mary up to sit with your mother, and I'll fetch you."

He picked up Nicole's case, and she followed him out to the truck with a rueful wave at Sadie. He didn't speak until they were headed down the long, winding road toward the ranch.

"I didn't expect to find you here," he said curtly.

"It wouldn't have looked right, to have Gerald and me under the same roof alone," she faltered.

He glanced at her. "Then how does it look to have the three of us under one roof?" he shot back.

She hadn't thought about that. She flushed scarlet and moved her gaze out the window. He'd left town because he didn't want to take her out, and now he was as remote as the clouds. She felt abandoned.

"Don't look like that," he said abruptly.

"Like what?" she muttered.

"Lost. Wounded."

She studied her hands in her lap.

"You get under my skin," he said abruptly. "I don't like it."

Her heart shifted uncomfortably. "You have the same effect on me," she said curtly, "and I don't like it, either."

"Then suppose we keep out of each other's way," he suggested.

"That might be wise."

He turned and looked at her just as she lifted her eyes to his. The truck almost went off the road. He braked to stop the truck, but his gaze didn't waver. She was young and sweet and she made him ache as he had in his youth, made him feel invulnerable and all male.

"If I touched you now, there wouldn't be any stopping for either of us," he said in a deep, slow tone. He reached out a lean hand and idly linked her fingers into his with a caressing pressure that was as arousing as a kiss. "I touch you, and my body aches. And if the way you're breathing is any indication, Kentucky girl, you're on fire for me."

She bit her lip, hard. But the tremors wouldn't stop. She tugged her hand away from his and he released it with careless indifference.

"Don't worry," he said with cool mockery, "I love my brother. His happiness comes first."

She frowned slightly. "I don't understand."

"Don't you?" He turned back to the steering wheel and put the truck into gear without another word.

She wanted to tell him that he'd gotten it all wrong, that she and Gerald were only boss and secretary. But he looked too unapproachable and she wasn't sure of him. Her feelings for Winthrop were new and a little frightening. She didn't want to have to face them.

During the next few days, as she helped Gerald plan the party in her honor, Nicole puzzled over Winthrop's cool behavior.

The night of the party, she dressed carefully in the hated gray jersey and did her face with a minimum of makeup. The band, a very good country-and-western one, was already in full swing when she went to answer the door with Gerald. Winthrop came in behind Sadie, glaring at Nicole and Gerald with coal dark eyes.

"Good evening, Winthrop," she drawled softly as Ger-

ald led Sadie off to the punch bowl, since she was the last
to arrive and there were no more guests to receive.

"Good evening, Miss White," he replied. His dark eyes
ran down her body like exploring hands, slow and very
thorough. He took off his Stetson, settled it on the hat rack,
then hung up his jacket.

Watching the muscles ripple under the white shirt he
wore, Nicole wanted to stand in his arms and feel him
holding her. It was a hunger that bordered on obsession.
She moved closer to him as the band swung into a slow
dance tune.

"I want to dance," she said quietly, aware of the guests
watching them.

He stared her down. "I don't dance anymore," he said
coolly.

She moved even closer, her perfume floating up into his
nostrils, her warmth teasing, seductive. "Hold me, Winthrop," she whispered, laying both palms slowly, hesitantly, flat down over the hard muscles of his chest. "You
want to and I want to. Everybody's watching." He started
to turn, but she blocked his path. Everyone stopped talking,
and she held her breath while he decided.

With a glance behind them and a muffled curse, he
pulled her into his hard embrace and began to move very
carefully to the slow rhythm of the music.

Nicky savored her small victory, closing her eyes in
wonder. Dancing with him was as sweet as she'd imagined
it would be. He began to move to the rhythm, a little clum-
sily at first, but quickly with more and more confidence.
She melted into him.

"There," she mumbled happily, "I knew you could."

"I could wring your neck," he said, forcing himself to
smile at her while other people joined them on the dance
floor. "You're brave in company."

"If we were alone, what would you do to me?" she

asked with open curiosity, her green eyes wide and twinkling.

The look in them softened him, just a little. She was a handful, but her heart was in the right place. His fingers edged between hers and caressed them as he turned her with amazing flexibility. He smiled then, the cold anger in his eyes melting into reluctant pleasure.

"What would you have done, Pollyanna, if I'd gone down on the floor with the first turn?" he asked.

"Oh, I'd have made sure I went down with you," she said matter-of-factly, "so that everyone would have thought I tripped you."

He pulled her against him and stood there for one long minute, fighting the urge to kiss her in front of everyone.

"Are we doing statue imitations?" she asked breathlessly.

His lips pursed. "I'm trying to decide whether to kiss you."

"Not in front of all these people, for heaven's sake," she burst out.

"These people—or Gerald?" he asked softly.

Her eyebrows went straight up with surprise. "Well, come to think of it, I'm not sure how he'd react to it," she had to admit.

Winthrop sighed, and drew her back against him. "Never mind, daffodil. Just dance."

All too soon the music stopped, and Gerald was there, waiting.

"My turn." He grinned. "Sorry, big brother."

Winthrop stared at his brother for a long minute, searching the younger man's eyes curiously. And for just a minute, he thought about refusing. Then he came to his senses. She was just a woman, for God's sake. If Gerald wanted her, he could have her, Winthrop thought angrily. He smiled, but there was no humor in it. He nodded with a mocking smile at Nicole and then walked slowly away to the punch bowl, pausing to talk to some of the other men on the way.

Winthrop didn't dance with her again, but Nicole felt his gaze on her wherever she went. Her eyes were on him just as much, when she thought he wasn't looking.

All too soon, the guests were leaving. Nicole had the crazy idea of being alone with Winthrop while Gerald took Sadie home. But he looked in her direction with an expression on his face that chilled her to the bone. It was as if he hated her. And because she was confused and a little hurt by his coldness, she asked if she could ride with Gerald and Sadie. They took one look at her face and agreed without protest.

"Isn't it cloudy tonight?" Nicole asked on the way back to the ranch.

"Snow clouds. Lord, I hope we don't get shut up with that horsey set from back East. They'll be here tomorrow." Gerald glanced at Nicole. "By the way, one of Winthrop's guests is from Kentucky. But I didn't catch his name."

Nicole consoled herself with the thought that there must be hundreds of horsey sportsmen in the world besides her father.

NICOLE LAY AWAKE staring at the ceiling for what seemed hours. Finally she got up and decided to make herself a cup of hot chocolate. The kitchen light was on. She opened the door and paused, stopping dead at the sight of Winthrop bending over the stove. He was wearing pajama bottoms, but no top. His chest was…incredible. Broad and bronzed and thick with a wedge of hair that covered his rippling muscles.

He turned, his dark hair tousled, and stared at her.

"I can't sleep," she confessed.

"I'm making some hot chocolate," he said. "Come in." He took the hot chocolate off the stove and poured it into the mugs before he put the pan in the sink to soak. He was limping rather badly, and she grimaced as he sat down with a hard wince.

"That's my fault, isn't it?" she asked gently. "I made you dance when you didn't want to. I'm sorry."

"I could have walked away from you if I'd wanted to," he said curtly. He took two pills, swallowing them down with a sip of the hot chocolate.

"But you didn't."

He turned, his dark eyes holding hers. "I like holding you."

Her face colored, and he smiled slowly. The silence was suddenly too sweeping, the loneliness of the deserted room staggering in its implications. They were alone. And he wanted her.

She felt him move before she saw him. He drew her up in front of him, holding her gently by her upper arms. "There's nothing to be afraid of," he whispered. "Nothing at all."

He bent his head, very slow and sure of himself. Nicole began to unwind, feeling the softness of his mouth along with its hardness, liking the delicate probing of his tongue just under her upper lip. She lifted herself toward him a little, put her hands against him and felt them tingle where they touched the thick hair that covered him.

His breath caught. He stopped and suddenly moved back. His eyes held hers, searching them. "I want more than this."

She couldn't look away. "How...how much more?"

His eyes went to her pajama jacket. "Nothing terribly indiscreet," he said quietly. He hooked his index finger into the V neckline of her pajamas and tugged her forward to him.

Her eyes went down to his lean fingers working the buttons with such deftness, and she couldn't look away. He undid them slowly, and then drew the fabric back from her high, pink breasts with a leisurely expertise that hypnotized her.

"God never made anything more beautiful than a woman's breasts," he said quietly, his voice very slow and deep. "Come here and let me hold you, Nicole. Let me teach you how beautiful it can be to touch skin against skin."

Her eyes closed at the first contact with his warm, hard body, and she cried out as her nipples stabbed into his skin, burying themselves in the damp, abrasive mat of hair that covered the hard muscles. He drew her very close, closing his own eyes as her soft body melted into him. He was aroused, and she knew it.

"It's exquisitely sweet, having you close to me this way." His arms tightened and trembled a little. So did his tall, fit body. "Nicky," he breathed on a groan. He began to rock her, fostering a new kind of intimacy between them, one that should have shocked her but was strangely familiar. She clung to him, letting him hold her, yielding to his strength.

She drew in a long breath, and he shuddered as he felt her breasts swell against his skin. "Give me your mouth."

She lifted her lips to meet his. He kissed her slowly, warmly, and even that was intimate, his tongue probing softly in her mouth.

He shifted her a little so that his hand could find the soft curve of her breast and tease it into arching toward those tormenting fingers.

"Do you want me to keep going?" he whispered at her lips.

"Yes," she whispered back, her voice breaking.

"Like this?" he murmured, with a teasing touch around the nipple, his fingers faintly callused and deliciously abrasive on her soft skin. "Or like this?"

His thumb rubbed suddenly at the tiny hardness and she cried out, a whimper of sound. His head bent to her body, and as she watched, fascinated, he arched her and opened his mouth and put it completely over her breast.

She thought that as long as she lived, she'd never get over the sensation. It went on and on, tearing at her, shaking her, making her too weak to move, to breathe, to think. His mouth slid from one breast to the other, and she moaned like a wounded thing.

Dazed, shuddering with sensation, she barely felt him move. And then she was on his lap in the chair, and he was holding her, cradling her.

"Shh," he whispered gently, his mouth soothing her now, touching her hot cheeks. "It's all right. Hush, darling, it's all right now."

He rocked her against him hungrily.

"You have exquisite breasts, Miss White," he breathed huskily. "As soft as satin, as warm as velvet. But if I don't cover them, you and I are very likely to become lovers within the next few seconds, right here on the floor." He sat her up on his lap like a big doll and proceeded to do up the buttons on her pajamas. When she was covered again, he drew her back down, holding her lazily while he pressed tender, undemanding kisses on her damp face.

"Any other woman I'd have in bed by now," he murmured. "But you aren't the kind of woman who can play around with sex."

"I wouldn't refuse you," she said slowly, choosing her words.

"I know. That makes it worse. I can't take the responsibility alone." He touched her mouth with a gentle finger.

"Responsibility?" she whispered.

"I could make you pregnant," he said gently. Her lips parted and the look in her eyes made him want to throw back his head and scream. His fingers trembled as they touched her face. "Nicky," he whispered.

"Do you want a son?" she asked in a husky, loving tone.

"Yes," he bit off. "I want one with you...."

In his eyes she saw the coolness of white sheets and the outline of two bodies in the darkness.... And all at once, she was standing and he was five feet away from her.

"I can't take you to bed one night and walk away from you the next morning. At my age, sex is a commitment, not a toy," Winthrop explained. "So suppose you go up to bed, and tomorrow we'll discuss terms."

"What kind of terms?"

He smiled slowly. "That would be telling."

She turned back to the door. "If it means I get to live with you, I'll agree to most anything," she said, and ran for it. Behind her, she heard rich, thunderous laughter, and by the time she got to the top of the staircase, she was laughing, too. Life was sweet and Winthrop had to feel the same way she did, because he was hinting at a lot more than a brief affair.

For an instant she had a twinge of guilt about not sharing her past with him. But there was still time, she told herself as she snuggled under the covers. Yes, there was time.

*

WHEN NICOLE WOKE UP the next morning, lacy white flakes were coming down like cotton out of the clouds, gently blanketing the trees and the grass. She moved to the window and sighed, vividly remembering last night and the newness of what she'd shared with Winthrop. Her daydreams were rudely shattered by the loud noise of a four-wheel-drive vehicle coming up the driveway with Winthrop at the wheel. The hunting party, she guessed. Suddenly she came away from the window feeling sick. She'd go back to Chicago alone, right now. She'd pack her things and get out while she could.

"Nicky!" came Gerald's voice outside the door. "Guess who one of our visitors is? It's your father!"

Along with that horror came a new one. She hadn't told

Winthrop who her father was, or that she'd renounced her inheritance. What was he going to think?

"I'll be right down," Nicole called back. Why did it have to be her father? she wondered miserably. Of all the sportsmen in the world, why him?

There were voices in the living room when she went downstairs, but the only face she saw was Winthrop's. The tender lover of last night was gone. His expression was hard, ice-cold.

"Look who's here," Gerald said, pulling her toward the big white-haired man in tweed.

"Hello, Nicky," her father said coldly. "Long time, no see."

"Not long enough," she replied, and the bitterness of the past was in her eyes.

"This is Carol Murdock," he said, introducing the willowy, very young redhead in ski pants and a mohair sweater under all the fur. "She's visiting with me for a while."

He laughed shortly. "We haven't spoken in two years, have we, Nicky? Nicky holds me responsible for her mother's death. And for cutting her off without a dime after the funeral," he added with killing precision. "Which one of these rich Christophers have you set your cap for?"

Nicole felt panicky. Her father was turning everything around. Winthrop's expression told her that he believed her father, and it grew even harder.

"I'm working," she said with what little pride she had left. "And I'm not chasing anyone. I don't suppose you knew I was here, of course," she asked her father.

"I haven't known where you were in two years," he replied shortly. "There's been a noticeable difference since you moved out, honey. I can balance the checkbook these days. I hope you find someone to support you, but it won't ever be me again." Dominic laughed, bending to brush a kiss across Carol's hair. "Your mother was enough."

"Don't you talk about my mother," Nicole said huskily. Her green eyes spit fire at him. "Don't you dare!"

"Do you have TV?" Carol asked suddenly, searching around. "It's so boring, just sitting."

Nicole was taken aback when Winthrop abruptly got up and led Carol off to show her the TV and VCR in the living room.

"Why did you make me out to be a cheap gold digger?" Nicole asked, searching the face that was so like her own.

"Just for the record," he said coldly, "I didn't kill your mother. She was no saint, Nicky, for all that you're trying to canonize her posthumously. She turned me out on the town as soon as she knew you were on the way, in revenge for what I'd done to her. Making her pregnant was a cardinal sin. Are you shocked, Nicky? Didn't you realize that people are human?"

Nicole listened, only half hearing him. Why should her mother have hated him for that? She was suddenly aware of Gerald, an unwilling eavesdropper to the argument. She shifted away from her father and tried to smile.

"Do you have anything for me to do?" Nicole asked Gerald, her tone conciliatory and faintly hopeful. He caught on quickly.

"As a matter of fact..." Gerald replied, and smiled vaguely. "If you'll excuse us..."

"Is he your partner?" Dominic asked Nicole, frowning.

"He's my boss," she replied coolly. "I'm his secretary."

Her father stiffened. "You're joking, of course," he said curtly. "No White has worked for a living for three generations—"

"Until now," Nicole interrupted. "You ought to try it. It has a humbling effect on a haughty spirit." She turned and left the room.

Nicole spent the rest of the day trying to avoid the other guests, and the snow continued to fall. At the evening meal

Winthrop sat at the head of the table with Carol on one side and Gerald on the other and completely ignored Nicole and her glum father. She was watching big dark eyes light up as he spoke to the nubile redhead, and hating the other woman for arousing the tender side of the man she could no longer reach.

"You wear your heart on your sleeve," Dominic said coolly. "Never let it show."

"A page right out of your book." She laughed shortly. "I suppose I'll be just like you when I'm your age. What a lovely future to look forward to."

"Stop sniping at me, Nicky," he said coolly, and his green eyes met hers. "All your regrets and all mine won't change the past. Neither will giving up your rightful legacy. Your mother wouldn't have wanted that. She had high hopes for you."

"Did she? I don't remember her being sober enough to discuss them in the past."

"Grow up, honey," he remarked. "Your mother was neurotic. She couldn't handle responsibility. In fact, neither could I. We were just kids when you came along, Nicky. Both of us. Kids playing house. And then there we were with a real live baby. We had to be responsible for you. That wasn't an easy task for two people who'd never known what it was to be responsible."

"What you and Mother had wasn't a marriage," Nicole accused him, all the hurt of the past coming back.

"We didn't love each other enough," he said simply. "Your mother and I were nice people, separately. We just weren't compatible. Who do you blame for that?"

For two years Nicole had blamed her father for her mother's untimely death, just as she'd blamed herself. But what if neither of them was responsible?

"I'm a black sheep, Nicky," Dominic said. "I always have been. But I never hated you, honey. I never could."

She tried to smile. "It seemed like it when you got here."

"I missed you," he said curtly, as if he hated even saying the words. "I missed Brianna. Everybody left me at one time. Damn it, how do you think I felt?"

He got up and stormed out of the room without even a backward glance. Nicole stared after him with confused emotions. He'd sounded, and looked, hurt. She rose, oblivious to the others in the room, and went upstairs to her room.

THE DOOR opened, cutting into her thoughts, and the comb paused in midair over her short, dark hair as Winthrop walked into the room and slammed the door behind him.

"You could have told me." His eyes narrowed on her face. "I asked you point-blank if you were related to Dominic White and you sidestepped the question."

She tilted her chin up and looked at him, drinking in the sight of his face, adoring it with her soft green eyes. "I'm not a bored heiress. Are you so afraid to believe what you feel, instead of what you hear? Can't you take my word for it? My father was getting even," she said, moving closer. "He was paying me back for walking out on him after Mama's funeral. He's over it now. He'll tell you the truth if you ask him!"

"I know the truth." He lifted his chin as she came closer, and the expression on his hard face was not welcoming. She pressed against him and his steely hands caught her, holding her away.

"Do I make you nervous, big, bad rancher?" she whispered, moving as close as his hands would allow. Her fingers went to his chest and her nails drew lazily across the cotton fabric. His heartbeat increased sharply.

"No," he denied. But something flickered in his dark eyes.

"Well, you make me nervous. You make me shake all

over when you touch me, and that doesn't have a thing to do with how much money you've got in the bank. And I didn't lie to you about being innocent. I am. And when we made love in the kitchen, I would have died for you.'' Her lips parted, welcoming, pleading, as she looked up into his eyes.

''Damn you, Nicky.''

''Winthrop.'' It was a moan, and he covered it with his lips.

It seemed to take a long time for him to realize what was happening. Her warm body in his arms drugged him. But minute by aching minute, the past came back. He eased his mouth away from hers, steeling himself not to care about the soft accusation in her drowsy eyes as she watched him pull away. ''No, thanks,'' he said quietly. He was as politely indifferent as if he were refusing a drink of water when he wasn't thirsty.

She looked up at him with slow comprehension. She'd banked everything on his desire for her; she'd seen it as her one way to reach him. But it hadn't. She'd lost.

*

SOMEHOW, Nicky got through the night. Winthrop had excused himself and gone out to help his men keep a check on the cattle. The snow had made the mountain roads impassable except with a four-wheel drive. But the hunters settled in with easy acceptance.

At dawn on the third day, the hunters piled into Winthrop's Jeep and headed down the valley. Gerald and Nicky worked alone in the study, leaving Carol to her videos.

''I'm worried about Sadie and Mrs. Todd,'' Gerald said abruptly. ''I tried to phone them an hour or so ago, and the lines are down.''

''Then let's go see her,'' Nicole said. ''Isn't there a four-wheel drive around here somewhere that we can use? I'll tell Mary where we're going.''

Gerald had the old Jeep idling when Nicole climbed in beside him. The vehicle sputtered and lurched as he put it in gear, and the chains on the heavy tires made a nice clanking sound as he shot down the mountain road. By the time they turned off onto the dirt road that led up to the Todd place, Nicky was regretting her decision to go with him. Gerald wasn't the driver Winthrop was, and as the heavy snow continued to fly at them, Gerald swung too wide around a curve and the Jeep suddenly left the road. It lurched crazily sideways and slid down onto a lodgepole pine. Nicky got a sudden and terrifying view of a sheer drop out Gerald's window.

With Gerald's help, she managed to lever herself up to the passenger door and gingerly open it. The Jeep pitched a little, and she caught her breath and shuddered, but the vehicle remained fairly secure against the pine. She managed to tumble out, then reached up to help Gerald.

They cleared the Jeep and collapsed onto the thick, soft snow, almost buried in it while they caught their breath.

''We're closer to the ranch than the Todds' place,'' Gerald said when they were standing in the road. But the snow was coming harder and thicker, and it was blinding, stinging their eyes. ''We can follow the road back...''

We hope, she added silently, because the blizzard wasn't letting up. She leaned into the wind and started walking. Beside her, Gerald kept up the pace. But when they'd gone a few hundred yards, the going got harder and harder. She concentrated on putting one foot in front of the other, watching her boot sink into the deep snow. It came over the boot top and down into her warm socks, wetting them, chilling them.

They rounded a bend, and found the road suddenly buried under a huge drift of snow. Nicole stopped, her eyes on the blanket of white around them, but there was no alternative route. They had to get through that drift or die.

"Oh, damn," she wailed, hating the hot sting of tears in her eyes.

"I'm so tired." Gerald sighed. He sank down with his back to the snowdrift. "So tired…"

"You can't go to sleep," she burst out. "We have to go on."

"How? The snow's too deep. We can't get through, Nicky." He closed his eyes, leaning back against the bank that angled against the snowdrift.

"Nice…."

Nicky shook him, but he was too weary to try anymore. She sank down beside him and sat there, looking around at the deadly white beauty of it.

Her green eyes went up to the sky. Well, it wasn't such a very bad place to die, she mused as drowsiness swept over her. She was near Winthrop, even though he didn't care anymore. Maybe he'd bury her here, and she'd be near him forever…

Something touched her. Shook her. That voice—it was deep and urgent and somehow familiar, but she didn't understand what it was asking. She tried to open her eyes, but it was just too much work. She slept.

Her head ached. She sneezed and the sound echoed around her. Was she dead?

She opened her eyes slowly. A canopy, pink, overhead. She turned her head and there was Winthrop. He was unshaven, his hair needed combing. He was sprawled beside the bed in a chair half his size, his booted feet splayed, his mouth open. He was snoring.

She stared at him for a long moment, memorizing him. "Winthrop." His name sounded rusty. She frowned, because it had hurt her throat to call him.

"You were damned lucky," Winthrop said, opening his eyelids. He glared at her out of eyes as black as night.

"Gerald?" she rasped.

"He's fine, thank God. I've had a hell of a night watching you fade in and out. You little fool, people have died in snowdrifts out here!"

"Oh!"

The exclamation was in response to the sudden, unexpected descent of his mouth, square over hers. His mouth opened against hers, lifting, teasing, his breath mingling wildly with hers while his hands caught hers and pulled them down to the bed beside her head, his fingers interlocking with hers.

"I could ravish you." He ground out the words huskily, and the eyes that glanced at her were blazing. He bent again, tormenting her mouth with his lips, brushing, lifting, teasing until she began to writhe on the sheets. He groaned her name, his mouth so tender, so exquisitely gentle with hers that tears ran hotly down her cheeks. He was the world, and everything in it. She loved him so.

Even as she thought the words, she whispered them under his warm mouth, breathed the truth against him, echoed her feelings like a prayer.

"No." He drew back suddenly. "Don't say it. I don't want that," he said quietly. "I'm sorry. But I...can't, Nicky."

"I can't help it," she whispered softly. "I'm sorry, too, but I do love you. I do, I do!"

"For God's sake, Nicky, I'm not a marrying man!"

Her face flamed when she realized where the conversation was leading. She stared at him, horror-struck. She hadn't meant that, but he'd assumed she was begging him to marry her.

"I...I didn't mean..." She searched his dark eyes quietly. "I'm sorry if I've embarrassed you. But you don't hate me anymore, do you?" she asked weakly.

"No, I don't hate you," he said quietly. He bent toward her, watching her face lift for him, her mouth part. He looked into her eyes while he kissed her, seeing the pupils dilate, the lids close drowsily. That excited him more, and he drew back before he got in over his head.

Nicole watched him get up, trying to hide her feelings. But he limped suddenly and she sat up, her breath catching. "Winthrop, you're hurt!" she burst out.

The caring note in her voice cut him to the quick. He glared at her. "I don't need a nurse," he bit off. "I can take care of myself. I've had years of practice."

He went out and slammed the door, leaving her stunned and hurt.

*

SOON AFTER Winthrop left the room, Nicole's father came in and took the chair Winthrop had vacated.

"Feeling any better?" he asked, and seemed to be genuinely concerned. Nicole could remember being sick as a child and having neither of her parents come near her.

"I'll be all right," she said. "I just feel a little tired."

"If Winthrop hadn't decided to call it quits early, the two of you would have frozen to death. He carried you over that drift all by himself, weak leg and all. I guess he's hurting like hell, from the way he limps, but he was determined."

She felt her heart leap with the pleasure that knowledge gave her. "He's quite a man."

"I think so," he agreed. "I told him the truth, by the way. Maybe," he added hesitantly, "you and I could exchange Christmas cards. Then, as time goes by, you might come to Kentucky to see me."

"Or you might come to Chicago to see me." She sighed.

"You know…in some crazy way, I loved your mother, even if we couldn't quite get our act together. She's pretty irreplaceable." His eyes fell. "God, it hurt when she died. I couldn't even tell you how it hurt."

"I don't think I would have listened if you'd told me then." She sat up straighter. "Thanks for coming up to see me."

"I'll check on you again, Nicky," Dominic said as he started toward the door.

Nicky must have slept then. She woke in the early hours just before dawn and glanced at the tall man sprawled again in the chair, grimacing as he breathed. His leg was probably hurting, and here he sat, when he could have been comfortable in bed.

Nicky got up, just staring at him. She touched his hard, warm cheek with her fingertips, tracing its high cheekbones. "Winthrop?" she whispered. "Come to bed."

He made a sound and his head turned, but his eyes didn't open. He let her tug him out of the chair, and he sprawled onto the bed with a mumbled protest. Then, with a mischievous grin, she crawled back under the covers and snuggled close.

The light streaming in the window woke her. She opened her eyes and found Mary standing at the curtains.

Mary paused beside the bed and bent to touch Nicky's forehead. "No fever. Good. You live yet." She pursed her lips at the clear indentation of a head in the pillow beside Nicky's. "You have a pajama party last night?"

Nicky grinned. "He was sprawled in the chair and groaning in his sleep. I got up and led him over here and tucked him in. He never knew."

"Poor man. Shame on you. You should not take advantage of the helpless." Mary grinned before she went out.

To Nicky's dismay, Winthrop didn't come back all day. She expected him every time the door opened. Mary brought breakfast and then Gerald came, followed by her father and Carol. When Mary came back after lunch to pick up the dishes, she cocked her head at Nicky's forlorn expression. "He cannot get up just yet," she said after a minute. "I think he may have pulled a tendon. I have made a poultice for it, which will take away the pain and make it heal. But in the meantime, he is an invalid.''

''It sounds as though he might need a little nursing,'' Nicky suggested.

''Perhaps.'' Mary shrugged. ''But put on your robe.'' Her dark eyes held Nicky's with subtle warning. ''He is still a man.''

''I love him,'' Nicky said simply. ''I wouldn't hurt him.''

She put on her long white chenille robe and went along to Winthrop's room, a little nervous about how she'd be received.

He glared at her from his bed, where he lay taut-faced with only a sheet drawn haphazardly over his lean hips for cover. ''What do you want?'' he asked curtly.

''I thought you might need something,'' she said, hesitating. ''How about some fruit juice?''

His dark eyes narrowed. ''How about telling me how in hell I wound up in bed with you last night?''

Her eyebrows arched. ''You were in bed with me?'' she asked with pretended horror. ''How scandalous!''

His lips made a thin line. ''It wasn't scandalous. Nothing happened! I don't ravish women in their sleep.''

''Ah, but you don't know what I might have done to you,'' she said, lifting her eyebrows mockingly. ''Anyway, you rejected me.''

''What were you trying to do?'' he demanded.

''You were groaning and I knew your leg was hurting you,'' she said with a smile. ''Since you seemed determined to sit up with me, I thought you should be comfortable. So I led you into bed, and you went with me just like a lamb.''

''Which wasn't what I felt like when I woke up,'' he replied curtly. ''Your gown was up around your hips and half off your shoulder.''

''It was?'' Her eyes were wide, trusting and innocent.

He sighed impatiently, and stretched lazily, watching her eyes drop to his chest with the movement. He liked the way it felt to let her look at him like this.

"You're a surprising girl, Nicole," he said, his voice dropping an octave, deep and sexy.

"Am I? I thought I was a gold-digging adventuress."

"That sounds bitter," he mused.

"I don't want a rich man, Winthrop. I have a job I enjoy, and I can make my own way in life. I was never looking for a…a meal ticket."

"I didn't know that. All I had left were my instincts, and they'd already let me down once. I haven't trusted a woman since this happened." He touched his knee.

"Were you in love with her?" she asked hesitantly, because it was suddenly important that she know that.

He met her searching gaze. "I wanted Deanne until she was an obsession with me. When she walked out, I thought I was going to bleed to death, and for two years I felt like a zombie. Is that love? I don't know. It's the most intense thing I'd ever felt, so maybe it was. But I'm over her now and I have no inclination whatsoever to go through it again."

Nicole sat down slowly on the bed beside him, her soft weight moving the mattress. "Love shouldn't be all physical." Her voice was as gentle as the fingertips that went hesitantly to his firm mouth and touched it. "It should be a sharing between two people. A bonding of thoughts and hopes and dreams. A linking of intangible things. Companionship. Friendship. Openness and honesty."

"You lied to me," he reminded her curtly. His fingers caught her wrist. "And you got too damned close," he said suddenly, every last bit of caution gone. His eyes glittered dangerously.

Before she could react, he levered her down onto the bed, on her back, and loomed over her with a purely arrogant look in his dark eyes.

"I don't want to be another one of your conquests," she told him, struggling.

"Sure you do. If you keep thrashing around like that, you're going to dislodge my sheet and the mystery of life will be over!"

She stopped immediately, glaring at him with wide green eyes. "You don't want commitment, remember?"

"I don't have to propose marriage to kiss you," he returned, bending.

"I have a cold—I'm contagious!" she squeaked.

"I have a sore leg, and that's not catching. But desire is," he whispered against her lips. "Shall I show you how easy it is to catch?"

He nuzzled her face with his, in soft, gentle caresses that wore her down all too easily. "Touch me."

Her hand faltered shyly, but he guided it over the hard muscles of his chest, letting her feel the silky hair, the ripple of muscle under rough skin. He traced her cheek with his fingers as he kissed her very lightly, and his hand slowly lowered to the buttons of her bodice under the robe.

"No," she protested.

"You want to be touched as much as I want to touch you." His fingers moved to the edge of her breast, tracing around it with maddening expertise, making her moan and stiffen suddenly in an explosion of unexpected pleasure.

"You belong to me. Mine," he breathed against her mouth. Her movements were exciting him, her little cries caught in his lips, making him hungry. "All of you. Here and here…"

He had her gown around her waist, and his whirling mind registered her complete abandonment to his ardor. He could do anything now and she'd let him. That realization was what slowed him down. He lifted his head quietly, looking at the helpless reaction of her body to his lovemaking.

"I'm afraid," she whispered.

"There's no reason to be frightened." He drew the backs

of his fingers against her, loving the way she tensed with pleasure. "I go just as high as you do when we make love. It's mutual, this chemistry. It has been from the very beginning."

"I won't have an affair with you," she said quietly.

"I wouldn't let you," he returned. He nuzzled her nose with his. "But I don't want marriage."

"I'll have to leave," she whispered, feeling her heart break.

"Inevitably," he agreed. He looked down at her as his fingers drew tenderly over her bare breasts and she trembled. "It knocks the very breath out of me to touch you this way," he breathed.

"You aren't the only one," she said shakily.

He bent and put his mouth gently on the soft curve, and then he drew back while it was still just a whisper of sensation. He helped her up, buttoned her gown and belted her robe with exaggerated indulgence.

As she left, Nicky managed a rueful smile at Winthrop, feeling disappointed and a little shy. His expression, on the other hand, gave nothing away.

*

THE HUNTERS went home on Saturday. Nicky found herself alone with Winthrop, who towered over her.

"You seem to have arrived at a truce with your father," he mused.

"I misunderstood a lot of things. Grief plays havoc with the brain," she said quietly. "Your knee…is it better?"

He half turned toward her. "Why? Were you thinking of offering me a massage?"

"I don't go around playing with men's legs."

"I know a lot of things you didn't do until I came along," he mused, and his eyes went straight to her yellow sweater. He tilted her chin up with a lean, strong hand and looked down at her. "I'm going out to check on my pure-bred herd. I'd take you with me, but you're a distraction, Kentucky girl."

"Listen here, Winthrop—"

"Say it again," he whispered at her lips, so close that she could almost taste him.

"Win...Winthrop," she obliged.

"Mmm," he murmured. His lips nuzzled hers, tempting them, urging her closer to him in the dim light of the hall. "Come up here..." He actually lifted her off the floor with two steely hands at her waist. "Now open that pretty mouth and kiss me properly."

He had the most incredible way of getting to her. She was lost and witless, drugged on his nearness. She gave him her mouth, parted her lips, and moaned when he deepened the kiss hungrily.

Winthrop finally lifted his head, his breath coming hard and quick on her faintly bruised lips.

"Do you like it that way?" he whispered roughly. "Or do you want me to be gentle with you?"

She trembled with reaction. "I like it...any way at all, with you," she whispered, clinging to him.

"Same here." He let her slide down his powerful body to the floor, savoring the feel of her against him.

Her eyes were wide and soft and drowsy, and he bent to brush her mouth once more with his. He was gone then, and she watched him until he was out of sight.

MRS. TODD HAD decided at long last to go and visit her sister in Florida, and it didn't really come as a surprise when Gerald announced at supper that he'd asked Sadie to marry him.

After they finished eating, Gerald excused himself, and Winthrop invited Nicole to go look at the colt with him.

"Isn't it late to be looking at horses?" she asked.

He glanced down at her. "Why? Are you afraid to be alone with me after dark?"

She hated that arrogant look. "Of course not!"

"Where is he?" she asked once they were inside the barn.

"Over there."

She followed his gesture and leaned over the gate, watching the little chestnut colt nuzzle at his mother's belly.

"Aw," she cooed. "Isn't he cute?"

Winthrop pushed back his hat with an irritable sigh. "Gerald says you and he are going back Monday to get the office shipshape so he and Sadie can get married Friday and have an extended honeymoon."

"Yes," she said absently.

He glowered down at her. "Look here, Nicole, we won't see each other again."

"Yes, I know." She looked up at him quietly.

"I'll always limp," he said unexpectedly.

"That's too bad."

"Is that all you can say?" he growled.

Her eyebrows arched. "What would you like? You're telling me what a bad risk you are, and I'm agreeing with you. You've been right all along, Winthrop. I need a younger man who doesn't limp, who wants marriage and children, so now I'm going to go back to Chicago to find one." She looked at the growing anger in his hard face. "That should satisfy you."

"Would you like to know what would satisfy me right now?" he asked under his breath.

"Not really. I'm tired and I'd like to go to bed."

"At last, we agree on something." He moved toward her.

"Oh, no, you don't. I'm saving myself for my future husband."

"Thank you."

"It won't be you," she told him doggedly. "You aren't a marrying man, remember? You don't want commitment."

"I don't know what I want anymore," he muttered.

"Well, I do," she said. "I want to go home. You only want my body. And that's not enough!"

"Will you listen to me?"

"No!"

She turned and ran for the house, easily outdistancing him. All he wanted to do was back her into a corner and seduce her. Well, he wasn't getting another chance to do that! She loved him, but she couldn't settle for a one-night stand. Not even with the only man she'd ever wanted.

*

WINTHROP wasn't around the next morning, and as the day wore on, he was still missing. Nicole had just finished setting the table for supper when the kitchen door opened and he appeared.

"Where's Gerald?" he asked.

Her heart was beating double time, but she wasn't about to let him know it. "He and Sadie drove Mrs. Todd to the airport. She left for Florida today."

"I know. I said goodbye before I went out."

"Sit down," Mary told them. "I will bring supper."

Winthrop motioned for Nicky to go ahead, and even pulled out her chair for her. He studied her intently while Mary brought in the main course, followed by rolls, vegetables and fruit. He stared at her for so long that her heart began to run wild and her breathing became quick and labored. "You might come back with Gerald for the wedding," he said abruptly.

Her heartbeat increased. But even as she heard him say the words, she knew that the minute she left the ranch, he'd forget her. His offer was just a sugar pill—something to keep her happy until she left. He didn't mean it.

"That would be nice," she said, without any real conviction.

"Nicky..."

Whatever he was about to say was lost, because Gerald and Sadie came back, and the conversation centered on the wedding. Bedtime came and there wasn't a single opportunity for any more discussion.

The next morning, before she had time to plan what she was going to say, she and Gerald were being driven to the airport. Winthrop was long gone, apparently out hunting again. Nicole didn't even get to say goodbye to him before she flew back to Chicago.

*

BACK AT WORK, Nicky found herself haunted by a particularly vivid ghost. Winthrop drifted around in her thoughts constantly so that she couldn't eat or sleep or rest. Gerald was surprised when she said she wouldn't be going back to Montana for his wedding, but once she explained her feelings of love for Winthrop, he understood.

Nicole settled into the office routine the day after Gerald's departure, fielding questions and phone calls. She wasn't prepared for the phone to ring and an angry, irritated Winthrop to be on the other end of the line.

"Where in hell are you?" he demanded coldly.

She stared at the phone as if it had grown teeth. "I'm...here. Working," she faltered.

"You were invited to the wedding," he reminded her.

"Yes, I know."

"Then why aren't you here?"

She closed her eyes and prayed for strength. "I don't think it's a good idea, Winthrop."

"Why not, for God's sake?"

"Because I can't live on dreams," she burst out. "And the sooner I face it, the better off I'll be. I know you mean well, but it…it tears the heart out of me, that's all. I won't come.''

She hung up quickly, before he could talk her into going to Montana. All the rest of the day she expected him to call back. But he didn't. She went to Kentucky and spent the weekend with a surprised and very different father and got back to her apartment feeling vaguely happy. But when a week went by with no word from Winthrop, she fell into a black depression. He didn't call. He didn't write. Christmas Eve came and Nicky gave up hoping that she'd hear from him. She wished her boss a merry Christmas, and went to Lexington for the holidays.

Her father met her at the airport with Carol beside him. "It's just like old times." Nicky sighed as they drove through town. "I always did love the way they decorate the city."

"Me, too. You ought to see the decorations we have at the house," her father said with a twinkle in his eyes.

"And your present," Carol added, also twinkling. "It was really hard to wrap, so I gave up trying and just stuck a bow on it."

When they got to the house, her father helped them out of their coats, then looked at Nicole. "Your present's in the living room. We'll go see about some hot cider while you open it."

"Aren't you coming?" she asked.

"Not just yet. Go on, now. And merry Christmas, sweetheart." He kissed her cheek and then went away, whispering to Carol.

Nicole opened the living-room door and stopped dead. Her present was sitting on the sofa, looking toward her furiously, with a glass of whiskey in one lean hand.

"Merry Christmas," Winthrop said curtly.

Her mouth flew open. He had a bow stuck on the pocket of his suit, and he looked hung over and a little disheveled. But he was so handsome that her heart skipped wildly.

"You've got a bow on your pocket," she said in a voice that sounded too high-pitched to be her own.

"Of course I've got a bow on my pocket. I'm your damned Christmas present." He got up and started toward her, limping just a little. "I can't eat," he said accusingly. "I can't sleep, I can't work. I spent a week up in the mountains trying to get you out of my head, and all I got was drunk. I'm hung over, bleary-eyed and half mad with wanting you."

"Oh, I'm so glad, Winthrop," she whispered. Her heart went wild. "Because I'm half mad with wanting you, too...oh!"

The tiny cry was lost under his devouring mouth. "You're mine now," he breathed into her parted lips. "You're going to marry me, lady. I've got all the necessary papers. All we need is a blood test, and that's scheduled an hour from now. We're going to have a Christmas wedding."

Tears stung her eyes. She looked up at him through a drowsy haze, her body intimately pressed to his, her eyes wide and soft and loving. "You don't want to get married," she whispered.

"Yes, I do," he corrected her. The look in his eyes was so tender that it knocked the breath out of her. "I just didn't know it until I let you walk out the door." He bent, brushing her mouth with exquisite gentleness. "I can't quite make it without you, Nicky. I've never been so alone. Come home where you belong. I'm too old, and too cynical, and not quite the man I used to be, but I...I love you."

"I love you, too," she breathed. "Deathlessly. Hopelessly. With all my heart!"

"God, I've been miserable without you!" He kissed her hungrily and she felt his hands at her hips, lifting her up into an embrace that made her shudder.

She looked straight into his dark eyes and imagined how beautiful it would be joining with him in loving union, softness to hardness, tender rhythm on cool sheets in the darkness. And she gasped again. "Oh, my," she whispered shakily.

"Oh, my, indeed," he whispered. He bent his head. "Merry Christmas, sugarplum."

She smiled back as she gave him her mouth. "You delicious Christmas present, you…"

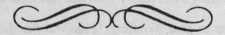

ALWAYS A BRIDESMAID

Patricia Knoll

Rejected! Shelby stared at the letterhead.

"Insufficient credit!" she sputtered. Her blue eyes skimmed down the page. "Well, maybe I don't have credit, but I've got cash!"

Across the room Mary Featherstone looked up from her sewing machine. She appeared to be buried in yards of the chiffon she was using to create four bridesmaids' dresses for a neighbor's wedding. Seeing her daughter's expression, she removed the pins from her mouth. "What's wrong, dear?"

Shelby waved the letter at her mother. "I've been turned down for that empty shop in Spanish Court by Mr.—" she glanced at the signature scrawled across the bottom of the stationery. "At least I guess it's a mister—A. J. Court."

"Oh, Shelby," Mary gasped. "And you were counting on it."

Shelby slapped the envelope from Court Properties against her palm. "So were you and the rest of the family. It would have been perfect for our business, with the florist, caterer and baker all right there."

"It was such a good idea, too." Mary's softly rounded face took on a dreamy look. "A business that arranges weddings."

Spurred by the disappointment in her mother's voice, Shelby shook her head. "We're not giving up! All our plans are made. With me arranging things and the whole family getting involved, I know we'll be a success. And Spanish Court is the perfect place."

Shelby snatched up the phone and punched out the number. "Don't worry, I'm just going to *talk* to Mr. Court."

"And say what?"

"That we've got money to pay the rent; we'll be successful, he doesn't have to worry..."

Shelby's convincing arguments frothed like soap bubbles until the receptionist came on the line and reported that Mr. Court wasn't in.

Shelby slumped in disappointment. "Where can I reach him?"

"Miss, it *is* noon," the frosty voice intoned. "Mr. Court is at lunch."

"Where?"

"I'm sorry." The secretary's voice echoed, faded, then returned. "He's out of the building."

"What? Could you say that again?" Shelby frowned. What was wrong with the phone? Phantom voices seemed to be on the line. When the voices faded, then became louder, her eyes widened. Of course, she thought. The secretary probably had a hands-free phone. If she turned her face away from it, her voice faded and the speaker picked up all sounds in the office.

A male voice was saying, "...take you out to lunch. Erica's okay? The seafood is terrific and the boss likes us to patronize—"

Shelby gasped with delight and quickly hung up the phone. Erica's was a new restaurant in Goleta, just north of Santa Barbara.

In less than twenty minutes Shelby was at Erica's.

Inside the restaurant's foyer, she was met by a hostess dressed in a dark red suit of raw silk. The hostess's welcoming appearance drew Shelby up to her full five feet, two inches and inspired a brilliant smile. "Mr. A. J. Court, please."

The woman's expression warmed even more, transforming somehow from politely welcoming to delightfully conspiratorial. "Oh, of course. Please come right this way," she said. "He was getting worried about you."

Stunned, Shelby blinked at the woman's retreating back,

unable to believe her good luck. Court had a lunch appointment with a young woman! Never one to look a gift horse in the mouth, Shelby followed. "I got hung up in traffic," she fabricated.

"HERE SHE IS." The hostess presented her young charge with a flourish. She stepped aside for Shelby to pass, favored them with a misty smile and glided away.

"Hey, wait a minute, Carmen," a deep voice protested. "This isn't—"

Knowing she had to do something quickly to avoid being thrown out, Shelby launched herself at the man who had half risen from his chair. "Darling! I'm so sorry I'm late." She wrapped her arms around his shoulders and gave the startled man a hug.

He reacted by glaring at her. "What the devil do you think you're doing? I've never seen you before."

Quickly, Shelby pulled out the chair opposite him and sat down. "I know I'm not the person you're expecting, Mr. Court. But if you'll just listen to me for a minute, I promise I'll leave before your date gets here."

As she talked, Shelby's misconceptions about A. J. Court were rapidly reforming themselves into reality. The man wasn't over thirty-five. He was lean and handsome in a harsh way, with angled cheekbones and straight dark brows that looked surprisingly delicate on his masculine face.

"Miss, my date is already overdue." His voice was precise. "She'll be arriving any minute, so you had better talk fast. I would have you thrown out of here, but I don't want to embarrass the owners. Who are you, anyway?"

"My name is Shelby Featherstone."

His gaze sharpened.

"I see you remember me."

"Yes. And the answer is still no. I won't reconsider."

"Why not? I've got money."

"You may have cash right now, but you have *no credit*,"

he said. "What kind of business is it, anyway? La Grande Affaire…seems a bit theatrical, don't you think? So does your name, for that matter."

"It's my real name!"

He glanced at his watch, signaling his impatience. "And what is your *real* business? From the title, I'd guess it's something I don't want taking place in my mall."

Shelby gasped. Did he think she was going to run an escort service? "I'll be arranging *weddings*. Just like it said on the application."

He shrugged. "Whatever you say. What are your qualifications for running such a business?"

"I've been a bridesmaid in five weddings," she answered with a firm nod.

He stared at her in astonishment before he threw his head back and hooted with laughter.

Shelby looked away, embarrassed. Her lips pursed as she waited for him to get over his outburst.

In spite of her wish to disappear inside the leafy fern beside her, Shelby couldn't help allowing her gaze to stray back to him. She was intrigued at the way laughter changed his face.

When his laughter finally wheezed into silence, he gasped, "Miss Featherstone, being a participant in a wedding is a great deal different from attempting to create a business of arranging them."

Shelby was forming a new set of arguments when the hostess appeared by the table with a telephone.

"I'm sorry to interrupt, Alex." She cast apologetic glances at both of them. "But this caller said it was urgent."

Court leaned back, allowing her to set the cordless phone down by his elbow. "Hello?" he barked into the receiver as the hostess moved away.

Shelby was amazed to see his face soften into a smile.

"What do you mean you can't get away, darling?" His

face settled into a frown. Shelby felt sorry for whoever "darling" was.

Now that she looked more closely, she could see that his crow-black hair had the faintest dusting of silver.

"I expected you here. I've already ordered our meals. I had this thing timed down to the minute. You were going to— No, dinner tonight is out. No, no, it's all right. I'll call you later."

He put a time limit on lunch? she thought in amazement, picking up a tiny cherry tomato. "Bad news?" she asked.

"Nothing I can't handle."

The hostess came to remove the telephone. As she turned away with it, she gave Shelby another warm smile.

"Now, where were we?" Court asked.

His hurry-up tone snapped Shelby out of her daydream. "You were about to rent me the space in Spanish Court."

"No, I wasn't."

"Mr. Court, I can make a success of La Grande Affaire. This business will be a success if given half a chance. You, better than anyone, know what kind of people patronize Spanish Court. Most of the clientele are wealthy professionals who would want a really stunning wedding, but don't have enough time to prepare it."

Court sat and stared at her. His gaze was fixed on her but had an unfocused intensity that told her he was deep in thought.

Coming from a big family, Shelby knew how to negotiate to get what she wanted. She also knew when to be silent and wait. Impetuous she was, without a doubt, but she wasn't stupid. She knew her chances of convincing him rested on the next few seconds. Nervousness fluttered in her stomach. Absentmindedly, she picked up the salad fork and began eating the salad that already sat on the table. Beside her plate was a napkin. She reached for it to spread across her lap.

"What the hell are you doing?"

Startled, Shelby looked up from the bowl, her hand clutching the napkin. Court reached across the table and snatched the napkin from her. With lightning motions of his fingers, he began unfolding it. "Where is it?" he muttered in disgust.

Shelby's hand flew to her throat as she watched him.

"Aha!" He lifted something from the folds and held it up.

It was a diamond ring!

Shelby's eyes grew enormous as she looked at the glittering stone, then at the hard-faced man holding it. She said the first thing that came to her mind. "Why, Mr. Court, isn't this a bit sudden? We just met!"

"Miss Featherstone, this obviously is *not* for you," A. J. Court said coldly, dropping the ring into his pocket.

Shelby's tongue clucked with sympathy. "You were going to propose to your date today, weren't you? Oh, how romantic. Does she like surprises?"

But something across the room caught Court's attention. "Oh, no," he muttered, turning back to her with an exasperated look. "I knew I should have gotten you out of here sooner." His hand shot into his jacket pocket. "Here," he demanded, pulling out the ring. "Put this on and pretend you're in love with me."

He ignored her protest. "The least you can do is help me out."

"Pretending to be in love with you would probably take more acting ability than I've got," Shelby fumed.

"Hush," he commanded. "Act happy."

The hostess, Carmen, was coming toward them, pushing a cart on which rested an ice bucket. It held a bottle of champagne. Behind her, supported by a cane, walked an elderly woman who was as classically beautiful as Carmen.

The two women, especially the older one, possessed a commanding presence that virtually drew Shelby from her chair as the small procession neared their table.

"Alexander, is everything well?" the older woman asked in a breathily husky voice.

"Very well, Erica. She has agreed to become my wife."

The woman clasped her hand and laid it along her own softly wrinkled cheek. "Oh, Alexander, this is wonderful."

Shelby was touched. The woman, apparently the restaurant's owner, must have ties to A. J. Court that went back many years. She saw him not as the powerhouse businessman he was but as a man she had known since his childhood.

"And what is your beloved's name?" Erica asked.

"Shelly Featherstone," he said, looking triumphant that he had remembered. "This is Erica Martinez. You've met her daughter, Carmen."

"My name is Shelby." She stressed the *B*. Her voice came out an octave higher than usual. "He loves to tease."

"Yes, he does," Erica agreed, her eyes shimmering with pleasure. She looked back at A.J. "You've done so much for us, Alexander. We want to repay you with this." She gestured toward the champagne bottle.

A.J. looked chagrined. "Erica, that wasn't necessary..."

"Of course it's necessary," Erica scolded. She turned to Shelby. "He gave us everything, has done everything for us. This restaurant—a dream I've had all my life—wouldn't exist if not for him."

"Really?" Shelby asked, bemused. "He gave you—*everything?*"

"He's so modest that he probably didn't tell you," Carmen broke in.

"You're a prince." Shelby fluttered her eyelashes at him.

Court flashed her a look that said he would deal with her later.

SHELBY ALLOWED HERSELF only a few tiny sips of champagne. She still intended to talk business and needed a clear head.

She sat back. "I want to know if you plan to rent me that space in Spanish Court?"

His face hardened. "I already said no."

Shelby straightened, prepared to begin her arguments all over again. "Listen, Mr. Court, you have no reason to..."

He looked pained as he rose to his feet. "Can we please talk about it outside? After you've given me the ring back."

"Afraid I'll throw it down and stomp on it?"

"How did you guess?"

With a sigh, she moved to slide it off. "Oh, no," she breathed. "It's stuck!"

WITHIN A FEW minutes they were pulling up in front of Shelby's modest home, his Jaguar closely following her Rabbit.

Shaking her head, Mary took charge, hustling her daughter to the kitchen. She filled a bowl with ice and water to soak Shelby's hand.

"There, safe and sound." Mary smiled minutes later, handing the ring back to A.J. He thanked her, slid the ring into a small velvet bag he had taken from his pocket and pulled the drawstring tight.

Shelby stared at her bare finger, her full lips curved into a gentle smile. She had never cared much for jewelry, but she loved the romantic idea of owning a symbol stating that somewhere in the world there was a man who loved her.

A.J.'s face was serious as he turned to Joe Featherstone. "I suppose you would like an explanation, sir."

Shelby hurried forward. "I'll tell you all about it, Dad. I think Mr. Court would like to get back to his office." She took A.J.'s arm and began propelling him toward the door.

He went willingly, nodding goodbye to her parents.

At the front door she stopped and put her hands on her hips. "I'm going to send my application in again for you to reconsider."

"You can send it, but that doesn't mean I'll look at it," Court answered, and headed toward his car.

"SHELBY," Mary said when Shelby reentered the kitchen, "Lynn Altman called."

Delighted, Shelby spun around. "She's home?"

"Has been for a week, but says she's been too busy to call."

"Yeah," Shelby's dad said, with a hearty chuckle. "Being the city socialite can really cut into the time you spend with your friends."

Lynn had been gone most of the spring and summer, so Shelby had seen little of her. The two girls had been good friends since grade school.

When the Altmans' housekeeper, Mrs. Moran, answered and said Lynn had just left, Shelby's smile of anticipation collapsed into disappointment.

"She asked me to invite you over Saturday night," Mrs. Moran told her. "She's having a party to welcome herself home and she was especially anxious for you to come."

"ISN'T THIS the guy you were engaged to for a couple of hours the other day?" Shelby's father held up the newspaper he was reading.

Shelby was sitting at the living room desk, papers spread around her as she attempted to draft an operating budget for her first few months in business.

It had been three days since Shelby had seen A. J. Court, and the memory of their crazy encounter hadn't dimmed.

His photograph was on the society page, included in a column about a benefit dance at the Museum of Modern Art. The caption identified A.J.'s companion as Marla Gaines, a docent at the museum.

Lynn Altman occasionally volunteered at the museum. Shelby wondered if she knew Marla Gaines.

"That him?" Joe Featherstone broke into her thoughts.

"Hmm? Oh, yes. It is. This must be his real fiancée," she said, then turned at a familiar sound. "There's the mail! Maybe the rental agreement has come."

On the porch, she all but snatched the mail from the carrier as he was about to put it into the box.

There *was* a letter from Court Properties. She ripped it open and scanned the enclosed letter.

Her application had been denied. Again!

*

LATE-SUMMER CHILL crisped the air so Shelby grabbed her full-length all-weather coat and pulled it on as she hurried out to Lynn Altman's party.

Waving goodbye to her dad, Shelby slid into her Rabbit and started for the Altmans' home. It took her fifteen minutes to reach the section of Santa Barbara where exclusive homes nestled among the hills.

Thinking of Lynn, Shelby wondered about the reason for her best friend's return. For more than a year Lynn had been involved in an on-again, off-again relationship with an Italian race car driver named Carlo Rosetti. Lynn's family had disapproved of him. The last time she and Lynn had talked on the phone, several weeks ago, the affair had been off. Carlo, it seemed, couldn't make a commitment. Lynn wanted a home and family.

Suddenly, Shelby's Rabbit hit a bump, rudely bringing her back to reality.

Shelby eased up on the gas pedal, but it was too late. As she rounded a corner, her tire hit a pothole and she heard the clang of a hubcap falling off. She glanced in her rearview mirror just in time to see the shiny silver disk roll away behind her car and disappear.

Disgusted, she pulled over and stopped. Stepping from the car, she hurried back about twenty yards and peered into the weeds that lined the road, fuming silently.

With a fat stick in hand, Shelby leaned over as far as she could and poked among the weeds, trying to estimate the path of the hubcap as it had spun away.

When she heard the sound of a car approaching, she didn't turn around but kept moving down the street, trying to keep her shoes clean.

As the car slowed then crunched to a halt on the graveled surface, Shelby stiffened. She wasn't sure she wanted help.

She grasped her stick in a threatening manner. Cautiously she looked around then groaned in dismay when she saw it was the last person in the world she wanted to see.

"Going fishing?" A. J. Court asked as he stepped from his dark green Jaguar.

Shelby refused to answer his barb. "I lost a hubcap," she replied, dropping the stick and pushing her hands into her coat pockets.

"I see." He looked back at her Rabbit. "Did you just come around that corner?"

"Yes."

"And hit that pothole?"

"That's right."

"You're looking too far back."

Minutes later, A.J. was holding up the hubcap. "I'll put it back on for you."

"Thank you very much."

He led the way to her car, put the hubcap in place and pounded it with the heel of his hand. When he straightened, he dusted off his hands and regarded her with an inquiring gaze. "Don't you want to thank me?"

"I already did." Shelby wrenched the car door open and slid inside. She sped up the street, leaving him standing, looking after her.

AT THE ALTMANS' door she was greeted by a smiling Mrs. Moran. The housekeeper had been with the Altmans since Lynn was in junior high.

Inside, Shelby greeted several people she hadn't seen in a long time and moved toward her hostess. Lynn gave her an enthusiastic hug, but was quickly distracted by other guests.

"Hey, lady, is this dance taken?" a voice growled in her ear.

Shelby sidestepped a couple who were making a beeline for the bar and turned to see Jeff Chambers, a friend from her high school days.

"It's not taken if we can fight our way through the crowd to where the dancing is," she answered, nodding toward the end of the patio.

"Hey, I didn't play football for four years for nothing." Jeff extended one elbow for her to hold and the other to clear a path. In moments they were through the crowd and on the dance floor.

Shelby smiled as Jeff twirled her around. She was glad to be with an old friend having a good time, and she lost herself in the fun until he took her through a particularly perilous series of steps. Gasping, she pulled away to tease him about his prowess as a dancer, but he was frowning into the crowd behind her.

"Hey, Shelby, do you know that guy coming toward us? He doesn't look too happy."

Shelby looked around, but since she didn't have Jeff's height advantage, she couldn't see over the crowd. "Maybe someone spilled a drink on him."

Shelby didn't have time to glance around again before she found herself being gripped from behind. A strong hand wrapped itself around her upper arm and a familiar baritone voice said, "Excuse me, I believe this is my dance."

Jeff seemed to pale at the dark-haired man with the grim face. "Uh, sure."

So much for the brave football hero, Shelby thought as Court swung her about.

"You've got more nerve than any woman I've ever

met," A.J. muttered furiously in her ear. He forced a smile and nodded to a couple dancing near them.

Shelby was stunned, unable to form a coherent reply to anything he was saying. Her feet moved automatically with his.

He placed his jaw near her ear. "Don't say anything until we get away from this crowd. I don't want an embarrassing scene."

"I don't, either," she said quickly, wishing she had thought to say it first. She followed A.J.'s lead as he danced her toward a less crowded corner of the patio.

His gaze darkened and his mouth pursed thoughtfully. "You know, gate-crashing isn't going to make me look any more favorably on your application."

Shelby's eyes widened. "Favorably! You've already turned me down."

"And I'm beginning to realize more and more that I was right. Why didn't you start nagging me about the shop when we met out on the road? I could have turned you down again and you could have gone right back home. You wouldn't have had to stage that little 'lost hubcap' scene."

"Staged it," Shelby squeaked, pulling away. She opened and closed her mouth a couple of times, unable to think of anything nasty enough to say to him.

"Well," he demanded. "What have you got to say for yourself?"

Before she could answer, A.J.'s attention was caught by someone across the room. "Damn," he muttered. "That's Randy Anderson, the society columnist. I guess it's time to seize the moment, as they say."

MOMENTS LATER, A.J. was holding up his hand, calling for attention, with Lynn at his side.

A.J. put his arm around Lynn's shoulders and drew her close.

Out of the corner of her eye, Shelby saw Randy Anderson moving forward, his reporter's interest obviously piqued.

"When Lynn decided to throw herself a welcome home party, she didn't know it would have another purpose," A.J. said, looking down at Lynn and smiling. He took her hand and drew a deep breath into his lungs. Shelby felt as if all the air had been drawn from hers. She didn't know what was going on, but a feeling of dread grew in her. Her heart felt as if it was bouncing between her throat and her stomach. She was light-headed with a feeling of inevitability when A.J. continued. "I...we decided to take this opportunity to announce our engagement."

As he spoke, A.J. looked directly at Shelby with an odd expression that seemed to be a mixture of defiance and regret.

Gasps and cries of delight rippled around the room. Guests applauded as A.J. leaned down and kissed Lynn lightly on the lips.

LYNN WAS SUPPOSED to be her friend, but she hadn't said a word about being engaged. Shelby's anger at A.J. was far less justified. And who was Marla Gaines?

Forcing what she hoped was a pleasant expression onto her face, she turned around. Lynn was smiling radiantly up at the tall dark man beside her. They were a striking couple, Shelby thought as she approached. Unconsciously, Shelby straightened her spine. "Hello, again, Mr. Court. Congratulations to both of you."

Lynn's soft brown eyes looked puzzled. Her gentle fall of blond curls shimmered as she turned her head. "You two know each other?"

"We've met," A.J. answered as he drew Lynn to his side and placed his arm around her waist. His eyes were on Shelby. He obviously didn't know that she and Lynn were old friends.

Just as she hadn't known that he and Lynn were in love.

"We just met recently," Shelby said.

"Oh, good, then Alex knows about your new business. I want you to make all the arrangements for my wedding." Shelby gasped and A.J. started. He jerked his arm from Lynn's waist and stared at her in surprise, but she rushed on. "It's going to be quite a large wedding. I'll have six bridesmaids. And I want you to be one of them."

"Wait a minute, Lynn…"

"I don't think that's a good idea," Shelby chimed in.

Lynn stopped speaking, the radiance beginning to fade from her smile. "What's wrong?"

"I think you'd better slow down on these arrangements," A.J. said. "You don't want to rush things."

The shock of the announcement, followed by Lynn's request, was too much for Shelby.

"I don't know, Lynn," Shelby put in. "I don't have things quite organized. You might want someone else."

"But I thought things were coming together so well. When I called the other day, your mom said you had found a shop and everything."

"Well, things didn't work out quite like I'd planned."

"I know." Lynn laid her hand on A.J.'s arm. "There's an empty shop in Spanish Court. You see, Shelby, he owns the mall. Anyway, I saw a vacant shop. Wouldn't it be perfect, Alex?"

Feeling as if someone had given her a heavy-handed clap across the back, Shelby tried to get her breath and think of something to say. A.J. didn't even bother to try hiding his fury as he said, "Yes—it would. Do you want the shop, Shelby? I'm sure it would be *perfect* for your business."

Because she had done nothing wrong, Shelby resented the angry glare he was giving her. Even Lynn was looking at him curiously, puzzled by his scathing tone. "I would *love* it," Shelby answered in a contemptuous tone that equaled his.

HALF AN HOUR LATER, Shelby felt that she had stayed long enough and began working her way toward the door. A. J. Court blocked her path before she even got away from the patio area.

"Leaving so soon, Miss Featherstone?"

Although Shelby was tempted, she decided she couldn't very well shove him out of the way in order to leave. "Yes. I promised my mother I wouldn't be out late."

His brow lifted. They both knew she was well past the age when she had to be in by curfew. He shrugged, his wide shoulders moving easily beneath the creamy linen of his jacket. "I understand. After all, why should you stay now that you've accomplished your objective?"

A slow simmering anger began heating up inside her. She placed her hands on her hips and tilted her head as aggressively as he was doing. "My objective?"

"You couldn't convince me any other way, so you ingratiated yourself with Lynn and made your need for a shop known. How did you find out about Lynn?"

The anger flared into blue sparks in her eyes. "Ingratiated myself, huh? Well, if that's true, I must have been a truly clairvoyant kindergartner."

A.J.'s lips quirked in a reluctant smile. Shelby studied him. There were a million questions she wanted to ask. How long had he known Lynn? Didn't the ring fit her finger?

"Who's Marla Gaines?"

His head swung toward her. "What?"

"No, who. Who's Marla Gaines? That lady you were pictured with in the paper."

His smile turned sardonic. "Been looking for me in the papers, hmm?"

Shelby's chin lifted. "I thought *she* was your fiancée."

Shaking his head, he moved back to her. "Just a lecturer at the museum. I guess she happened to be standing next to me at that charity event when the photographer came around. I don't know her."

Shelby felt an odd rush of relief. He wasn't engaged to that woman after all. A rush of guilt followed. Instead, he was going to marry Lynn.

He was engaged to marry one of her best friends. She and A.J. would have to be friends, too—for Lynn's sake.

THE RESTAURANT salad bar looked sadly depleted when Shelby and Lynn finished and carried their loaded plates to their table.

"So," Lynn said brightly. "When can I talk about my wedding gown?"

"Oh, Lynn..." Shelby looked at her friend in dismay. She knew it was a bad idea to take on the job. "I don't know."

"Why? What's the matter?" Lynn asked, worried.

Shelby shook her head. "Things just aren't...worked out yet...the shop and all."

As Lynn's eyes searched her face, Shelby felt herself turning red.

"I thought you and Alex were working out the details about the shop."

"We are."

"Well, then, what's the problem?"

"It's going to take a while to get the place organized."

Lynn fluttered her fingers airily. "Don't worry, I'm not in that much of a hurry. We haven't even set a date yet."

"Where did you meet him?" Shelby asked suddenly.

Lynn started, her eyes snapping to Shelby. "You mean Alex?"

Shelby shook her head in puzzlement. She had never seen Lynn so dreamy. "Yes, your fiancé—remember him...?"

"He was one of Dad's protégés," she replied. "He's been such a help this past year. After Dad died, he helped out with the lawyers...everything. He came to San Diego with papers to sign because Mother wouldn't come back here. We can trust him.'' Lynn chewed slowly on another bite of salad. ''I feel safe with him,'' she concluded.

Safe? Shelby nearly choked on a crouton. Safe with the thorough masculinity that was so much a part of him? Safe with his keen mind and quick wit? Safe with the hard-driving businessman who could be such a dangerous adversary? Her own feelings were exactly the opposite. She found him exciting and disconcerting, not dependable and friendly.

Lynn held up her left hand. ''He brought the ring over yesterday,'' she said, watching the light wink in the stone. ''He was having it enlarged. I don't know how he knew it would be too small.''

Shelby did. Under the table, she folded her hand so her thumb could rub over the place that had been chafed by the ring he'd intended for Lynn.

''Lynn, you can tell me to mind my own business if you want, but what happened to Carlo Rosetti?''

Carefully avoiding Shelby's eyes, Lynn laid down her fork and pushed her plate away.

Shelby watched as Lynn's fingers stiffened at the edge of her plate. ''Weren't you in love with him less than two months ago?''

''He's not ready to settle down.''

''And you are.''

''Yes.'' Lynn's voice was very low. ''Racing is his life.'' She looked up, her eyes lively. ''It's very exciting. Watching him race was wonderful—but frightening. My heart was in my mouth the whole time. Not knowing if he would win or lose or—''

Shelby nodded, encouraging her to keep talking.

The animation faded from Lynn's features, replaced by an unusual gleam. ''My parents didn't approve of him, and he thinks I've got too much money. He's from a very poor family," she added.

Shelby nodded. "I can see where that would cause problems."

"It didn't have to," Lynn said fiercely. "We could have overcome it. If he'd been willing to compromise and make a commitment." One slim hand balled into a fist. "He just won't make a commitment."

"And A.J. will?"

Lynn blinked. "Oh, yes, Alex would."

AS PROMISED, the assistant manager of Court Properties had given Shelby the keys on Monday. Her parents and several aunts had spent all week helping her fix up the shop.

"Shelby, have you decided what kind of sign you're going to have outside?" Mary asked, pausing in her work.

The family thought the interior design was great, but when it came to discussions about a tasteful but eye-catching theme for the outside, everyone had a different opinion.

At the sound of footsteps, the family swung their heads toward the door.

A. J. Court stood in the entrance, looking over the shop's interior with interest.

"Nice," he said.

Shelby's jaw dropped. Hadn't they left each other, daggers drawn, just a few days ago?

"The shop looks good, Shelby," he complimented.

He couldn't have said anything that would have pleased her family more.

"Thank you," she stammered. "We'll be finished in a week. Our only problem is a sign for the outside."

"I've been thinking about that," he said. "I was wondering if you might consider a name change."

"A name change?" Shelby repeated in a carefully neutral tone. Here it comes, she thought.

"You look skeptical," he said with a wry twist to his lips. "Wait until you've heard what it is."

"I'm listening."

"Since your last name is so unusual and your business will basically be run by the women in your family—" He glanced around at the sweaty, disarranged females. Automatically, they each straightened their clothes or smoothed their hair. "Why don't you call the shop Featherstone Brides?"

There was a moment of silence while the family mulled over his suggestion, then smiles broke out all around.

"That's a wonderful idea," Mary twittered. "Why didn't we think of that?"

Shelby was about to speak up when the phone rang.

"I'll get it," she called, leaping forward.

"Hello?"

"Shelby, is that you?"

"Hello, Lynn? Yes, it's me."

"Is Alex there? He said he was going to stop by your shop this afternoon."

"Yes—yes, he is." Shelby turned and waved the phone at him. "It's Lynn."

He took the receiver.

"You did what!" A.J. bellowed. "The Los Angeles paper? Do you really think that's a good—"

Shelby moved away before she heard any more of the conversation, which had sounded like a lovers' quarrel. She felt unreasonably disheartened at the thought of Lynn and A.J. being lovers. Of course they were. They were engaged.

"I hope everything's okay, Mr. Court," she heard her mother say as the family packed up to leave.

WHEN THEY WERE alone, A.J. turned to Shelby. "I'd better be going, too."

Shelby smiled. "Thank you for coming by, and for suggesting the new name."

He nodded, giving the room one last look. His hand was reaching for the doorknob when he turned back. "I had a dinner date scheduled, but it looks like I've been stood up again." He gave her an abashed grin. "I hate to eat alone. Would you join me for dinner?"

She glanced down at her shorts and baggy T-shirt. "I'm not exactly dressed for—"

"Nothing fancy," he said quickly. "We can go to McDonald's. I haven't eaten there in years."

"Well..." To her mortification, her stomach growled.

Shelby smiled sheepishly and nodded.

THEY HAD BOUGHT a couple of Big Macs and some fries and driven to the beach. At this time of day in the late summer, the area was almost deserted.

Shelby had left her shoes in A.J.'s car and persuaded him to do the same. He had been reluctant, but she was very convincing, even talking him into shedding his coat and tie and rolling up the legs of his slacks. He complained that he looked ridiculous. Privately, Shelby thought he looked casual and sexy. They had perched on the top of a group of rocks to eat.

"How did you and Lynn's dad meet?" Shelby asked.

"I hit his car one night when he and his wife were driving home. I had been drinking." When Shelby gasped, A.J. added, "I was the only one hurt."

"You were injured?" Shelby asked, appalled at the thought of him being in pain.

"Not in the fender bender we had, but Sanford packed a hell of a right punch!"

Shelby fell back on the sand as she laughed, picturing short, pudgy Mr. Altman "duking it out" with A.J. "Did you feel as if you'd been attacked by Santa Claus?"

"How did you guess? Anyway, when we got to know each other, he made me realize I was wasting more than money, so I went back to school. He started me in business, too. He was my mentor and friend," he said in tones of deep affection.

Listening, Shelby smiled. She had really liked Mr. Altman.

She lay in an abandoned sprawl, wearing dirty clothes and bare feet. Her big blue eyes were soft with pleasant memories. A.J. grinned back at her, then his smile faded. His look became intent. Slowly, as if afraid she would bolt, he reached out and touched a silky brown strand of hair. Shelby froze, staring up at him. He looked faintly puzzled for a moment.

Very carefully he arranged each of her curls against the sand as though he was a photographer about to immortalize her on film. Shelby didn't move—barely breathed. Her heart was pounding in her ears, sending blood in a mad rush through her. His touch was as gentle as a breeze, his face as intent as that of someone searching for gold. He lowered himself onto one elbow beside her until his face was only inches from hers.

His palm found her cheek, the pad of his thumb journeying across her cheekbone and up to the corner of her eye. Shelby's eyelids trembled shut. His touch seemed to burn while comforting her at the same time.

"If you want to pull out of the arrangements for this wedding, I'll be glad to pay whatever fee you ask," he said quietly.

It took several seconds for his words to soak into her befuddled brain. Her eyes snapped open. "What?" she breathed, blinking in astonishment.

"Tell Lynn whatever you want—the shop isn't ready yet, you've got too many clients, your sister's having a baby— I don't care—just pull out."

The sensual fog he had created around her was clearing as fast as mist before the sun. She sat bolt upright, her eyes snapping furiously. "I can't pull out, unless it's what Lynn wants, and I know she doesn't."

"Shelby," he said with great patience, apparently oblivious to her anger. "This wedding isn't what you think."

She scrambled to her feet and clapped her hands onto her hips. Belligerently, she glared at him. "Isn't what I think? It's two people saying their vows before their assembled friends and family, isn't it?"

He stood up beside her, his long sinewy body making it seem like one easy motion. "Not exactly."

She pointed an accusatory finger at him. "You don't think I know what I'm doing. You feel coerced into renting me that shop. You think I'm going to fall on my face and take your wedding plans down with me."

His eyes were sparkling now with a familiar angry light. "Believe it or not, Shelby, I really don't doubt your abilities," he said, folding his arms across his chest. "I'm doing this for your own good!"

She took a breath, trying to think rationally. "If you're going to make some kind of decision about your wedding plans, I think Lynn had better be in on it."

"As far as she's concerned, the decision is made," A.J. answered grimly.

"Then there's nothing further to discuss. If you're not happy with my work, you can dismiss me. But at least *see* my work."

A.J. lifted his hands in a gesture of defeat. "I tried," he said. "Don't blame me if this doesn't turn out as you expect."

Shelby stared at him.

"You know, Shelby," he went on, "you're just as persistent as I thought you were the day we met."

"And you're just as bullheaded," she snapped. "I don't know what Lynn sees in you!"

Immediately she knew she had gone too far. She tried to back away, but he stepped close and took her arm. He drew her forward, his warm hand sending shivers over her flesh. A.J. put his face close to hers and she stared at him, her eyes huge. Although dark was closing in fast, she could see his face clearly. Sensual awareness arced between them like an electric shock. His knowing look told her that he knew she felt it.

His voice was low when he spoke. "Oh, you don't, do you?"

"FEATHERSTONE BRIDES," Shelby whispered, looking at the new sign above her shop door. Delighted, Shelby shut the door. This was the second week her shop had been open.

Everything was perfect, and Shelby felt satisfaction in knowing she had been right about the location.

Moments later, a man appeared at the store front. Thinking he must be a potential client, Shelby greeted him with her most winning smile.

"You work here?" he asked, his eyes never leaving her face. He had an accent she couldn't quite place.

"Yes, I'm the owner..."

"Shelby Featherstone?"

"Why, yes. Have we met?"

He gazed at her for a moment from beneath thick, brooding brows before answering. "We have a mutual friend—Lynn Altman. I am Carlo Rosetti."

Shelby's eyes widened and she swallowed a gasp. Guiltily, her gaze darted around the mall as if she thought Lynn or A.J. might materialize from behind a potted palm.

A corner of his mouth quirked. "I see you have heard of me."

"Yes, uh, yes," she stammered.

"May I speak with you?" he asked.

"Yes, please come in." She finally managed.

CARLO HAD a wonderful smile. It spread his lips wide, giving him an open, approachable look.

"Sit down. We'll have some fresh coffee."

She scurried into the back room and poured two mugs of coffee while her mind ran through a dozen different reasons for his unexpected arrival.

"You are wondering why I came," he stated when they were seated.

"Yes. How did you know about me?"

From the pocket of his Italian cut sports jacket, he took a newspaper clipping. She unfolded it to see Lynn and A.J.'s radiant faces smiling up at her. Randy Anderson's column describing the engagement party accompanied the photograph. The end of the article mentioned that all arrangements would be made by Shelby Featherstone.

He stared at the article for a moment, his expression severe. He poked a finger into A.J.'s face. "I want to know about him. This man, Court. Do you know him?"

"Well, yes, I do, but I really don't think I should be discussing him with you. Have you talked to Lynn?"

"I want to hear from someone else," Carlo answered, his voice low and fierce, his eyes flashing. "Her view would be colored by—love." He practically spat the word. "What is he like?"

Shelby hesitated. He was going to insist if she didn't tell him.

"He was a friend of Lynn's father," she began. Carlo sat listening, his very stillness evidence of his concentration. "He's in real estate investing and development." She gestured toward the window. "He owns this mall and many other properties."

Carlo nodded, obviously filing away every shred of information. "But what is he like?"

Shelby racked her brain, trying to figure out exactly what he wanted her to say. "He's tall with dark hair and green eyes..."

"No, no, no!" Carlo shot to his feet. "I want to know what kind of man he is."

Shelby watched him prowl restlessly between her desk

and the window. "You mean you want to know if he's good enough for Lynn?"

He stopped and gave her a straightforward look that became a bit sheepish. With a half-apologetic nod he agreed.

Shelby gazed at him in dismay. She had the feeling he wouldn't go until she told him what he wanted to know. She took a deep breath.

"He is helpful and sympathetic, I guess you might say," Shelby began. No it went beyond that. "Compassionate."

"A wimp," Carlo snorted, tossing his head like an angry bull.

"Not at all!" Shelby declared, incensed.

"It sounds as if he has made another conquest besides Lynn." Carlo's eyes were shrewd.

Color ran up under Shelby's skin. She hadn't meant to be so transparent. "I simply think he's a good man, with a sense of responsibility."

Furiously, Carlo paced toward her. "And Lynn has told you I have none?"

"No! She never said anything like that!"

"Is that why she dumped me?"

Shelby blinked in confusion. "She dumped *you?*"

His powerful shoulders heaved upward. "She might as well have. She refused to see me again unless I was considering a future for us."

And he didn't like ultimatums, Shelby finished for him silently. Her heart went out to him although she felt terribly guilty about discussing Lynn and A.J. with him. "Do you really think you should tell me—" she began, but his Latin temper was on fire.

Carlo's suddenly fierce look had Shelby shrinking back against the sofa. He swept out the door, leaving Shelby gasping as if she had just been picked up and dropped by a tornado.

She slumped against the sofa cushions and theatrically put the back of her wrist to her forehead. The man was like a seething volcano. No wonder his relationship with Lynn had been rocky. Lynn!

Shelby leaped for the telephone, wanting to warn Lynn that Carlo was in town and would probably try to contact her. She punched out the number, but there was no answer at the Altmans' home.

*

"DO YOU KNOW where Lynn is?"

The shop door shuddered on its hinges as A.J. swept in the next morning. He shut the door with a thud that rattled the glass, and rushed over to Shelby's desk.

She jumped, smearing ink across the wedding plan sheet she was working up for a new client.

"Where Lynn is?" he repeated. "She didn't come home, and the housekeeper is worried."

Immediately the image of Carlo flashed into Shelby's mind.

"No," Shelby said, carefully avoiding his eyes as she dabbed at the ink streaking across her planning sheet. "I don't know where she is. But...someone else may." Slowly, she told him about Carlo's visit.

As she talked, A.J.'s expression became more and more grim as if something was twisting inside him. His mouth angled down and his brows pulled together in irritation. "This happened yesterday?" he demanded to know, sweeping back the sides of his jacket and thrusting out his chin.

"Yes." Shelby twisted her fingers through the strand of pearls at her throat. "Do you think Carlo found her?"

A.J. sighed and rolled his eyes heavenward. "I should be so lucky."

Shelby clamped her hands on her hips. "You think seeing him will get him out of her system once and for all?"

"Let's just say it might settle things," he said enigmatically. "Come on, we've got to find her."

"We?" Shelby asked cautiously.

Turning, he began to pace again. "Yes, we'll have to brainstorm to come up with some idea of where she is. I'm responsible for her."

"A.J., she's a grown woman," Shelby said, slipping her hands into the pockets of the gray suede jacket that matched her skirt. "She's responsible for herself."

Her steady gaze watched his restless pacing around the room. She was worried, too, about Lynn's state of mind.

"Does she have a favorite place she likes to go when she needs to think?" he asked.

"Maybe the Altmans' summer cabin?" Shelby suggested.

"Never heard of it." He drew a pen and small pad from his jacket pocket. "Is it near here? Give me directions."

Shelby frowned, her blue eyes thoughtful. It was strange that he didn't know about the cabin. He had been helping Mrs. Altman with financial matters since her husband's death. Perhaps mention of the cabin had simply never come up. "It's in the Angeles National Forest. Very remote. About four hours from here."

A sigh of exasperation gusted through A.J.'s teeth. "Have you been there?"

"Years ago. We went skiing."

"What makes you think she would be there now?"

Shelby shrugged. "She's always loved it."

"Do you know the phone number?" he asked, moving toward the telephone.

"No phone. It's remote—and rustic."

A.J. swept around Shelby's desk, heading for the telephone. "I'll call my office and tell them I'll be gone the rest of the day. Can you get someone to come in and watch the shop while you guide me, or do you just want to close up for the day? I realize it's an inconvenience since it's only 2:00 p.m., but it can't be helped."

"Guide you?" Shelby sputtered. "Close up shop?"

"Of course," he said, his green eyes regarding her as if he had made a perfectly reasonable request.

A.J. SLOWED as she gave directions to the cabin perched on a cliff rim several miles from the town of Big Bear.

Both of them slumped in disappointment when they finished jolting over the rutted drive and stopped before a cabin that had the name Altman painted on a small plaque beside the door. Lynn's car wasn't parked out front, and there were no lights on against the gathering dusk and steadily worsening fog.

"Now what?" Shelby asked.

A.J. was already sliding out from behind the wheel. "Now we find a way to get inside to see if she's been here."

"You mean breaking and entering?"

"I'll have a locksmith come out first thing in the morning to fix whatever we damage."

"Oh, great," Shelby fumed, getting out of the car and following him to the front door. "It's not enough that you make me leave my shop and come up here on a wild-goose chase, but now you're making me an accessory to a crime!"

A.J. grunted in satisfaction when he discovered the key under a loose board of the porch. "I'll have to talk to Sharon Altman about this. It's very careless."

"No kidding," Shelby said earnestly. "She should be more careful. There's no telling who might just walk in."

A.J. scowled at her, turned the key in the lock and pushed the door open.

Shelby's gaze raked eagerly around the room, but A.J. stood for a moment on the porch, frowning back at the fog.

Shelby took off her jacket and laid it with her purse on a table by the door.

As always, Mrs. Altman's superb taste showed even in a home seldom used. The furniture, a sofa facing the huge fireplace and several easy chairs, was heavy but simple.

"Where's the light switch?" A.J. asked, feeling along the wall.

"Guess again," Shelby answered, making her way cautiously through the gathering gloom toward a small table by the window.

"What do you mean?"

She picked up a kerosene lamp and a box of matches and held them up. "I told you it was rustic."

Glancing about for any signs of recent habitation, Shelby ran her fingers over the mantel, then the hearth. The fireplace was swept clean and logs laid in place. Only the touch of a match was needed to send the logs into crackling flame.

A kerosene camp stove stood in a corner of the room, along with an icebox that required a huge chunk of ice to keep things cold. Both stood open and empty.

As A.J. lit the lamp and adjusted the wick, Shelby could see that the pantry doors were tightly closed and that no empty cans were in the trash container.

"Well, I guess that answers our question," she sighed, turning to him. "Lynn hasn't been here. We'd better— What are you doing?" she asked, when she saw he was bending down before the fireplace.

"Lighting the fire, obviously."

"But we've got to go. It's getting dark!"

He sighed, his lips flattening in a rueful grimace. "I'm afraid we're not going anywhere for a while. Look at that fog." He nodded toward the window.

Automatically, her gaze followed his. Outside the world was covered with a thick, white blanket.

"But we can't stay here." Her voice rose with a tinge of hysteria. "I thought you were worried about Lynn."

"I am." He knelt at the hearth and struck a match. Within moments, tongues of fire licked up to take possession of the seasoned wood.

A.J. stretched his hands toward the blaze. His head dropped forward and he let his shoulders slouch.

Nervousness began to sizzle and crackle not so cheerfully along Shelby's spine. "If we don't go right now the fog will just get worse. I've got to get back…"

"We can't drive in that, Shelby. We can't take a chance on unfamiliar roads…."

"You should have thought of that before you dragged me up here!"

"How was I supposed to know this would happen?" he snapped, then seeing her genuine distress, he softened. "The fog might let up any minute and we'll have a better chance of getting out of here safely."

"*I'm* getting out of here now," she said, grabbing up her jacket and purse and wheeling toward the door with some vague idea of making her way to the main highway.

"Shelby, wait!"

Frightened, she looked back to see A.J. bolt after her like a track star at the starting gun. His headlong charge spurred her to hurry. She swung the door open and started down the unlit steps, damp from the dew-laden fog.

Shelby's low-heeled pumps slipped and she teetered for a moment on the edge of the top step. When her arms flew wide, as she tried to regain her balance, her jacket and purse went flying in one direction and her feet in the other. With several sickening bumps, she tumbled to the bottom of the steps.

A.J. was beside her in seconds. "Shelby, are you all right?" His voice sounded shaken.

"I think so."

"Once, just once, I wish you'd think before you act."

The gentle touch of his hands as he ran them over her checking for injuries belied his grumpy tone. She gasped and jerked away when he touched her left knee and when he got to her arm, his hand came away bloody.

"Ooooh," she moaned, closing her eyes.

"You can't tell me you're one of those women who faints at the sight of blood."

"Of course I am. That's *my* blood. But I'm used to it," she said with a sigh, struggling to sit up.

"Let's get you inside. That's a nasty scrape."

He looped her arm around his neck and slipped his arms beneath her.

Shelby clutched at him as he swept her into his arms, turned and headed back up the stairs.

He deposited her carefully onto the couch, took off his jacket and rolled up his shirtsleeves. "What do they do for water around here?"

"There's an electric pump outside."

Within minutes, A.J. was kneeling beside her, placing a cold cloth on her knee and wiping off the worst of the blood on her arm.

"You're going to have to take that off," he told her, leaning back on his heels.

Her blue eyes huge, Shelby gazed up at him. "You mean my blouse?"

"Of course," he answered matter-of-factly.

Shelby clutched the neck of her blouse with her good hand.

A.J. sat back on his heels and gave her a smile that grew into a full-size grin. "Why, Miss Featherstone, you don't think I have designs on your honor, do you?"

"Well, n-no, but—"

"Then take it off, or I will."

"You'll have to find me something else to wear."

"Like what? A bedsheet?"

"I don't know!" she snapped, feeling ridiculous. "Look

in the bedroom. Maybe Mrs. Altman or Lynn left some clothes.''

With an aggrieved sigh, A.J. got to his feet and went into the bedroom. Shelby heard a great deal of drawer opening, door slamming and muttering. Finally he came out with two pieces of cloth clutched in his hands. He held up the first one. ''How about this?''

It was a Mickey Mouse T-shirt, probably a relic from Lynn's college days.

''It'll look perfect with my skirt,'' Shelby assured him.

He handed it over and turned his back without being asked. To her embarrassment Shelby discovered she couldn't maneuver her sore arm out of her torn sleeve. ''A.J.?''

''My eyes are closed, Lady Godiva.''

She cleared her throat. ''I need help.''

He swung around. Seeing her flushed face and averted eyes he made quick but careful work of getting her into the shirt. Shelby repressed a shiver as his fingers touched her arm. When they finally had the shirt arranged, A.J. rolled up the sleeve to expose her upper arm and picked up the basin of water.

Turning her toward the light, A.J. clucked his tongue in distress.

''What is it?''

''I didn't see this before, but you picked up several large splinters from that porch step.''

''Splinters? How big?''

''I just want to know, can you barely see them with the naked eye?''

''A little larger than that...and there are several of them.''

She groaned. ''You mean the kind where people say 'Hold still while I pull out this teeny-tiny sliver. Maybe we can sell it to someone who needs a mast for a clipper ship.' That kind of splinter?''

"My, how you exaggerate," he said admiringly, getting to his feet. "They're not that big—not quite. I'll have to see if I can find a pair of pliers, I mean tweezers, or a needle."

At the word "needle" Shelby sank with a moan into the sofa cushions, then gasped because she had involuntarily bent her sore knee.

He was back in a moment with the tweezers. Just as he was about to touch them to her skin, she reached up and grabbed his wrist. "I'd better warn you, A.J., I'm not good with pain."

A.J. FINISHED cleaning her scrapes and wrapped her upper arm in bandages that he had found in the bathroom. He dropped the cloth he had been using back into the basin and went out onto the front porch. After a few moments he returned, carrying her suede jacket and purse. "I'm sorry, Shelby. The fog is so thick I can hardly see the car from the bottom of the steps. I almost had to crawl around on the ground to find these," he said, indicating her things. "We'll have to stay here all night." He laid the two articles on the table and gazed at her regretfully.

She would have been more upset if she thought he'd done this on purpose. But they were caught in circumstances they couldn't change. "I guess it can't be helped," she said, gaining a quick look of approval from him. "Do you suppose there's any food around here?"

He laughed. "That a girl, back to normal already."

She gave him a haughty look, made slightly ridiculous by her outsize shirt and bandaged arm. "I do not appreciate comments about my appetite."

"Then you shouldn't have such a big one," he retorted cheerfully, going to the pantry and pulling out several cans. "We've got a choice here. Chili, chili, and oh, yes, chili."

"Why don't we have chili?"

AFTER DINNER, Shelby settled on the sofa before the fire, while A.J. piled the dishes in the sink and then brought the last of some wine he'd managed to find and their glasses. "We might as well finish this off."

He sat beside her and lifted his wineglass to view the color. Backlighted by the fire, the wine looked like melted rubies.

"Shelby, it's wonderful being with you tonight," he said quietly, taking her completely off guard.

He gazed at her. One side of his darkly handsome face was softly lit by the fire, the other was in deepest shadow. He was strong but caring, wise but witty, harsh but gentle. It didn't seem to matter now that they had butted heads at every encounter.

Because she was in love with him.

The realization brought a surge of delighted awareness, followed by sickening dread. This wasn't right. She started to get up from the couch, not sure what she intended to do, but his hand shot out to stop her.

"Where are you going? It's too early for bed."

"I—I, uh, I don't know." Despair closed her throat on the words she should say. Words about needing sleep, going home tomorrow, finding Lynn, taking care of her business...

"Sit still." He pulled her down beside him.

He slipped his arm around her and gave her a friendly hug.

Shelby shivered, turning toward him. Her wide eyes and long lashes bespoke innocence, while the look she gave him was one of very feminine awareness.

His face was only inches away, his lips a mere whisper from hers. The invitation couldn't have been more obvious.

A.J.'s arm tightened and he lifted his other one to feather his finger through her short curls. "I apologize." His voice was suddenly very husky, as if he was having trouble getting the words out or forgetting what he meant to say.

"Apologize? For what?"

"For...oh, never mind." He slid his hand around to clasp the back of her head and closed the gap between their lips. His lips moved on hers with a thoroughness that left her gasping.

He kissed her again and again, murmuring low, unintelligible words to her. The sound of his voice was as exciting and hot as his lips on her mouth...her eyes, cheeks and ears.

"There's a word for a woman like you," he murmured against her throat.

"What is it?" she gasped, head thrown back, her face suffused with joy.

"Zaftig."

She turned her face to kiss him. Her husky laugh puffed against his cheek. "Doesn't that mean plump?"

"It means exciting, rich, fulfilling...ah, Shelby, why didn't I see you before?"

She wanted to clutch him to her and at the same time push him away. She felt the need to clasp her arms over her chest to stop the tingling that had started there. But she could do nothing about the heavy wanting that settled low in her body. There was only one satisfaction for that. A satisfaction she could never have.

Why hadn't he seen her before what? Before becoming engaged to Lynn?

Panicked sanity finally urged her to jerk away from him. She gasped in pain when she twisted her injured arm. "Don't, A.J. We mustn't do this. You're *engaged* to one of my oldest friends!"

She leaped to her feet but stumbled when her knee gave way. He was beside her in a flash, reaching to help, but she backed away. His face was as stricken as hers. He ran a shaking hand through her disarranged hair. "Shelby, let me explain. This has gone on long enough...."

"Never mind," she commanded, holding her hand out

in front of her, her face confused and full of self-loathing. "Don't make it any worse than it already is!"

She turned and ran into the bedroom, threw herself across the bed and burst into tears.

AFTER CRYING for what seemed like hours Shelby had fallen asleep in her clothes. Her suede skirt would probably never be the same.

She would never be the same.

The problem with making a dramatic exit, she decided, was that one had to get up and face the same problem in the morning. And what a problem it was. She had fallen in love with another woman's fiancé.

Shelby threw her arm over her eyes and indulged in some well-deserved self-loathing.

She heard A.J. stirring about in the other room, so she got up, carefully nursing her sore arm and knee and slipped into the bathroom where she used some makeup and a hairbrush to make what repairs she could to her ravaged face.

A.J. was in the kitchen and when he heard her open the bedroom door, he spoke without turning around. "Coffee's ready. I'm not very hungry, but help yourself to what food there is. I think I'll take a shower before we start back."

His voice sounded perfectly normal but when he turned around, Shelby saw his face was as drawn and grim as her own. "Thank you, but I'm not hungry."

While he showered, Shelby took a cup of coffee and limped outside, where she anxiously scanned the sky. The visibility was good enough for them to be able to get out safely, she decided with relief.

SHE SMOOTHED her face into blankness and stood up quickly when A.J. emerged from the bedroom. His hair was damp and he was rolling the sleeves of his wrinkled shirt up to his elbows. He glanced around swiftly. "How is your arm? And knee?"

"Fine." She avoided his eyes, leaning over to pick up her jacket and the tattered blouse.

"Let me see," he said from right behind her. His fingers were gentle as he touched her puffy knee then grasped her elbow and checked her wounds. "The swelling should go down soon. It'll be all right. Looks like I got all the splinters, too."

His hand was warm on her arm, his thumb tender on the inside of her elbow, his scent was that of soap. Their eyes met. His were as anguished as her own but held a longing that shook her. Trembling, she pulled away and stepped back.

He didn't move. "Shelby." His voice was suddenly hoarse. "We've got to talk."

Horrified, she scurried toward the door. "No, there's nothing to talk about. We'd better go."

"Shelby!"

The look she gave him said the discussion was closed. His lips thinned for a moment in displeasure, but he followed her outside. After locking the door, he put the key back in its unsafe hiding place.

As they pulled away, Shelby gave one last glance at the cabin. Her feelings about it had undergone a radical change. Happy girlhood memories had been forever changed to ones of embarrassment and pain.

Once they got out of the lingering fog, A.J. drove fast, and Shelby was happy to have him do so.

He swung through town and pulled in at Spanish Court where Shelby had left her car. When A.J. stopped the Jaguar, she almost tumbled out onto the sidewalk in relief.

"Shelby, wait." A.J.'s voice was low and urgent.

She had stopped, halfway out of the car, with her back to him. Slowly, she turned her head to look back over her shoulder. "What is it?"

"About last night..."

Her thick lashes fluttered down over eyes dark with misery. "Don't talk about it."

"We've got to."

"It never happened."

"It did."

"It *shouldn't* have."

A.J. gripped the steering wheel and clenched his eyes shut. "Dear God, I don't know *what's* happened. Things have gotten so damned complicated. Listen, Shelby," he pleaded, opening his eyes. "I want to apologize...."

"Don't." Her voice wavered and her blue eyes were huge and hurt as she backed out of the car.

"Wait—" he called after her, but in an instant Shelby was out of the car, clutching her things to her, limping through the mall.

*

"SHELBY, I couldn't believe it when Alex told me the two of you had gone running off to the cabin looking for me." Lynn Altman swept into Featherstone Brides.

Shelby felt a surge of guilt. Telling herself that nothing had happened didn't help. She had *wanted* something to happen.

Shelby took a deep breath. "Lynn, Carlo Rosetti was here Thursday."

Lynn didn't meet her eyes. "I know."

"So he *did* contact you?"

"Yes."

"He asked me about A.J. He was jealous and angry when he left here."

Lynn's soft mouth curved in a smile that Shelby had never seen there before. It could only be described as smug. "I know," she said again, then her smile faded. "He called me. We talked.'' She seemed to drift off into her own thoughts.

Appalled, Shelby gaped at her friend. ''Then what happened?''

Lynn started out of her dreamy look. ''Happened? Why, nothing. We still don't see eye to eye.''

Lynn looked as if she was going to explain, but apparently changed her mind. ''I want to discuss our gowns. You look wonderful in that shade of blue,'' Lynn said, indicating Shelby's dress.

A wave of sick dread began to churn in Shelby's stomach.

The bell toned quietly, and Shelby froze when she saw that it was A.J. He came in quietly and shut the door.

A.J. walked over and kissed Lynn's cheek. She smiled briefly. ''I thought we could have a drink if you're finished here,'' he said. ''I got a phone call today that we've got to talk about.'' He shot a guarded glance at Shelby.

''All right. I just have to pay Shelby.'' Lynn drew out her checkbook and made her first payment to Featherstone Brides. A.J. watched with a frown.

Lynn said goodbye and allowed A.J. to take her arm as they moved toward the door, her eyes scanning the slip of paper in her hand. She turned back and held up the receipt, bewilderment and humor on her lovely face. ''Is this a joke, Shel? A receipt signed by Shelby Court?''

''WHAT DO YOU THINK of this one?'' Shelby asked.

With no thought to possible grass stains on her yellow skirt, she sank onto a small hillock overlooking a stream that meandered through the center of Sandrock Park. Sighing, she took off her three-inch-heeled pumps and rubbed her aching feet. She and Lynn had been searching out the perfect wedding site. Sandrock was the third park they had visited that day, along with two churches and a particularly beautiful section of beach.

Shelby struggled with jealousy. Lynn, who had always been quiet and amenable, had become animated and determined, even vivacious in the past few days, while Shelby had become withdrawn and pensive.

"This is perfect," Lynn finally decided, twirling around in an excited pirouette. "This is exactly what I want." She came back to Shelby and plopped down contentedly. "Now," she added under her breath. "If I can just get the groom to see it my way."

An incredible pain knifed through Shelby and she sat up suddenly. "This place doesn't have an aisle," she snapped, unwillingly peeved at the image of A.J. and Lynn together. Ashamed, she reached for her shoes and slipped them on. Out of the corner of her eye she saw a movement and glanced to her left. She gasped and drew back as Carlo Rosetti rushed out from behind a wide-trunked oak.

"So—" he said, contemptuously. "This is where you are going to marry Alexander Court!"

Lynn, who had been half dozing on the grass, lost in her happy daydream, leaped up with a shriek.

"Carlo! What are you doing here?"

Carlo stalked across the grass in short quick strides. His handsome face was twisted with anger and passion. "I have been following you as you have gone from place to place, finding the perfect spot for your marriage," he shouted, mimicking Lynn savagely.

"You've been listening to everything we said," Lynn accused, raising a shaky finger and pointing at him.

"Yes, and I'm tired of listening, tired of watching you make plans to marry this…Court." He practically spat out A.J.'s name as he reached out to grab Lynn's arm. Although he and Lynn were almost the same height, he seemed to loom over her. In contrast to Lynn's elegantly tailored pantsuit, he was dressed in old jeans and a T-shirt. His muscles flexed like steel cords as he drew the stunned blonde toward him.

Shelby leaped to Lynn's defense. "Let go of her, Carlo."

"Stay out of this, Miss Featherstone," he growled, without turning his head.

"I won't," she said, grabbing on to his arm. It felt like iron and would probably be as difficult to pry loose, she thought. Lynn wasn't helping at all but was staring at Carlo, wide-eyed. Shelby looked around frantically for help. The park was deserted.

"You ran away from me last week," he said to Lynn, ignoring Shelby completely. "I wanted to talk to you."

Lynn opened her mouth but all that came out was, "I—Carlo…"

"Can you blame her?" Shelby sputtered. "You probably scared her out of her wits."

Carlo shook Shelby off as casually as if she was a leaf clinging to his forearm. His dark eyes bore into Lynn's. "*Did* I frighten you?"

She shook her head, her face becoming pink. "Not—not really."

Carlo's voice was low and intense when he spoke again. "I came after you. I wanted to talk to you—I still want to—about Alex Court." His face grew anguished, his black eyes full of pain. "I know he is not good enough for you."

"Not good enough for her!" Shelby exclaimed, flabbergasted. "Why, I'll have you know he's a wonderful man! He's good and thoughtful—but tough," she admitted for fairness' sake. "He has compassion and understanding and—" Her tirade stumbled to a halt as she realized that Lynn was staring at her, openmouthed.

"Why, Shelby," she gasped. Understanding seemed to rush over her. "I had no idea."

Mortified, Shelby stared back at her friend. Now her secret was out. She had betrayed their friendship completely.

Shelby held out a shaky hand, hoping that Lynn could forgive her. "Lynn, I'm…sorry. I never meant to hurt you."

"Shel," Lynn whispered, "I never suspected."

Carlo's eyes darted from one girl to the other, and he smiled with sudden determination.

He whirled Lynn around and forced her to look at him. His dark eyes snapping, he said, "You're coming with me."

Chin up, Lynn faced him. "You know what I want...."

Carlo's face was suddenly so fierce, Shelby thought he might strike out. She took a protective step toward Lynn, who didn't flinch at the look on his face.

"You mean marriage."

"That's right."

They stared at each other, eyes battling. Finally, he nodded. "If that's what it takes."

He grabbed Lynn's left hand and snatched off her engagement ring. She squealed in surprise and jerked her hand back as Carlo shoved the solitaire at Shelby. "Here, give this back to Court. Lynn won't be needing it."

Still holding on to Lynn, Carlo began running. Lynn took leaping strides to keep up.

"Hey, wait a minute!" Shelby, who had been frozen into immobility, snatched up her purse and started after them. The combination of high heels and a sore knee slowed her too much, though. Carlo, dragging Lynn with him, soon disappeared over the next hill in the direction of the parking lot.

By the time Shelby reached the bottom of the next hill, they were roaring away in Lynn's white Triumph, with Carlo driving. "Call Alex!" Lynn yelled out as they sped away.

SHELBY CLUTCHED her purse, with Lynn's ring inside, and reached up to knock on A.J.'s front door. She had intended to call him as Lynn had said, but somehow she didn't feel right about it.

How was she going to break the news to him? Possible

explanations and apologies had formed in her mind as she drove but when A.J. swung the door open and stood staring down at her, her mind went blank.

He had removed his suit jacket and loosened his tie. Obviously, he had just run distracted fingers through his hair because the black tendrils were mussed, standing on end.

"Shelby." His lips formed her name, as his green eyes took a quick, thorough, catalog of her features. "What's wrong?"

She didn't know what she was going to say. He looked awful, his face drawn into lines that added years. Surprise crossed his face, and then he began to smile. Sick dread churned in her stomach because she knew that momentarily she would be responsible for taking that smile off his face. "May...may I talk to you?"

He stepped back, swinging the carved door wide. "Of course. Come in."

He indicated the sofa. "Sit down. Would you like something to drink?"

Miserably, she shook her head. "A.J., this isn't a social call. I have something for you...."

The eager delight on his face faded to a wary regard. "What is it?"

With shaking hands she reached into her purse and pulled out the ring. Her words tumbling over each other, she plunged into a recounting of the afternoon's events.

Robotlike, A.J. extended his hand as he listened. She dropped the ring into his palm and watched his fingers curl over it.

His stunned look brought tears spurting to Shelby's eyes. Oh—she could just kick Lynn and Carlo for hurting him like this!

A.J. pulled Shelby into his arms and comforted her.

Pity and love overwhelmed her and she wrapped her arms around his waist, offering what comfort she could.

"A.J., I'm so sorry. I can't believe Lynn and Carlo did such a thing!"

He didn't answer, and it was several more seconds before Shelby realized that he wasn't crying at all—but laughing!

Shocked, she jerked her tear-streaked face back and stared up at him.

"Thank God they did," he gasped, his eyes bright with tears of laughter. "I didn't know how much longer I could go on with this!"

Shelby thought he might be hysterical, but to her amazement, she realized that he was truly relieved. Finally she managed to say, "I'm—glad you're taking it so well."

When his laughter had finally wheezed to a stop and he stood, hands on hips, grinning down at her, she said, "Let me get this straight. You're not upset that your fiancée eloped with another man?"

He drew a deep breath and expelled it in a long sound of relief, looking happier than she had ever seen him.

"I would be," he said, "if she had really been my fiancée."

Shelby gaped at him. She was silent for a full minute. "What do you mean?"

A.J.'s amusement faded when he saw how pale her face had become. He took her arm, led her toward the sofa and forced her to be seated. "Sit down. I'd better explain."

She flounced onto the couch. "Yes. You'd darn well better!"

"You already know how I fooled Erica," he began.

Shelby frowned. "What's that got to do with it?"

He held up his hand. "I'm getting to that. Lynn and I had an agreement. She was supposed to help me trick Erica. That's why the ring was in the napkin." He pulled the ring out of the pocket he had dropped it into and turned it around in his fingers. "The plan was for her to slip it on as soon as she got there, to make it look as if we were already engaged, had been planning marriage for a while."

Involuntarily, Shelby's right hand covered her left, as she remembered the brief time she had worn the ring.

"The ring belonged to my mother," he said, and added wistfully, "It was the first thing of value my dad ever bought after our farm started making a profit. I kept it for my wife to wear."

Shelby saw his eyes on her and laced her fingers together.

"Anyway," A.J. went on, "Lynn was going to help me and I would pose as her fiancée to get Carlo's attention."

Shelby started to speak, but he held up his hand. "Let me finish—" his dimple quirked up "—and then you can yell at me." He paused and began pacing across the room. "My idea was that if Lynn and I just leaked word of our engagement, if Lynn even suggested she was considering marrying someone else, Carlo would come around. Oh, I know, her parents, especially her mother, didn't like him. And Carlo thought she deserved to marry a rich, successful man. But Lynn was determined to have *him*."

Shelby jumped up, clamped her hands onto her hips and stalked up to him. "Then why that big announcement at Lynn's welcome-home party? *That* was certainly more than a 'suggestion' that you two were going to marry."

A.J. spread his hands wide. "Because Anderson was there. Lynn couldn't locate Carlo, so.. ."

"She was trying to flush him out," Shelby concluded, pursing her lips.

"Yes, I had no idea you and Lynn were close friends until later."

Seeing the wistfulness on his face, hearing words she had never expected to hear, Shelby almost softened toward him, but she stiffened her resolve. She had suffered guilt and remorse—for nothing!

"You could have told me the truth later," she pointed out angrily. "Lynn was acting so strange I didn't know what to think. You were trying to buy me off—make me quit. Why?"

"Because I thought exactly this kind of thing would happen. Carlo isn't the type of man to get dressed up in a monkey suit and get married in front of five hundred of Lynn's nearest and dearest friends. I told her that, but she was looking at the whole thing through rose-colored glasses. She wasn't supposed to plan a real wedding at all."

"But you and Carlo had never met. You don't know his personality…." Shelby closed her eyes briefly and sighed. "You had him investigated, didn't you?"

"Hell, yes," A.J. growled without revealing a shred of conscience. "She was my best friend's daughter. I couldn't let her marry some jerk. Carlo turned out to be a good man, if somewhat hardheaded."

Shelby took a turn around the room, her steps short and angry. "But why didn't you tell *me* what was going on? It wasn't fair to keep me in the dark like that. All kinds of plans were in motion…."

"I know." His gaze slanted down guiltily. "But I had promised Lynn I wouldn't tell *anyone* the truth until Carlo saw reason. Then, after the night in the cabin, I almost told you, but you wouldn't listen."

Shelby shook her head. "But you knew it was all a farce—and my business, my reputation was at stake. It wasn't fair to keep this from me!"

He took a step toward her. "I know, but by yesterday I began to see that things were going to work out."

So many conflicting thoughts were buzzing around in her head that she couldn't think. "Do you have any idea what guilt I went through?" she burst out. "I agonized—hated myself—because I had fallen in love with my friend's fiancé!"

When she realized what she had just admitted, her hands flew to her mouth as if she could call the words back. Her eyes were huge, peeking over the tips of her fingers. Turning, she fled the room, heading toward the front door, appalled at what she had just blurted.

A.J. was after her in a flash. "Don't run away from me, Shelby!" He caught her at the door and spun her into his arms. "Hell, what a way to tell a man that you love him," he muttered, his green eyes dark and fervid, his voice intense. "But I should have expected it from you."

His mouth came down on hers and Shelby forgot that she was supposed to be angry with him. Passion flared between them, and she wound her arms around his neck, remembering only that she loved him.

He broke away, breathing hard, and placed his forehead against hers. "I love you, Shelby," he said. "I thought this mess would never be straightened out so I could tell you that."

She snuggled into his arms, relieved and delighted that the barriers between them were finally down. "I was sure I would never hear *you* say *that*." Her hand stole up to pinch him hard on his ear.

"Ouch!" he yelped. "What was that for?"

"For deceiving me and making me agonize and hate myself for loving you."

His expression grew suspiciously innocent. "I never actually lied to you. There were just certain things I couldn't tell you."

She gave him a haughty look. "Don't let it happen again."

"I promise." He paused, his eyes solemnly searching her face. "Now I want a promise from you."

"What?"

He lifted the solitaire. "Marry me."

Shelby's eyes filled with tears as she stared at the diamond and then at him. "Marry you?"

"You've got most of the plans made, don't you?"

"Plans?" Shelby couldn't seem to stop parroting his words.

"For the Altman-Court wedding—now the Featherstone-Court wedding." When she didn't speak, he rushed on. "Hey, is it the ring? I can get another one. I can understand why you wouldn't want to wear one that someone else had worn, and—"

She stilled his quick words by standing on tiptoe to kiss him. "This ring will do fine." Her face was very grave as she said, "It was always mine, A.J."

He grinned suddenly and lifted her hand, slipping the ring on easily and kissing the place where it rested. "Yes, it was, wasn't it? And now it even fits."

Harlequin Romance®

From first love to forever

takes you there.

Save $3.00 off the purchase of any 4

SILHOUETTE *Romance*™

series titles.

Visit Silhouette at www.eHarlequin.com
T5V1CSRUSR
© 2001 Harlequin Enterprises Ltd.

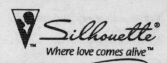

Where love comes alive™

From first love to forever

takes you there.

Save $3.00 off the purchase of any 4

series titles.

Visit Silhouette at www.eHarlequin.com
T5V1CSRCANR
© 2001 Harlequin Enterprises Ltd.

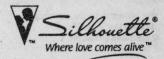

Silhouette®
Where love comes alive™

Harlequin Romance®

Capturing the world
you dream of

Save $2.00 off the purchase of any 3
Harlequin Romance®
series titles.

$2.00 OFF!
any three Harlequin Romance series titles.

```
5  65373 00009  0   (8100)0  10736
```

Visit us at www.eHarlequin.com
T5V1CHRUSR
© 2001 Harlequin Enterprises Ltd.

HARLEQUIN®
Makes any time special®

Harlequin Romance®

Capturing the world
you dream of

Save $2.00 off the purchase of any 3
Harlequin Romance®
series titles.

$2.00 OFF!
any three Harlequin Romance series titles.

```
52603293
```

Visit us at www.eHarlequin.com
T5V1CHRCANR
© 2001 Harlequin Enterprises Ltd.

HARLEQUIN®
Makes any time special®